SPECIAL MESSAGE TO READERS

THE ULVERSCROFT FOUNDATION
(registered UK charity number 264873)
was established in 1972 to provide funds for research, diagnosis and treatment of eye diseases. Examples of major projects funded by the Ulverscroft Foundation are:-

- The Children's Eye Unit at Moorfields Eye Hospital, London
- The Ulverscroft Children's Eye Unit at Great Ormond Street Hospital for Sick Children
- Funding research into eye diseases and treatment at the Department of Ophthalmology, University of Leicester
- The Ulverscroft Vision Research Group, Institute of Child Health
- Twin operating theatres at the Western Ophthalmic Hospital, London
- The Chair of Ophthalmology at the Royal Australian College of Ophthalmologists

You can help further the work of the Foundation by making a donation or leaving a legacy. Every contribution is gratefully received. If you would like to help support the Foundation or require further information, please contact:

THE ULVERSCROFT FOUNDATION
The Green, Bradgate Road, Anstey
Leicester LE7 7FU, England
Tel: (0116) 236 4325

website: www.foundation.ulverscroft.com

Katie Fforde was born and brought up in London but has lived in Gloucestershire with her family for the last thirty years. Her first novel, *Living Dangerously*, went on to be chosen as part of the WHSmith Fresh Talent Promotion. There have been over eighteen novels since, as well as some grandchildren. Her hobbies, when she has time for them, are singing in a choir and flamenco dancing. Katie Fforde is President of the Romantic Novelists' Association.

THE PERFECT MATCH

Three years ago, Bella Castle left her hometown nursing a broken heart over Dominic Thane, the man she fell in love with but couldn't have. Now she's made a life for herself in the country, working for an estate agent. She loves her new home, her new job, and her new boyfriend Nevil, who also happens to be her boss. They seem to be the perfect match for each other. But although Nevil's just proposed to her, he's been strangely preoccupied recently, and Bella can't understand why. Then Dominic turns up unexpectedly, throwing all her plans and good intentions into disarray. And Bella begins to question if her new home really is where her heart is . . .

Books by Katie Fforde
Published by Ulverscroft:

LIVING DANGEROUSLY
THE ROSE REVIVED
WILD DESIGNS
STATELY PURSUITS
LIFE SKILLS
THYME OUT
HIGHLAND FLING
ARTISTIC LICENCE
PARADISE FIELDS
RESTORING GRACE
FLORA'S LOT
PRACTICALLY PERFECT
GOING DUTCH
WEDDING SEASON
LOVE LETTERS
A PERFECT PROPOSAL
SUMMER OF LOVE
RECIPE FOR LOVE
A FRENCH AFFAIR

KATIE FFORDE

THE PERFECT MATCH

Complete and Unabridged

CHARNWOOD
Leicester

First published in Great Britain in 2014 by
Century
London

First Charnwood Edition
published 2015
by arrangement with
Century
The Random House Group Limited
London

A catalogue record for this book is available from the British Library.

ISBN 978–1–4448–2489–6

Published by
F. A. Thorpe (Publishing)
Anstey, Leicestershire

Set by Words & Graphics Ltd.
Anstey, Leicestershire
Printed and bound in Great Britain by
T. J. International Ltd., Padstow, Cornwall

This book is printed on acid-free paper

To my sister Jane Gordon-Cumming and
her husband Edwin Osborn, with love
and many thanks for the inspiration.

Acknowledgements

Huge thanks to Catherine and Richard Crawshaw of Besley Hill in Stroud who were so enthusiastic about this project and extremely helpful. All the mistakes (and there will be some!) are my own but you were both brilliant.

Major thanks too goes to my sister Jane and brother-in-law Edwin who helped me in so many ways, even when they weren't aware they were doing it. I'm so happy we now live so near each other!

Enormous thanks as always to the amazing sales team. Also Jen Doyle, Rebecca Ikin and Sarah Arratoon in marketing, who perform their alchemy with such cheerfulness and good humour. Thanks are always due to the amazing Charlotte Bush and Amelia Harvell who are so professional but even more fun.

To my wonderful editors Selina Walker and Georgina Hawtrey-Woore who are also so kind and understanding as they urge me on to better efforts.

Also Richenda Todd who controls the fine detail but doesn't touch my jokes.

And of course, Bill Hamilton from A M Heath, always a rock.

There will be many people I should have thanked but please trust that I am not ungrateful, just terminally forgetful.

Thank you all!

1

Bella Castle took a breath and put on a smile she hoped would hide her frustration. She and her clients were standing in front of a little gem of a house and yet it had just been deemed unsuitable.

'It might be a good idea to have some sacrificial boxes too, ones that you don't mind if they don't get ticked,' she said gently. 'While it's useful to make a checklist, you don't want to be ruled by it or you'll never find a house.'

Bella had grown very fond of the Agnews over the eight months she had been trying to find them somewhere that fitted their requirements, but she did sometimes find them exasperating. They had small-stately tastes with semi-detached money. Big rooms, large garden, views, a garage, a restricted search area and a reluctance to compromise made them something of a challenge. This particular garden, filled with roses and other summer flowers, was deemed 'too small and too much on the flat' although a level garden was one of their top priorities.

Mrs Agnew raised her eyebrows. She knew she was fussy and could even laugh at herself, but she hadn't so far managed to compromise. 'OK, I'll have 'rose-covered arbour' as my sacrificial box. Darling?' She looked at her husband.

'What about the 'wildlife in the garden essential'?'

Mrs Agnew shook her head. 'I couldn't

compromise on the wildlife.'

'No need to,' said Bella briskly. 'There's always wildlife.' She said this with a certainty she hoped masked her ignorance, but given they were in one of the less populated parts of the Cotswolds, she was fairly confident.

'Then I'll have 'model-train room' as mine,' said Mr Agnew, who was slightly less fixed in his ideas of the perfect home.

Mrs Agnew chuckled gently and then looked wistful. 'Will that make it easier to find our dream home?'

Bella laughed. 'I'm sure it will.'

She was aware that she was very lucky; living with her godmother, Alice, who had a house the Agnews would die for, made it possible for her to stay in this desirable area in a way she could afford.

She watched them drive away from the charming house that she'd been convinced would be perfect for them and then got into her own car. She *was* disappointed. There was another family who'd been unlucky on a house that had gone to sealed bids and if she found just one of these clients somewhere to live she'd be content. She was about to set off back to the office when her phone went. It was Nevil, her boyfriend and her boss.

'Any good?' he asked, after the briefest greeting. 'Don't tell me,' he went on, 'it made her 'feel hemmed in'.'

Bella felt instantly protective. These were her clients and only she was allowed to consider them fussy. 'Come on, Nevil, if a house isn't right, it isn't right, and that last property I showed them was a bit claustrophobic.'

'So what was wrong with this one?' he said. Bella could picture him, one eyebrow raised, pencil poised over his pad, which he mostly used to doodle on.

'Too flat,' said Bella.

'Ye Gods!'

'I'm going to come back to the office now. There are a few bits I need to see to,' she said quickly, before he could go on about her favourite clients any more.

'No! No need to do that, sweetie,' said Nevil, going from irritating boss to conciliatory boyfriend in an instant. 'It's four o'clock — you push off home. I'll see you tomorrow.'

Nevil wasn't usually one for suggesting she 'pushed off home' and she was a bit taken aback. 'Oh, OK then.' She paused. 'I might call on Mrs Langley.'

'Good plan! See if she's finally decided to put her desirable six-bed on the market. God, she must rattle around in there.' He chuckled. 'Sorry, hon, there I go again — always the estate agent! You go and see your old lady. And pick up some flowers on the way, keep the receipt and take the money out of petty cash.'

Bella wished she hadn't mentioned Mrs Langley. Nevil, though well meaning, didn't understand that garage carnations didn't really set the heart racing. 'To be honest, she's got a garden full of flowers, but it's a sweet thought.'

'Get her some chocolates then — something nice.'

'Nevil, it's OK. I'm sure when she's ready to

move she'll let us know.'

'It's good of you to keep up the pressure though, Bells,' said Nevil. 'It shows your dedication to the job. I do appreciate that.'

As she set off in her car Bella thought about Nevil. He did get it wrong sometimes but his heart was in the right place. She found she was smiling. She'd been very lucky to find a new job in an estate agency in a very pretty market town only forty-five minutes away from her hometown, run by a man who, while not exactly pretty, was easy on the eye.

Mrs Langley had been a client who had been very easy to please, basically because, after a long chat, Bella had discovered she didn't really want to move and told her so. It had been a huge relief to Mrs Langley, who wanted to stay with the garden she had spent nearly fifty years creating. Bella had told her how simple it would be to turn the morning room into a pretty bedroom and how, with the utility room next door, she could have an en-suite and that she need never go upstairs again if she didn't want to. They had been firm friends ever since and whenever Bella called she was guaranteed a cup of tea and a piece of cake. Bella found she often needed cake in her business. Being an estate agent required an awful lot of patience.

Nevil was aware that Bella called relatively often but he didn't know that Bella never brought up the subject of moving unless Mrs Langley did first, and then it was to reassure her that it wasn't a good idea unless she really wanted to, no matter what anybody said.

* * *

Bella and Mrs Langley sat in the flower-filled garden at the rickety iron table on rickety iron chairs saved from being desperately uncomfortable by faded cushions that smelt faintly of old shed. A little way away from the house, it was Mrs Langley's favourite spot, close to a creaking arbour and threatened by a huge rambler, which, now it was June, bore hundreds of tiny, very fragrant flowers that scrambled beyond the arbour and up into the nearby tree. Bella couldn't help thinking how much the Agnews would love it, if only they were millionaires and Mrs Langley wanted to move.

Bella was handed a cup and saucer and a plate. 'You must have known I was making lemon drizzle,' she said, indicating the cake.

Bella sighed happily. 'You know I adore everything that comes out of your oven but lemon drizzle is a bit of a favourite.' She took a mouthful.

'My nephew's been in touch,' said Mrs Langley after a few moments' contented silence.

Bella swallowed and paid attention. It had been Mrs Langley's great-nephew — although she missed out the 'great' when she referred to him — who had wanted Mrs Langley to move. Bella had always feared repercussions. It seemed Mrs Langley did too.

'Oh?'

The elderly woman nodded. 'Yes. He's going to stay the night here and wants to take me out for a meal. That's nice, isn't it?'

She sounded just a bit desperate, as if needing Bella to think well of the stranger who had wanted his great-aunt to move out of her beloved home of fifty years and go somewhere 'more suitable'.

'It is,' she agreed brightly. 'Make sure you go somewhere really good. I suggest you get him to take you to the Dog and Fox. It has a lovely conservatory you can eat in, with wonderful views of the garden.'

Mrs Langley wasn't distracted by the thought of another gardener's herbaceous borders. 'I'm worried he's going to ask me to move again.'

Bella leant forward. 'Did he say anything about it?'

Mrs Langley shook her head. 'No, but — you know — I worry.'

Bella was firm. 'You don't have to move. There's no reason why you should. I'm sure if you tell him you want to stay put he'll say no more about it. After all, when you told him the first time he didn't mind, did he?'

Mrs Langley nodded. 'It's just, you know, my brother — his grandfather — was very forceful. It might be an inherited trait. Last time I wrote a letter. I might not be so brave when I see him face-to-face.'

Bella put her hand on her friend's. 'No one can force you to move. If you did become too frail to live on your own you could have a companion. It's not as if you haven't got plenty of room, after all.'

'That sounds terribly expensive. I may live in a valuable house but I don't have much of an income.'

'You could have the sort of companion who does it in exchange for a room. Some nice woman to be here at night, check you're OK and then go off to work.' Bella patted the soft, age-spotted hand. 'But you're a long way from that. Anyone who can bake as well as you do doesn't need anyone making their Horlicks for them.'

Mrs Langley chuckled, seeming cheered up. 'That's true!'

'And if there's any argument, I'll tell him there's absolutely no market for lovely old houses with loads of character with gorgeous gardens.'

Mrs Langley smiled. 'I'm sure he'll believe you.' She paused. 'Have you time for another cup of tea and some more cake?'

Bella looked at her watch. 'I'm meeting Alice's train at about half past seven. So yes, that would be lovely. As long as I'm not holding you up?'

'I'd be very glad of the company and I won't need to eat later if I have more cake now. One of the joys of growing old is that you don't feel obliged to eat healthily any more, if you don't want to.' She put a slice of cake on Bella's plate.

'So when is he coming? Your nephew?' asked Bella.

'Next week some time.' Mrs Langley put out a hand. 'I don't suppose you'd like to come out with us? I could suggest . . . '

'I'd be more than happy to,' said Bella, 'but wouldn't it look a bit odd if you asked if you could bring your estate agent along?'

Mrs Langley laughed. 'If I put it like that it

would look very odd but I'd refer to you as my friend. Which you definitely are.'

'You could say you needed me to assist you to the bathroom. He'd be bound to say yes then. But I think you should give him a chance first. If he arrives at the house and is instantly measuring rooms and tapping walls you could ring me, and then tell him about needing bathroom assistance.'

Mrs Langley sighed. 'Then he'd say I definitely need to move.'

'Nonsense,' said Bella. 'You could have grab rails and all sorts. Your home is perfectly suitable for you if it's where you want to live.' She glanced at her watch. 'I should go fairly soon. Is there anything that needs doing while I'm here?'

Bella hadn't actually mentioned it to Nevil, but one of the reasons she called so often on Mrs Langley was so she could do the little bits and pieces her old friend found difficult. He might not have approved, feeling she was keeping a very valuable potential client in her property longer than was right.

'Well, the hose has fallen off the tap again, if you wouldn't mind . . . '

'Of course I don't mind. I'll water the greenhouse and then put the hose back on. I wish you'd let me work out a better watering system for you.'

Mrs Langley looked anxious. 'You know I hate change.'

Bella smiled sympathetically. 'But if it meant you could go on growing tomatoes longer, it would be worth it, wouldn't it?'

'I suppose so. I just wouldn't want my nephew to think I couldn't cope with the watering any more.'

'I'll look into it. Nothing will happen until after your nephew's visit, I promise you.'

'I must say,' said Mrs Langley after a bit of thought, 'if there was a way of keeping my greenhouse going that didn't involve watering cans, I would be interested.'

'Of course there is. I'll ask around and let you know.'

A little later, only slightly damp, Bella got into her car and set off for the station. She knew just whom to ask to sort Mrs Langley out with a watering system that involved nothing more energetic than turning on a tap.

2

Alice settled back into her seat on the train with a happy sigh. She had her Kindle, her things about her, and shortly someone would bring her a cup of tea. Or even a glass of wine. First-class travel — at least on the train — was within her budget at last and she loved it. When she turned sixty, Alice had resolved that she would stop suppressing her itchy feet and travel more. She just needed to work out how. Going up to London more often was a start.

As the train had obligingly been ready for boarding early, she was well into this month's book-group choice before people who didn't share her idea of punctuality began to board the train.

Alice had arranged her bags so she wasn't taking up much space and carried on reading. She didn't look up until she became aware of someone plumping down in the seat opposite and a briefcase landing on the table. Then she glanced up and smiled to indicate she didn't feel she owned the entire four seats before returning to her book.

The man took a bit of time to settle and Alice stopped reading in order to look at him properly. She was an inveterate people-watcher and, she soon discovered, he was well worth a glance. He was, she reckoned, younger than her — fifties probably — but had an energy about him that was more youthful. He wore a very nice suit and a tie that challenged the suit with its flamboyant colours and slightly skewed angle.

Alice wondered if, at sixty, one was expected to stop looking at the opposite sex with interest. Probably, she concluded, which was rather a shame. Not that she was constantly on the lookout for attractive men or anything, but felt that if she did notice one, she should probably leave the looking to younger women.

Yet the man opposite kept drawing her attention away from her Kindle. He was restless, opening his briefcase, taking things out, shutting it again, looking at his watch. He caught her glancing at him and smiled apologetically.

'I wonder when the trolley will come round,' he said.

'We probably have to set off for that to happen,' said Alice, 'but that's due any minute now. Ah, here we go.' She looked out of the window, enjoying the moment when you couldn't quite tell if it was the train moving or the platform.

It was a while before the trolley did come, and when it rattled to a halt beside them, Alice's travelling companion seemed excited. The attendant looked at Alice expectantly but as she wanted time to consider her options, this seat-side service being new to her, she suggested the man went first.

'What can I have for nothing?' he asked.

Impressive, thought Alice. She'd have been much more circumspect.

'Tea or coffee, hot chocolate, cake, biscuits,

crisps,' said the man in charge.

'Not a sandwich and a bottle of wine?'

'No, sir,' the attendant said firmly. 'You have to pay for those.'

'But I left my wallet in the office and I haven't much money.'

Alice retired behind her Kindle. In spite of his insouciance it must have been embarrassing for this man wanting to stock up on free food and drink like this.

'I'm sorry about that, sir, but I'm afraid there's nothing I can do.'

'And you're sure I can't have a sandwich if I don't have any of this other stuff?' he asked, gesturing towards the biscuits, cake, fruit and crisps with a disparaging hand. 'The value of them put together must come to the same as the cost of a sandwich.'

'I'm sorry, sir. Only the free things are free. The rest has to be paid for.'

'But the sandwiches have a very short shelf life — you probably have to chuck them at the end of the trip. The other stuff lasts ages.'

'I said I'm sorry — '

Alice could bear it no longer. 'Can I buy you a sandwich and a bottle of wine? I've got my wallet.'

The man looked at her with eyes she now saw were blue. 'I couldn't possibly let you do that.'

'Why not? It's not exactly a four-course meal at the Ritz. The bottles of wine are tiny. Let me pay.' Alice tried to sound authoritative. She felt her age should give her a bit of gravitas. Although maybe her newly highlighted hair would detract from that.

The man looked longingly at the sandwiches and then back at Alice. 'No. It would be wrong.'

Alice decided not to argue any more. 'OK.'

Relieved to be no longer dealing with the man who wanted everything for nothing, the trolley attendant turned to Alice.

'Right, I'll have two sandwiches, two bottles of wine' — she glanced up at her companion — 'red, I think. Oh and some crisps and a bottle of water.'

Once she had paid and the trolley had rattled off, she handed a sandwich and bottle of wine to her companion. He sighed.

'I give in,' he said, 'because I'm starving. But I insist on introducing myself. I'm Michael McKay.'

'Alice Aster,' she said and took his hand. He looked at her intensely for a moment and she realised it had been a while since a man had really looked at her. She found she liked it.

'Do you mind if I start?' he said.

'Not at all.' She responded to the warmth of his smile and decided this sort of thing was not forbidden for women over sixty. Seventy might be another matter.

Michael McKay ripped open the package and consumed the sandwich in three bites. Alice, who had had lunch, didn't open hers. She suspected Michael would want that too. She did open her wine though and a packet of crisps.

'I can't tell you how grateful I am,' he said, accepting the second sandwich when she handed it to him. 'I was so hungry. I realised as soon as I got to the front door of the office I'd left my wallet in my desk drawer, but I'd have missed the train if I'd gone back for it.' Then he made a face. 'Actually, I probably wouldn't have missed it but I'd have worried that I would.'

Alice nodded. 'I like to be early for trains too. We have that in common.'

'So, where are you headed? Reading? Or the Far West?'

Alice chuckled. 'Well, not the really far west but beyond Swindon. Stroud, actually.'

'I get off at Kemble.'

'Oh, posh Kemble,' said Alice laughing. 'Such a pretty station.'

'The scenery around Stroud is lovely too,' he said politely.

'It is indeed. I've lived there on and off for over thirty years.' She realised this made her sound terribly old but that didn't matter. Did it? Briefly she wondered if buying French beauty products off the internet in order to look younger — as she did — was a bit pointless if you more or less told everyone you'd reached bus-pass age.

'So, can I have your address?' he asked.

Alice was not a fearful woman. She believed in people and felt that most of them were well meaning. But she knew that if she let slip to anyone she knew — particularly her god-daughter Bella, who had a slightly maternal attitude towards her godmother — that she'd given her address to a man on a train she would be in big trouble.

'Why are you asking?'

He looked at her as if she was mad. 'So I can send you a cheque.'

'You're surely not suggesting you write a cheque and post it to me for the price of a sandwich and travel-sized bottle of wine?'

'But of course I am.' He paused significantly. 'It was two sandwiches.'

Alice couldn't help laughing. 'That's ridiculous. Tell me how you're going to get back to London tomorrow if you haven't got your wallet.'

'You're changing the subject.'

'Yup.' She laughed gently. 'You must see it's ridiculous to worry about such a small amount.'

His blue eyes pierced hers. 'I can't owe money to people. I'm constitutionally incapable.'

'Well, that's just silly!'

She could tell instantly that he was not in the habit of being laughed at much, but felt it was good for him to experience it, all the same.

'Is it? Most women I know are only too delighted to be paid for.' He had stopped looking affronted and a small smile was gathering at the corner of his eyes.

'And some are perfectly happy to pay for themselves and for other people — men even.'

'So you're one of these modern women?'

It was rather lovely to be described as being modern. She smiled warmly at him.

Just then the ticket inspector arrived at her side and — being law-abiding and unsure of the rules — she felt obliged to produce her Senior Citizen railcard, which Bella had insisted on referring to as her Old Person's railcard in a very disrespectful way. This would teach her to flirt with younger men, she told herself.

'Well, at least you'll feel better about me buying you a snack,' she said, 'now you know I'm old enough to be — well, your aunt, at least.'

The intense blue gaze was back. 'Oh I could never think of you as an aunt.'

Alice found herself blushing. It had been a while since anyone had chatted her up, and she wasn't even sure he was. As she didn't know how to respond she picked up her Kindle. 'I think I ought to carry on reading now. It's my book group soon.'

'Are you enjoying the book?'

Alice thought for a moment. 'Not awfully.'

'Then don't read it!'

'That would be taking anarchy too far,' she said sternly and turned her attention to the least accessible of last year's Booker Prize long list. Inside, she was smiling.

* * *

Bella was there waiting for Alice when the train pulled into Stroud a little later than scheduled.

Bella waved as she caught sight of her godmother amongst the small crowd coming out of the station. Alice was easy to spot in her drapey turquoise silk outfit that managed to be elegant and casual at the same time. With good bone structure and well-cared-for skin, she was someone Bella felt proud to be associated with.

She kissed her godmother on the cheek. 'Good day? Oh, no need to ask. I can see you had a lovely time! I'm afraid I haven't cooked. Fancy fish and chips?'

'Sounds lovely.'

'So how was travelling first class?'

'Brilliant!' Alice said.

Bella frowned slightly. Had Alice done something different with her make-up, or was she actually blushing?

3

A few days later Nevil and Bella were sitting in Alice's garden. They had a bottle of wine and a takeaway pizza. Alice had disappeared into her sitting room and they were alone.

'So, how's my little Curly Top, then?' said Nevil, filling Bella's glass.

At the same time that Bella wondered if she could tell Nevil she hated his nickname for her she realised he was in a very good mood, so she decided to overlook the reference to her hair, which was indeed on the curly side.

'I'm well — which you do know seeing as we've been working together all day.' She smiled.

'You know I like to keep personal stuff out of the office.' He smiled too.

He was, Bella thought, very good-looking. He had pleasant, even features, nice dark-blond hair, which fell over his forehead when he got excited, and he always looked smart. He was a few inches taller than she was and they made a good pair. Her dark curls complimented his fairer looks.

'You've been in very cheerful lately,' she said. 'You didn't moan when you realised the photocopier was out of paper. You didn't even moan because you had to actually do photocopying!'

Nevil laughed. 'I was a bit annoyed about that, but as I had asked Tina to go out for sandwiches it wasn't her fault she wasn't there.'

Bella was a bit surprised at this mellow attitude. He was very good at his job and, he frequently told her, you didn't get to head your own estate agency — even as part of a franchise — before you were thirty by being Mr Nice Guy in the office. Mr Nice Guy was for clients only.

'I think you're softening up in your old age, Nevil,' she said with a smile.

'Not at all,' said Nevil, not rising to her teasing. He was, after all, only thirty-two. 'I'm just happy to report that it won't be long before you and I can get a place together.'

'Great!' said Bella, hiding her dismay by picking up the bottle and topping them both up.

'Doesn't it drive you mad living here with your godmother? I mean she's lovely but — well . . . ' Nevil had good manners, it was part of his professional persona, so he left his sentence unfinished.

Bella considered how to explain, even though she felt she shouldn't have to. 'It's fine. There is plenty of space here, and she doesn't give me a curfew or anything.' Actually Bella really liked sharing Alice's house. They fitted in very well with each other and considering how long Alice had lived here on her own, this had surprised them both. She had been a lifeline when Bella had needed one and she was delighted that Alice enjoyed sharing her home with her. Living with Nevil might be a lot harder — given his feelings about small chores in the office, he was unlikely to be willing to push the hoover round himself.

'Well, anyway, you won't have to be doing it too much longer.'

'How come?'

'I could tell you, but then I'd have to kill you.' Nevil grinned.

Bella supressed her irritation at this expression and decided not to press him. He would tell her when he was ready. 'OK. Do you want the last bit of pizza?'

'Don't you? It's yours really.'

'You go ahead. I'm trying to cut down anyway.'

Nevil picked up the pizza and took a large bite and smiled at her. 'Good choice.'

Bella watched him eat it and wondered if it was weird to prefer living with an older woman to the thought of living with her boyfriend. And while she was asking herself this she wondered if he was implying she was fat. She wasn't, she knew that, but when she'd first walked into his agency looking for a job she had been skeletally thin — for reasons she tried to forget on a daily basis. Maybe he liked very thin women.

Her brain flicked back to why she had been so thin, why she had suddenly left her hometown to live with her godmother and take a job she was very lucky to get. Heartbreak or a new love was the best diet aid. However, now she was settled. She had a job she loved and colleagues she got on really well with, and — well, Nevil, who was — most of the time — a really good boyfriend.

'Has Alice thought how much this house would fetch if it went on the market?' Nevil asked, chewing away on his pepperoni.

'Don't think so. I don't think she wants to move. In fact, I know she doesn't. It is big for just the two of us, but it was her family home. And she's done so much to the garden over the years.'

'What is it with these women — like your Mrs Langley — insisting on living in enormous houses just on their own? The amount of money they have tied up in those properties is crazy.'

'But there's no real reason they should move if they don't want to. The time has to be right for these things.' Bella laughed. 'Though of course it would be fabulous to have the houses on our books.'

Nevil seemed not to have heard her. 'Will Alice manage on her own when you move out?'

'Of course! She's only sixty.' She was just about to say, 'But I'm not moving out,' when she stopped herself. If Nevil found the right house, it would be natural for them to move in together.

'I was just thinking what's best for her.'

'Of course.' She smiled, but she knew he wouldn't be able to help calculating the commission on a house as big as Alice's. 'Do you fancy finding something nice to watch on telly? We could go into my sitting room and snuggle up on the sofa.'

Nevil didn't seem tempted by this cosy suggestion.

'Not really. I think I should get off. Things to do and all that.'

After they had shared a pepperoni-flavoured kiss goodbye, it occurred to her that he'd become quite busy after hours recently, and briefly wondered if he was seeing someone else. Otherwise why pass up on what could amount to an invitation to stay the night? He had already stayed a few times, so he knew it wouldn't be awkward. But then she realised that while cheating on her wasn't an impossibility, it wouldn't make him so chirpy. Also, if he'd lost interest in her, he'd just dump her; he wouldn't talk about moving in together. No, it must be something else. She didn't intend to spend too much time worrying about it.

* * *

'Oh, I am glad you've rung, dear,' said Mrs Langley the following afternoon. 'My nephew wants to meet you!'

Bella, who had tracked down a man to fix up an irrigation system for her, was ringing to give Mrs Langley the details. She hadn't been expecting this.

'Does he? Why?' Then she thought she knew why. It was because he thought she was persuading his great-aunt to stay in her house and not sell. 'Does he want to tell me off?'

'I don't think so, dear. He just said, 'I'd be very interested to meet this young woman you talk about so much.''

'Oh.' She wondered why Mrs Langley kept talking about her, but was rather touched. 'So how is it going?'

'Well, we've decided he should stay with me whenever he needs to be in the area. He might work here permanently He's been here three nights already.'

'And that's all right for you?'

'Do you know, I rather like it! It's nice to cook for someone other than myself and he's very handy about the house.'

'Well, that's good. So he's not bossy and overbearing then?'

There was a pause. 'No, he's not, though he does have an air of authority, if you know what I mean.'

'But he's not trying to bully you into selling?' Bella persisted.

Another pause. 'No. He wants to know how well I manage. But in a concerned way, you know?'

Bella didn't know but she was reassured.

'And I'd really appreciate it if you'd come and have a drink with us — before dinner. My nephew works very hard and could do with some young company.'

'Well, I am young,' Bella agreed. 'And I'd be delighted to come. Only I'd be coming for *your* company.'

Mrs Langley laughed. 'You realise there won't be cake?'

Bella chuckled. 'In which case, Mrs Langley, I'm afraid I have to refuse — '

'Please call me Jane! I think we know each other well enough by now.'

'All right, Jane. I'll come, even if there isn't going to be cake.'

The arrangement was made and Bella went to join Alice in her sitting room. Nominally, Bella had the morning room for her own use but she hardly ever went in there, except to clean it or on the rare occasion Nevil stayed over. She and

Alice liked to spend their evenings together, if they were both in.

Now, Alice was sitting in front of the television although it wasn't on. Bella was surprised to find her here. She was more often to be found in the garden at this time of day, especially when the sun was shining.

'Do you need a cuppa? Glass of wine?'

'I've had an email,' said Alice.

Bella waited for more detail but none came. 'And? It's not like you've never had one before, is it? Although if it's offering you a trillion US dollars if you send all your bank details, it's probably a scam.'

Alice laughed. 'No! It's a proper email. From a person.'

'So?'

'It's from a man.' Alice swallowed. 'The man I met on the train . . . '

'Which train? When? You've never told me about this!' Bella wasn't so much shocked as slightly taken aback. Why hadn't Alice mentioned it before?

'It was the other day. I didn't mention it because I suppose I felt a bit stupid.'

'Alice! It's OK to meet people on trains you know, even when you're ancient, like you.'

Alice laughed gently. 'Well, that's good because he's emailed me. He wants us to meet up.'

'But that's amazing and lovely! Maybe I'd better get a train somewhere . . . '

'But you've got Nevil!'

'I know I have. I was only joking. Tell me about this man!'

Alice said, 'Maybe I will have that cuppa. You?'

'I'll come with you. We can sit in the kitchen.'

Bella made tea, wondering about Alice's man and, as always, thinking that her kitchen was just about perfect. Bella got to see a lot of kitchens in her job, some of them very grand, but none of them came up to the standard of Alice's. Handmade units that didn't look as if they belonged in a showroom, a huge table for sitting or eating round, a dresser crowded with china and the sorts of ephemera that proper kitchens accumulated over the years, a Rayburn and a jolly good ordinary cooker. The view over the garden and a comfy sofa added to the abundant charm.

'So?' she said, having put a mug of tea and some biscuits in front of her godmother. 'Tell your Auntie Bella everything!'

'Well,' Alice began, obviously quite pleased to talk about it. 'He came and sat opposite me and hadn't had lunch. He'd left his wallet in his desk drawer and . . . I bought him a couple of sandwiches. He was terribly reluctant to accept them.'

'Was it because you're a woman?'

Alice shrugged. 'He didn't actually say that specifically, but he did say that the women he knew liked men to pay for things.'

'Old-fashioned,' said Bella.

'Possibly, but not that old. I think I might have flirted with a younger man. He wanted my address, but I knew you'd have told me off, so I eventually gave him one of those lovely cards you did for me for my birthday with my email address on it.'

'But they also have your postal address on them.'

'I somehow managed to overlook that.' Alice bit her lip. 'And he must have done too, or he'd have just sent a cheque.'

'Noo! He didn't send a cheque because he wanted to see you again. He must like you.'

'Well, I hope he does. I was very nice to him.'

'I don't mean 'like' in the same way you like the postman. I mean — well — fancy you.'

'Don't be silly, darling.' Alice had no difficulty in dismissing this suggestion. 'He was years younger — possibly only in his early fifties. Although I am very bad at guessing people's ages.'

'So why does he want to meet up then? When he could just send you a cheque? Or just forget about it?'

Alice frowned. 'Well, obviously he's barking. Maybe I'd better not meet him.'

Bella laughed. Her godmother never accepted that she was an attractive woman. Personally, she wasn't at all surprised this man wanted to meet her again.

'It's wonderfully *Brief Encounter!* Havc you made an arrangement? A where and when?'

'No. He wants me to suggest all that.'

Bella considered Alice. It was obvious from her added sparkle that she did not want to be talked out of this. 'Well, I think you should meet him. He sounds lovely! And when did you last go out with a man? Not since I've been living with you, that's for sure.'

'Not for years — at least, not one who's not an

old friend I've known for ever and wouldn't have if he was on toast and garnished with parsley. But I don't think I'd know how to behave!'

'Of course you will! You'll just have a drink, chat for a bit, go through and eat, chat some more. Really, it'll come perfectly easily to you.'

'I was joking, actually. It's just being with a man I don't know — it might feel a bit awkward.'

Bella became a bit more sympathetic. It had been a while since she'd been on a date as such herself. 'I'll keep texting, so you can tell me if you're unhappy and I can sweep in and rescue you.'

'Or I could just walk out and drive myself home?'

Bella nodded. 'There is that option, but mine is more exciting.'

Alice laughed. 'You're not shocked at the thought of someone as old as me having a date?'

'Of course not! I think it's fab!' But privately she was a bit surprised.

Reassured, Alice became more cheerful. 'So where should we meet? He's asking me to suggest a venue. He lives in Kemble.'

Bella considered. 'Lunch or dinner?'

'Dinner. He works in London.' Bella's pause made Alice worry. 'Maybe I should suggest coffee, at the weekend?'

'Dinner should be all right, but we must think of the right place.'

'Yes. Definitely nowhere remotely romantic. I don't want him to think it's a date,' said Alice.

'I think it is a date, actually, but I agree you

don't want anywhere romantic. He might turn out to be a munter when you see him again.'

Alice's expression became a bit dreamy. 'I don't think that's going to be a problem.' She paused. 'On the other hand, I expect the light in first-class carriages is very flattering and he'll get an awful shock when he sees me again.'

Bella began to giggle. 'I don't know much about first-class carriages but I shouldn't think they worry about flattering the older woman when they design the lighting.'

Alice glared. 'When you're sixty, you won't be making 'older woman' jokes, trust me.'

'OK, I believe you, but where would be the best place for you to go?'

After much discussion, Bella went on Twitter and asked for suggestions. Having considered these, they checked out websites and eating-out guides and eventually came up with a gastro pub.

'But it has rooms!' objected Alice. 'He might think — '

Bella wouldn't let her finish. 'He won't think anything of the kind! Now email him with the details. It's not too far; you can get a taxi if you want to drink. Or you can ring me and I can be with you in twenty minutes.'

Alice went to her study and turned on her laptop. Oddly, given the difference in their ages, she felt reassured by Bella's positive reaction. She was convinced it would be one dinner and then she'd never see Michael McKay again, but their meeting on the train and their subsequent conversation had been invigorating. She would enjoy the dinner too, she was sure.

4

A couple of evenings later, Bella walked across Jane Langley's expansive lawn, sent there by the notice on the gate: 'In the garden'. She felt a bit like the Boden poster girl, but she thought the print dress was probably appropriate for drinks with her friend — whom she must remember to call Jane — and her nephew. Pretty but respectable was the look she was going for. She had picked a bunch of flowers from Alice's garden and put them in a jam jar so Jane wouldn't have to find a vase. Even though Jane had a garden full of flowers Bella felt she couldn't arrive empty-handed and she knew Jane would appreciate them.

She could see them sitting where the rose grew up into the tree behind, on the chairs where she and Jane had often sat, drinking tea and eating cake. But as she got nearer, she realised Jane's nephew looked familiar. Two steps on and she recognised exactly who he was and wished, with all her heart, that she could stop, turn and run back across the lawn to her car. There, sitting in a lovely sunny garden she knew well, was the reason she had left her hometown and her first job.

'Darling! How pretty you look!' said Jane Langley as Bella approached.

Dominic Thane stood up.

Two steps later Bella was face-to-face with her past.

'Dominic says you two know each other,' said Jane Langley. 'What a coincidence!'

'Yes,' said Bella, trying to smile. 'Hello, Dominic.' Just for a moment, their eyes locked. He glared at her with such dislike it made her catch her breath. She'd worked hard to get away from him, physically and emotionally, and seeing him again, entirely unexpectedly, was a shock, especially given his reaction to her. She sat down without waiting to be asked. It was either that or fall over. She put the flowers down without even handing them over.

Dominic passed her a glass of champagne from the tray on the table. Jane was looking at her a bit oddly, she realised. Bella took the glass. 'Are we celebrating?'

'Dominic brought it. Isn't it kind?' Jane frowned. 'Are you all right, dear?'

'I'm fine!' said Bella, sounding to her own ears a bit strangled, hoping no one had noticed she had yet to make eye contact with Dominic since sitting down.

'Shall we have a toast?' he said. 'To the reuniting of family members and old friends.'

He raised his glass to his great-aunt and then looked across at Bella, but she didn't look back. If they'd been friends once, the look he had given her told her they were anything but friends now. But why? How on earth had that happened? She hadn't said goodbye to him when she'd left, but surely he wouldn't care about that? And certainly not three years on!

Bella's first sip of champagne at least made it possible for her to talk normally. 'So, er — Jane, when did you last see Dominic? You might have told me, but I've forgotten.' It wasn't the best opening topic of conversation, but it was the best she could do.

'He was a page boy at a family wedding when I last saw him,' said Jane. 'He looked enchanting. It was before he took after all the men in his family and his hair went white the moment he reached thirty. Then it was as dark as his eyes.'

'I prefer to call it silver, not white, Aunt Jane,' said Dominic and suddenly laughed.

A jolt went through Bella and she took another desperate sip. Her body was letting her down. It had just been a schoolgirl crush — nothing had happened between them! Not unless you counted a kiss under the mistletoe that might have — but probably hadn't — contained a hint of something more. Her brain told her it was just because the moment Dominic laughed, his rather severe features were transformed into something very attractive. His silver hair highlighted his dark eyes, framed with brows and lashes that were equally dark. It was only her body responding. Her brain was in charge; it would be OK.

No one spoke and Bella sipped her drink, trying to think of something to say, wishing someone else would.

'The garden's looking lovely, Jane,' she said at last, sounding like an actress who was ad-libbing rather unimaginatively.

'Thank you. Since the weather has obliged I've been able to get quite a lot done,' said Jane. 'Oh, and thank you for sending that lovely young man. He's set up a brilliant system so I can water my tomatoes without doing more than turn on a tap.'

Bella smiled. She'd thought the lovely young man was to be a secret, but obviously her old friend felt it was all right to mention him in front of Dominic. 'I'm glad it all worked out OK.'

'And he's quite happy to come and do some of the heavier things for me if I want him to. I have got Keith, who does the lawns, but he's not really a gardener. I can't trust him. But Aiden knows his stuff.'

'Oh good,' Bella said, deciding to leave the conversation instigation to the other two. If she went on she'd end up asking Jane what she thought of the latest goings on in the *Archers*.

'Would you like some more champagne?'

Bella looked up. Dominic's expression was as cold as his laughter had been warm a moment ago.

'Yes please,' she said quickly. She was not going to get through this without some sort of support, and alcohol would have to be it.

Much to her relief Dominic and Jane began talking about family members and Bella was left to her own thoughts.

Was it just coincidence that had brought Dominic into her relatively new and comfortable life? He couldn't have been following her, surely!

Or did he want to tell her off because she'd stopped Jane selling her house? If so, why wait until now? She had done that less than a year after she'd moved here. No, she was being paranoid, she decided. He didn't dislike her and he wasn't following her.

'So, are you here for long?' she asked when there was a break in the conversation.

'I'm joining a practice in the area. As a solicitor,' he added.

Bella's heart lurched. She hadn't forgotten he was a solicitor — they'd both worked for the same large estate agent, but here? Nevil's estate agency wasn't big enough to have a separate legal department; they used local solicitors, and that would mean she and Dominic could easily run into each other.

Still, if Nevil brought up his name she'd say something damning about him, and that would be the end of it. It would be far too embarrassing to have to work with him again.

'Oh?' she said. 'That's interesting.'

'It should be. I'm very excited, about it.'

He didn't sound terribly excited, but he always had been cool and unemotional.

'He was going to rent while he looked for somewhere to buy, but it seems silly to do that when my house is so big,' Jane explained. 'You live with your godmother and it works well, doesn't it?'

This was a nasty shock. She would have to time her visits to Jane more carefully. As Jane was looking at her appealingly, she quickly nodded. 'It works brilliantly, but I'm very well house-trained.'

'But you could find him a nice house, couldn't you?' Jane went on.

'I might be able to, but don't forget' — she laughed lightly, sounding slightly shrill — 'other estate agents are available.'

'I'm very well aware of that,' said Dominic and he frowned. His very dark brows, in stark contrast to his silver-grey hair, looked like clouds gathering before a storm.

What Bella longed to know was whether he'd be bringing his wife with him.

'What sort of house would you want?' asked Jane. 'A family home? Period features?'

Bella couldn't help smiling as she realised her long chats with Jane had rubbed off on her language.

'I'd like something to do up and, yes, period details would be good. I don't want a new-build.'

'How many bedrooms?' asked Bella, glad to be on firm ground again.

'It would really depend on the property.'

'More than two?' She couldn't help herself asking.

'Definitely.'

She still didn't know about his wife. Not that it would make any difference, not now.

'Well,' said Jane, who was beginning to relax, 'you can't expect Bella to find you a house if you don't tell her how many bedrooms you want.'

'I'm not particular. And I'm not in a hurry. If it's OK with you, Aunt Jane, I'm happy to keep staying with you.'

Bella didn't like this plan much. 'I think you should rent. If you're a cash buyer, you can go into a rental property, learn about the area, which parts you like best, and then you'll be in a good position to proceed if the right property comes up.'

Dominic raised one of his thundercloud eyebrows. 'That's me told!'

'No,' said Bella firmly, 'that's you advised. Of course no one is obliged to take advice if they don't want to.' She got up. 'Now, I'd better go. You've probably got a table booked.' She bent down and kissed her friend's cheek. 'Thank you so much, Jane. It was charming, even if there wasn't cake.'

She straightened up. 'Goodbye, Dominic. It was — interesting meeting you again.'

Then she walked across the lawn, her back stiff and her chin up, wishing her heels didn't keep sinking into the grass.

5

Alice was sitting in her kitchen, ostensibly doing the crossword, actually thinking about Michael and trying to stop feeling so giddy about the prospect of what was really a thank-you dinner. She looked up as she heard Bella's car pull up outside, glad to be interrupted. 'Hi love!' she called when she heard Bella's key.

Bella came into the kitchen looking wretched.

Alice was disturbed. 'Are you all right? What's the matter?' She couldn't think what could have happened to make Bella so sad in the course of drinks with an old lady. 'Mrs Langley hasn't died, has she?'

Bella shook her head, almost laughing at Alice's somewhat melodramatic suggestion. 'Nothing as bad as that, thank goodness, but not good.'

Bella looked as if she needed to talk. 'Big drink? Cup of tea?' Alice suggested.

'Tea, please.' She pulled out a chair and sat down.

'Did the nephew make a pass?' Alice asked after she had put the kettle on, trying to make Bella smile or at least stop looking quite so down. 'Put his hand on your knee while you admired the peonies? Bore you senseless?'

Bella managed half a smile. 'No.'

'Well, that's something. Does this emergency need chocolate? I've got some in the freezer.'

'It's OK.'

'So tell me what happened with the nephew.'

Bella sighed deeply.

Although she'd never said anything, Alice knew that when Bella had come to live with her three years ago, she hadn't given her every single detail of why. 'Yes?'

'It wasn't what he did, it was who he was.'

'And who was he?'

'Dominic Thane. The married man I left my hometown because of.'

Alice sat down quickly.

'And he obviously really dislikes me!'

'I know you told me a bit about it at the time, but run it all by me again. I think I must have forgotten a vital detail.'

Bella shook her head. 'I don't think you have. I was in love with Dominic — he was in our legal department — which was awful because he was married, but I did think I was keeping it together, trying not to be alone with him — much.' She looked up. 'I thought I'd get over it. It was only a crush, or so I thought, but then he announced his wife was pregnant and I knew I had to get right away.'

'Had anything ever happened between you? I'm just not sure your crush would have lasted if you hadn't had any encouragement.'

'Oh, I don't know . . . '

'Yes?' Alice prodded gently. Then she got up to find the brandy anyway. She needed one even if Bella didn't.

'Well, there was a kiss — under the mistletoe so quite respectable — at a Christmas party.'

'It would have been unusual if you'd had mistletoe at a summer barbeque,' said Alice.

Bella winced slightly. 'And it went a bit askew — you know it happens, you don't aim right, you shift a bit and suddenly it's on the mouth.' She looked up sheepishly. 'It went on a second or two longer than it should have done, and ever since I've wondered if it really was by mistake — on his part.'

Alice sipped her brandy. 'I don't think these things happen by mistake. Not really.' She paused. 'Was there anything else that gave you even a hint that he might have — liked — you?'

Bella thought for a long time. 'Well, we did work well together. And we shared a sense of humour. We got each other, you know?'

Alice nodded. 'I know.'

'Which is why I had to leave, really. I wasn't certain I could trust myself not to — you know — engineer meetings, make him coffee 'just because I was having one' and things like that. But I did leave, which was the right thing to do. And although I didn't say goodbye to him personally — I couldn't face it — we didn't have a row or anything. But this evening . . . ' She thought back to his hostile expression. 'It was if he was really angry with me, and I haven't a clue why.'

Alice handed her some brandy. 'It does seem very unfair.'

'It's a complete and utter mystery!' Bella sipped the brandy without seeming to notice. 'And now here he is! Just when everything is all going so well. I'm not going to leave again! Besides, I've got Nevil. He wouldn't want to leave everything he's built up here.'

'No reason why he should — or you should. You can avoid Dominic, can't you?'

'Of course! It shouldn't be a problem.' Her mind obviously elsewhere, Bella picked up the brandy bottle and added some more to her glass. 'I do wish I knew what kind of baby he had. You know — girl or boy — and if it was all OK.'

'You didn't find out from one of your old colleagues?'

Bella shook her head. 'I thought about asking, but I didn't want anyone to think that my leaving was anything to do with Dominic, or that I took that much of an interest. Maybe I was a bit paranoid.'

Alice shrugged. 'Unless you were friends with his wife, it might have looked a bit odd.'

'We'd met a couple of times at office parties — the boss was keen on us all getting together — but I wouldn't call her a friend.'

Alice nodded. 'So why are you so curious? If you're over him?'

'I am over him, definitely, but it's a part of the story I don't know and I think I need to.'

Alice realised that Bella wasn't over Dominic at all, but was making a very good effort at convincing herself she was. 'It should be easy enough to find out, surely.'

Bella shrugged. 'I don't know. He wouldn't tell Jane how many bedrooms he wanted in the house he's looking for.'

Bella looked so glum Alice couldn't help smiling. 'But she would know about the baby. Ask her!'

'That's a good idea. As long as I can ask without it looking weird.'

'Trust me, no one would think it odd if you asked if Dominic had children. It's a perfectly normal question for an estate agent to ask.'

'I'll ask then. I suppose I just feel so shaken, I've lost my sense of what's normal and what's not.'

Bella finished her brandy and got up. 'I feel loads better now, thank you, darling Alice.' She smiled. 'The next thing is your big date!'

Alice shuddered. 'I don't know if I'm looking forward to it or not!'

'Oh, Alice! Of course you are! It's a lovely romantic thing. If he just wanted to pay you back he'd have sent you a cheque. Or even the cash.'

Alice had heard all this from Bella before and she had to admit she was right. 'I know. And I suppose I am excited. It's just so out of my comfort zone.'

'Comfort zones are for getting out of,' said Bella.

Alice didn't reply for a few moments. 'Yes. Yes, they are. And I have been yearning for a bit more excitement recently.'

'Oh? Isn't living with me exciting enough for you?'

Alice gave Bella gentle push, glad to see she had cheered up enough to tease her. 'It's very exciting and I love it but I have lived in this house for a very long time. The garden is on its third incarnation. Maybe something else needs to change.'

Bella looked confused.

'It's all right,' Alice went on, 'I'm not going to dig up the lawn and put in a swimming pool. You get yourself something to eat and find something comforting on telly. You've had a difficult evening.'

Bella relaxed. 'I think I will, if you don't need me to help you decide what to wear or anything.'

'Not now! And I'm going up early so I can read in bed. I still haven't got through the book-group choice and I daren't confess to not having finished it again.'

Bella gave Alice's shoulders a squeeze. 'Thank you for being my therapist — and for the brandy. It really did help.'

* * *

Once in bed, Alice thought about her god-daughter, glad that Bella seemed so much better now. It must have been a shock, seeing the man she'd run away from in her friend's garden. But she was strong, she had a good life now, and was sensible enough to be able to focus on her future and not allow herself to be thrown off course by this.

Having put her mind to rest about Bella, Alice allowed it to return to its current default setting, which was thinking about Michael and their date. She had lied to Bella when she said she had wanted to read — although not about not having finished the book. Really she wanted to go through her wardrobe and think about Michael and their meeting.

Of course she wanted to see him, hugely, but

she hadn't been on anything remotely resembling a date for years. And when she cast her mind back to that occasion she realised she hadn't fancied the man at all. She'd been more interested in what the food would be like at the restaurant. This time it was different. The only thing that spoilt her pleasurable anticipation was the fact that Michael was younger than her. She'd never been attracted to a younger man before and she felt that sixty was rather late to start.

If any of her friends had expressed a similar anxiety she'd have reassured them instantly. Age was just a number and who cared who was born when, after all? But other people were different — it was fine for them. This was *her* thinking about going out with a younger man. She wondered briefly if 'fear of being a cougar' was a recognised phobia and, if it was, what the treatment was likely to be. Being shut in a room full of nearly naked teenagers probably. She shuddered even while she chuckled.

6

The following evening, Bella checked Alice's phone was fully charged and that she knew exactly where Alice was going. She had also made sure that Alice had cash and a credit card separate from her wallet in case it got stolen from her bag. Alice knew for a fact that had their situations been reversed, Bella would have found such over-concern an intrusion, but she accepted it meekly, mostly managing to conceal her amusement.

'If you want to drink just ring me and I'll pick you up. You probably won't enjoy yourself if you're counting alcohol units in your head,' Bella had said.

Before she drove off, Alice allowed Bella to check that she had looped the strap of her handbag round the gear lever, to stop an opportunist thief grabbing it at a red light.

'I am going for a quiet meal in one of the most crime-free areas of the country,' said Alice mildly.

'You need to get into practice. Your next hot date might be in London!' Bella retorted, winking.

Bella had already approved Alice's outfit and helped her with her make-up. Alice still thought fondly of the days when she called tweezers 'eyebrow-pluckers' because that's all she used them for. Now she had to check for stray hairs before she even started on her foundation.

They were both very pleased with the outcome. Alice had gone for a well-loved outfit that was pretty but didn't look like she'd tried too hard. A linen dress with a non-matching slubby linen cardigan seemed about right. She'd had her hair done the day before and Bella had painted her toenails. She was as ready as she was ever going to be.

Alice waved at Bella, standing on the doorstep, and drove away.

When she reached the pub she found there was one very smart car in the car park already. She really hoped it was Michael. If she'd been meeting a woman she wouldn't have minded arriving first at all. She would have just sat and read or caught up with messages and emails on her phone. But she felt that it would look rather desperate to be sitting there if she was meeting a man.

She put her shoulders back and walked into the pub with an air of confidence that was mostly fake. She didn't want to look anxious and he might be looking out of the window.

She saw him the moment she crossed the threshold. He leapt to his feet. He was smiling.

'Alice! You came! How lovely!' he said and kissed her cheek. He seemed extremely pleased to see her.

'Of course I came,' she said, instantly feeling better, her nerves replaced by excitement. 'We had an arrangement!'

'Well, yes, but you never know with people. You might have thought better of it.' He looked down into her eyes for a moment and she was very glad she hadn't backed out.

'I suppose so.' She smiled back.

'Shall we have a drink in the conservatory? Or would you like to go straight to the table?'

'Let's have a drink in the conservatory,' said Alice, thinking she might as well ring Bella for a lift after all.

'Champagne? Pimm's? Gin and tonic? They have a cocktail menu if you fancy something with an embarrassing name.' He paused. 'But I don't think it would be at all comfortable.'

Alice chuckled. She knew exactly what cocktail he was referring to and appreciated him not saying it out loud. She wasn't remotely prudish, but he didn't know that, and she liked the fact he hadn't wanted to risk offending her. 'A glass of champagne would be lovely. The trouble with Pimm's is it tastes so innocuous and then you find you can't stand up. Champagne always works for me.'

'I so agree.'

He ushered her ahead of him, not actually touching her but with a guiding hand hovering over her shoulder. It made Alice feel cared for.

'This is a nice spot,' he said. 'I had a recce earlier.'

A second later Alice was sitting on a very comfortable sofa looking over a perfectly cut lawn which fell away towards distant hills that seemed to undulate forever. 'What an amazing view!'

'It's wonderful, isn't it? I think those are the Black Mountains we can see.' He laughed. 'Of course we can't see a lot of industry and stuff in between, but it does give a lovely impression.'

The waitress appeared with some menus. 'Would you like drinks?'

'Oh yes,' said Michael. 'Champagne for my companion and I'll have ginger ale.'

'I know you do drink,' said Alice, when the waitress had gone, 'so why ginger ale?'

'I've always believed it's important to get your girlfriend drunk but to stay sober yourself.'

She couldn't help laughing. 'I'm not your girlfriend! We've only just met!'

'I know, but I'm planning ahead.'

He looked at her, his intensely blue eyes seemingly trying to absorb information about her. His attention went to her head in a way not even the strongest cocktail could have done.

'You're mad, but in a good way,' she said as soon as she could speak. She didn't tell him she was far too old to be a girlfriend in case for some reason he'd overlooked this fact.

'So, what have you been up to since I forgot my wallet?' he said.

'Nothing very exciting. I counselled my lovely god-daughter, who lives with me.'

'Lucky god-daughter!'

'Her name is Bella and I know she feels lucky. I have quite a big house so we can share without getting under each other's feet.' She realised that Bella would have told her she shouldn't have mentioned that her house was big, because then Michael might chase her for her money.

'That sounds nice. I live alone. I like that on the whole.' He made a face. 'I'm divorced. Two grown-up children. All fairly amicable.'

'I'm single, never been married, no children,' said Alice, feeling it was only fair to be equally frank.

'Any particular reason you never married?' The way he said it didn't seem nosy, just interested.

'It never felt right. One of the few men I fell in love with was married, so that wasn't to be. Another's career took him out of the country and I wasn't prepared to give up my own career to follow him. I was the sales director for a small company and it was a really interesting job I loved. The others didn't seem worth giving up my independence for.'

'I'm glad we're both single,' said Michael, as the drinks and the menus arrived. 'Even if it is just coincidence.'

'Yes,' Alice agreed slowly, 'but not exactly a spooky coincidence.' She was thinking of Bella, and how the man she ran away from turned out to be her friend's great-nephew. 'It's not like we share the same birthday or anything.'

'We might! When is your birthday?'

'The twenty-seventh of September.'

'Oh, well, mine's not then, but I'm sure we have lots of other things in common.'

* * *

By the time they had spun out the evening with extra cups of coffee in the conservatory, they discovered they did have a lot in common. Alice found Michael very easy company and she hadn't laughed so much in ages. She even let him pay for dinner without a fight.

Eventually she forced herself to look at her watch. It was nearly midnight. 'Oh my goodness! I should go!'

'Must you?'

'Yes! Apart from anything else the waiters want to clear up. I'll phone Bella.' She reflected for a moment. 'I didn't have all that much to drink but I don't want to take the chance.'

'On the other hand, I didn't have anything to drink. I can drive you home.'

It didn't take her many seconds to decide that this was absolutely fine. 'I'll just text Bella to tell her she can go to bed.'

'Goodness me! She waits up for you?'

By now Alice didn't feel obliged to pretend she had a hectic social life. 'Not usually but young people are very cautious, and frankly, in our case, the adult/child relationship is reversed. She said she'd pick me up.'

Alice got out her phone and saw several missed messages. She decided not to read them now and just sent a text. *Getting a lift home. Lovely evening. Don't wait up*. The chances of Bella not waiting up were slim, but she should find the message reassuring.

As they drove through the summer night Alice reflected that the joy of being escorted home by a charming, attractive man was as strong now as it ever had been.

'It is a lovely house,' he said, as he brought the car to a halt in the drive.

He'd got out and walked round to open her

door before she'd even located the door handle, which seemed very well concealed. As he handed her out she decided she wasn't ready for him to kiss her goodnight properly. He obviously felt the same, because although he gave a brief hug, he just kissed her cheek.

'It's been a really wonderful evening,' he said. 'I do hope you enjoyed it as much as I did.'

'I probably did,' she said, laughing gently. 'Thank you very, very much. It was lovely.'

'It was,' he said. 'Absolutely perfect.'

'Not many things are perfect, but that was.'

'I'll be in touch very soon,' he said. Then he kissed her cheek again.

* * *

'No need to ask if you had a good time!' said Bella as Alice came in and dropped her bag on a chair.

'I had a very nice time, thank you.' Alice tried to sound serious but she couldn't help giggling.

'Do you want to tell your Auntie Bella all about it? Over a nice cup of cocoa?'

'If you make me tea I'll give you edited highlights,' Alice agreed.

'So?' Bella asked a few minutes later. 'What was so special about him?'

'He made me laugh!' said Alice. 'And he seemed just as interested in me as I was in his life. That's rare, I find.'

Bella sipped her tea thoughtfully. 'Yes it is. Very rare.' She tried to remember when Nevil had shown an interest in her as a person, separate from him. Had he ever?

While Bella locked up and wiped crumbs from the worktop, she reflected that Alice seemed to be having more fun than she was at the moment. If only Dominic hadn't reappeared in her life, then she'd be happy jogging along with Nevil. But Dominic reminded her of the fireworks love could produce, and seeing Alice obviously enjoying sparklers, if not actual rockets, made her feel discontented and thoughtful.

She looked around at Alice's lovely kitchen — her eclectic collection of storage jars on the shelf above the Rayburn, the postcards and birthday cards pinned to a spare wall behind the fridge. It revealed her personality and Bella knew that if she and Nevil lived together it wouldn't be her favourite things that decorated the kitchen, it would be his.

She wondered then what Dominic would be like to live with, and realised with a start that she hadn't managed to erase her feelings for him quite as thoroughly as she'd thought.

7

Bella put the phone down and rubbed her ear. She was in the office and had just had a very long conversation with a woman who was wondering why she'd had no offers on her house although she'd had a good number of viewings, so Bella had arranged to go over and talk to her about how to make her house more sellable.

She was making notes on just how to do this when Nevil passed her desk.

'Can you pop into my office for a moment?' he said.

'Business or pleasure?' asked Bella with a twinkle.

'Oh, you know me — always business! And now, please, I've got a lot on.' But he gave her his charming smile, reminding her why she'd been so attracted to him in the first place.

Bella had managed to put the drinks with Jane Langley and Dominic Thane to one side. She couldn't help thinking about it, like a hand going to a sore place before you remember you shouldn't touch it, but she had rationalised it all and concluded that she had done nothing to make Dominic angry, and so she must just put it out of her mind and get on with her life.

Now she picked up a notebook in case it really was business and followed Nevil into his room.

Unusually for him in the office he drew her into his arms. 'So, how are you? We don't seem to have seen each other properly for ages!' he said.

'You've been so busy! We both have.'

'Then let's go on a date! I'll take you out to dinner somewhere nice.'

'I'd love that!' said Bella, remembering how much fun Alice had had with the man she'd met on the train. It had been like that when she and Nevil had first got together. Maybe it could be like that again. Maybe they'd go back to his house afterwards.

'We have lots of catching up to do.' He kissed her cheek.

'Is that all you wanted to see me about? Arranging a date? You could have phoned!'

'I wanted to do it in person.' He kissed her again and then ran his hands over her body, ending with a squeeze of her bottom. 'Hmm, definitely plumper than it was.'

Offended but not wanting to show it, Bella wriggled out of his grasp. 'So when would you like to go out?'

He caught hold of her hand. 'Tonight suit you? I'm very busy for the rest of the week.'

He looked at her earnestly for a moment and Bella said, 'Fine,' and smiled. Just then the phone rang.

'Oh!' said Nevil. 'I must take that.'

'OK,' said Bella.

Nevil picked up the phone. 'Hi there! Can you hang on a minute?' Then he held the receiver to his chest and made shooing gestures to Bella. Slightly hurt, she left the room.

Why was it that lately, just when she was

beginning to feel as if she might fall in love with him completely, Nevil did something that niggled her? She'd been quite busy herself and it was a bit annoying to be summoned to his office when really he just wanted to ask her out. He could have done that at lunchtime — or even sent her an email or text. And he'd been so secretive. He never usually minded her overhearing his telephone conversations.

She walked through the back of the office to the car park thinking. If she'd been completely in love with Nevil any opportunity for them to be together would have been welcome, however inconvenient. But was being in love a sensible condition for an adult in full command of their wits? Probably not. It certainly hadn't done her any good in the past. That 'in love' thing was really a crazy obsession that meant you couldn't do anything except think about the person you were fixated on. It was more like a horrible virus than an emotion. It didn't help you make good decisions either and she could only be grateful that her morals meant going after a married man was out of the question. Otherwise she might well have made the most almighty fool of herself. So she wasn't in love with Nevil in that crazy way, but was that a problem? She sighed. It was probably an advantage. What they had was based on sensible things like companionship and friendship. There was sexual chemistry too, just not an insane amount.

* * *

Mrs Macey's house had originally belonged to her father. She had lived there since she was a bride, over fifty years, she told Bella, and they had not been people to go in for decorating. Their last attempt at updating had been when large brown swirls were the *dernier cri du chic* and no ceiling was complete without Artex swirls to match those on the carpet. It made the already small house look even smaller and darker and altogether very unappealing to the first-time buyer.

In spite of Bella's most flattering and tactful efforts, Mrs Macey was not open to suggestions about how her chances of selling could be improved but she did accept that no one had made her an offer and wanted Bella to help.

'What I love about this house is the view!' said Bella as she walked up the path to the front door where Mrs Macey was standing, arms folded, waiting for her.

'Well, it's pretty enough, but people still won't buy my house.'

'I promise you, Mrs Macey, when you make a few very minor alterations, they will. People need to be guided in the right direction.'

'I thought that was your job. You're supposed to sell my house for me. You'll be getting enough from me when you do. You think you'd make more effort.'

Bella smiled. She liked a challenge, and Mrs Macey's house would have a lot going for it if only it wasn't in such bad decorative order. 'I'm going to make just a bit more effort and so are you, and between us we'll get you living with your daughter by Christmas!' It was rather an ambitious promise but she went with it anyway.

'Christmas! It's still only June! I want to be moved by Michaelmas!'

Bella realised that Mrs Macey had never been through the process of selling a house before and didn't have any idea of how long it could take. She smiled reassuringly. 'The end of September is rather optimistic and the whole legal thing takes a while, but if you work with me — and a couple of workmen I know — we might just do it.'

Mrs Macey shook her grey head. 'I'm not spending a fortune on work I'll never get the benefit from.'

'Ah, but you will get the benefit! Your house will sell. Now let's see what really needs to be done.' Bella decided that Mrs Macey probably preferred straight talking. 'Have you still got a cat?'

Mrs Macey frowned. 'My Tibby died last back end,' she said.

'But her memory lingers on! I think we need to get rid of all these carpets. They smell. People think the house is damp.' Without waiting for permission, Bella bent and lifted the corner of the carpet in the hallway. As she'd thought, under it were stone flags. And yes, they were damp.

'I'm not paying for a new carpet!' Mrs Macey was weakened but still fighting.

'You won't need to down here. People love these flags. We'll just get rid of all the carpets, give the floor a good wash and put down a couple of rugs. Rag rugs would be best,' Bella added, her fondness for interior design getting the better of her. With luck they could make the damp look as if it was because the flags had just been washed.

'I'm too old to go pulling up carpets. And then what would I do with them? I expect if I left them in the garden, to keep the weeds down, you'd say they made the place look untidy!'

Bella smiled again. 'You're absolutely right, I would say that. What I suggest is that I get my man in, let him do all the heavy work — take away the carpets, maybe give the place a lick of paint here and there, fix a few things — and you'll sell this house in a brace of shakes.'

'And how much would it all cost?' Mrs Macey was suspicious, especially of estate agents. Everyone knew they were a bad lot.

'Five hundred pounds, but you'd get that back from the price of the house.'

'How do you know? How can you be so sure? I don't want to be here another winter with no carpets, do I?'

'That won't happen,' said Bella, her mental fingers crossed. 'This house is an undiscovered gem.' She knew it was — she'd written the details herself.

'Lots of people have discovered it,' said Mrs Macey, 'they just haven't seen it as a gem.'

'They will if you go along with my suggestions.' Bella was genuinely convinced this was true. It was a really lovely cottage, tiny and with no damp-proof course or central heating, but in a lovely spot. It was a perfect love nest for a young couple starting out.

'You seem very sure of yourself, young lady, but supposing you're wrong? Supposing someone comes in here and says, 'No carpets, I won't buy it.'?'

Bella became firm. 'People are mean. If they don't like the carpets they'll try and beat you down, make you take less than the asking price. Trust me, less is more.' It certainly was when you were talking about swirly brown monstrosities that stank. 'If we work together to get this place shipshape, spend a bit of money on it, it'll sell — '

'In a brace of shakes. I know, you told me.'

Bella was in an in-for-a-penny-in-for-a-pound mood. 'And if you really want a quick sale, you'll let us get rid of the kitchen.'

Mrs Macey and Bella went into the kitchen together. Broken Formica units the shade of old mustard were topped by piles of saucepans and crockery. An electric cooker with only two plates stood next to a dresser loaded with china animals and a faded dinner service, just too new to be 'retro'. It was a mess. The best part for Bella was the deep window sill where two old clay pots full of scarlet geraniums stood above the Belfast sink but which was marred by rows of empty jam jars, many of which had dead spiders and flies in them.

When she'd had her clean-up, she'd take new photographs and just have the pots and the deep sill. It could look straight out of *Country Living* magazine.

'I know it's hard for you to imagine,' said

Bella. 'But if you let my man take out all these units, pull up the lino, clean the floor, and just leave your cooker, the sink and a table and chairs and the geraniums, it'll be snapped up. And I know you've got a table upstairs that would do perfectly.'

Mrs Macey muttered, but she hadn't shown Bella the door yet. Bella pressed on. 'If we just spent a bit of time and money — not very much of either — you'll have people fighting each other for it. You might even get more than the asking price!'

As Mrs Macey had been very impressed by the asking price as it was, not having kept up with the rocketing hikes in the market, this appealed to her. 'Well . . . '

'Would you like me to talk to your daughter? Maybe you could stay with her while the work is done?'

'It's not easy to get there. Her Pete'd have to come and collect me . . . '

'I'll drive you!' said Bella, knowing that Mrs Macey's daughter lived three-quarters of an hour away. 'And I'll make sure everything is all right here while you're gone.'

At last Mrs Macey was satisfied and the arrangements made. Bella felt a bit sorry for her son-in-law, who probably wasn't up for having his mother-in-law to stay before the annexe she was to live in was complete, but they'd all appreciate the extra Bella was sure the house could achieve if only a few basic things, including the lingering smell of cat, was dealt with.

Exhausted but content, when she got back to her car Bella pulled out her phone and called the man who would turn Mrs Macey's house from hovel into extremely desirable cottage full of original features. 'Jim,' she said when he answered. 'How is my absolutely favourite person in the entire world?'

Jim chuckled. 'I'm busy, Ms Flatterer, how are you?'

'Well, thank you. I've got another job for you. Are you really busy?'

'I am. Your blokey has got me doing all sorts, but I've always got time to fit you in.'

Bella frowned. No one was supposed to know that she and Nevil had a relationship outside the office but apparently they did. She decided to ignore the reference to it. 'It's not actually a big job. More getting rid of stuff than joinery.'

'That should be OK, then. So, how long have you and Nevil been an item, then?'

'Oh, well, not all that long. And we're not really an item — it's very early days.' This was a lie — they'd got together quite soon after she arrived, but she couldn't help feeling now that it had been some kind of rebound thing. And emotionally it didn't feel as if they'd gone beyond the initial attraction. 'Now, to get back to Mrs Macey's — it's a gorgeous little cottage, groaning with original features, hiding under a whole load of tat.'

She went on to detail what was required. Jim gave her a day when he could do the work and Bella made another call to Mrs Macey's daughter.

As she drove slowly along the lane from Mrs Macey's house, she thought about the area. Now it was a wooded valley, but once it had been the site of a brick works and the half-dozen houses that overlooked the valley had originally been built for the workers. Before the turn-off to the lane there was a small village green overlooked by a well-respected primary school. A short walk away there was a church and a pub. If only the little hamlet had a shop it would have been the perfect place to live, but shopping still required a car drive of twenty minutes to the nearest small town. But aesthetically it was delightful, and convincing buyers they wanted to live there wouldn't be difficult.

Satisfied the house would sell easily once it no longer stank of damp and cat pee, she drove back to the office, glad that she'd got to know Jim. Before she arrived at the estate agency Nevil used to get tenders from builders, which took ages, as most of the jobs were very small. But Bella came across Jim when he was doing work for Alice, made him her friend, and had given him all the work since.

She was annoyed that he knew about her and Nevil though, because Nevil had been so adamant that no one should. Bella didn't like having to keep secrets, and yet somehow she seemed to have a few of them herself.

She hadn't mentioned Dominic's reappearance in the area to Nevil, because she felt it wasn't absolutely necessary. In the same way, while she had told him she'd left her hometown because of a man, she hadn't given him any details. She was grateful now that Nevil hadn't pressed her for them, possibly sensing she didn't want to talk about it.

So, when they met up this evening, while she'd tell him that Mrs Macey had agreed to do a few things to fix up her house, she wouldn't add that she, Bella, was taking Mrs Macey to her daughter's while the work was done. Or that, if she possibly could, Bella would help Jim with the work, to make it cheaper for Mrs Macey and so she could 'play house' with this 'undiscovered gem'.

'Where is the property again?' he asked when she got back to the office.

Bella felt he should know this, but told him anyway.

'Ah . . . ' he said.

'Ah what?'

'Nothing! At least, nothing I can tell you about now.'

'Maybe this evening?' asked Bella. Nevil might be too busy to tell her everything this minute, but they were having dinner together later. Plenty of time to talk then.

8

'I don't understand why he can't pick you up,' said Alice, as Bella got into her car that evening. 'Why should you both have to stay sober?'

'We're not eating that locally, is why. Nevil wants to try this place over beyond Gloucester. And it's good for me to stay sober. I don't mind. Have a nice evening!'

As Bella drove away she realised she didn't know what Alice's plans were. She didn't have her gardening clothes on, so maybe she was going out? She felt now that she should have asked, but she'd been preoccupied by what Nevil might want to talk to her about.

The restaurant was right on the river and specialised in fish. It was reached via a very long muddy lane — such a long lane, Bella discovered when she got out of the car, that it wasn't on mains drainage. Had it not been for her job, she might not have recognised the slightly sweet smell as being 'eau de septic tank', but it registered instantly. There were downsides to knowing things, she realised as she burrowed for her smarter shoes in the passenger well and put them on. Then she went into the restaurant.

She found Nevil in the bar with his briefcase open, examining some papers. He put the papers in the case as she approached, got up and kissed her cheek. 'You look nice. Have you eaten here before? The fish is excellent.'

Bella kissed him back. She didn't much like fish, and as they'd started going out soon after she'd arrived, she thought he might have known it was unlikely she'd been to this restaurant before. 'Hello, Nevil,' she said.

'Shall we go straight through to the table? I don't want to be late as I've got some things to do afterwards.'

'Not just a quick drink first? The view from here is so lovely.' She wasn't sure it was lovely but it was certainly dramatic. The Severn seemed as wide as the sea and the light on the water gave it an unearthly look.

'The view from the dining room is pretty much the same. We've got a window table. Thank you!' he said to the waitress. 'We'll go through now if the table is ready.'

'Fine,' said the young woman. 'If you'd like to follow me.'

When they were settled at their table, and Bella had confirmed that the view wasn't quite as good as from the bar, the waitress said, 'Would you like something to drink?'

'Yes,' said Nevil, 'I'll have a glass of wine. Do you want one, Bells? Or would you rather have something soft? Elderflower? Cranberry?'

'I'd like a glass of white wine and a glass of sparkling water, in two separate glasses, please,' she said to the waitress.

'Oh, fine,' said Nevil, a bit surprised. 'Can we get some menus?'

When their drinks and menus arrived, Bella had a large sip of her wine. She savoured it and then topped up her glass with sparkling water. As

Nevil hadn't bothered with a toast she didn't feel obliged to. He also kept the waitress so she could take their order.

'Bells? What are you going to have?'

Bella would have liked a bit longer to look, but just went for the non-fish options. 'I'll have the chicken liver pâté, then the steak, medium rare, new potatoes and salad,' she said briskly.

'Oh, don't have the pâté, it's terribly fattening,' said Nevil.

Bella gave him a questioning look and said smoothly, 'That's all right. I'm not on a diet.'

'But, darling, you want to look good in your wedding dress. She'll have the smoked salmon.'

Bella wondered if she was going to faint for a moment. 'I'll have the pâté,' she said firmly, wishing she hadn't added water to her wine already.

Nevil shrugged. 'You'll regret it later!' Then he went on to give his own order. 'You look a bit taken aback, sweetie,' he said when the waitress had gone away. 'I suppose I should have told you in a different way but we know each other too well to have to worry about the niceties, don't we?'

Bella felt you could know someone a lifetime and you'd still need to have this spelt out. Had he just proposed marriage? She had no idea how to answer him. 'Um . . . '

'It makes sense, doesn't it?' Nevil continued. 'We were going to move in together anyway, my parents loved you that weekend when I took you down. If we got married — say next year — we'd have time to get established before your biological clock starts ticking and we have a child.'

Bella sipped her drink, partly to give herself time to think what to say, and partly because her mouth had gone dry with shock.

'You're all right about this, aren't you?' said Nevil. 'I know I kind of assumed . . . '

'It is a bit of a surprise.' And she couldn't decide if it was a good surprise or a bad one.

'Oh.' Nevil seemed crestfallen. 'Sorry, I just thought . . . ' He paused. 'Maybe I didn't think!'

Bella felt a rush of compassion. She put her hand on his. 'Now I know what you have in mind, I'll consider it.' She gave him her fondest smile, not sure if she meant it or not.

'We've got lots of time to think about it. The venue I have in mind is booked up until this time next year anyway.'

'This is a lot to take in.'

'Of course. You'll have to tell your parents, and break it to Alice — although you say she'll be all right?'

'It's not just those things . . . '

'But we have plenty of time.' He grinned and she smiled again, still totally at a loss.

At that moment, to Bella's relief, their starters arrived, which absolved her of having to say anything for a few minutes. Nevil seemed unaware of just how much of a bombshell he had dropped.

The moment the food was in front of them, Nevil started shovelling up his whitebait. 'This is jolly good!'

Bella nodded and spread some pâté on a bit of toast.

'Toast?' he said. 'Carbs? Still, I'll let you off this once. Plenty of time to get you into shape after all.' Another batch of tiny fish went into his mouth. 'I think we'll agree we don't want you looking like a meringue. Just something very simple and stylish.'

Bella couldn't believe he was talking about her wedding dress, when she hadn't actually agreed to marry him. Teasing, she said, 'Actually, I think I'd like a crinoline, with lots of beading, like on that programme about gypsy weddings?'

He was so stunned that she got another generously laden bit of toast into her mouth before he realised she was joking. 'You are a one, Bells! Now, tell me, how did you get on with Mrs Macey?'

So relieved to get off the subject of her notional wedding dress, Bella was enthusiastic. 'Oh, brilliant! She's going to stay with her daughter while the work's going on. We're going to rip out the kitchen and the carpets. I might ask Jim if he could skim the Artex although he may not need to do that. And then I think a very simple look for the kitchen.'

'You're going to leave it with no kitchen?' Nevil frowned. 'Kitchens sell houses, you know that.'

'I do know that,' said Bella. 'But they don't have to be fitted, do they? Mrs Macey's is crying out for something really basic but lovely. Just the cooker that's in there, the Belfast sink, a table and chairs and her old dresser. With the geraniums on the window sill it'll look like something out of the Flopsy Bunnies. You know?

Those lovely Beatrix Potter pictures?'

Nevil shook his head and scooped up the rest of his fish. 'Honestly, Bells, I know you're brilliant at your job, it's one of the reasons I want you to be my wife — we make a good team — but I do think you're a little bit barking.'

Bella put down her toast, her appetite suddenly gone. She wasn't sure if she wanted to marry Nevil, but what was the alternative? If she turned him down she might have to leave and start a new life all over again. Did she really want to do that? Couldn't she live in peace a little bit longer?

At least she didn't have to make any decisions immediately. Nevil just assumed she'd go along with it. She could do that, for a bit, anyway.

* * *

As Bella drove back down the muddy lane a few hours later, away from the river and towards the main road, she realised that because of Nevil's announcement that they were getting married, she had completely forgotten to ask him about all this work he was getting Jim to do, and his mysterious phone call that she couldn't listen to. He usually asked her to get Jim in for things, as he reckoned Jim gave her a better price, and he didn't often keep a dog and bark himself, as he so flatteringly put it. So what was it he wanted him to do?

And unless it had been a personal call — what sort of personal call would be private to her? — it was a business one, so why wouldn't he want her to overhear that? It was all a bit of a mystery.

In fact, Bella thought, as she turned onto the main road, the whole evening had been very unsettling indeed.

9

The following morning Alice was standing by the kettle looking oddly guilty when Bella came into the kitchen.

'You're up early!' she said.

Bella yawned. 'I finally gave up trying to go back to sleep. Then I heard you.'

Alice smiled and got out mugs. 'So what kept you awake?'

Bella rubbed her hair vigorously trying to get her brain to work. 'The fact that Nevil and I are apparently getting married.'

'Good God!' said Alice, spinning round. 'Did he propose, then?'

'Not really.' Bella sighed deeply. 'He just sort of announced it.' She sat down at the table. Talking to Alice about it would help sort out her thoughts. 'He implied he was giving me plenty of time to get off those extra pounds.'

'What extra pounds?'

'I'm not sure. But he thinks I've plumped up a bit.'

'Well, he's wrong. For God's sake! You're not going to marry a man who says you're fat when you're not, are you?'

'No! I mean, no . . . ' Bella laughed at her own vehemence. 'He was probably only joking. I'm sure he doesn't really think I'm fat.'

Alice pursed her lips. Bella knew she was deliberately not expressing her opinion. Alice had never said she didn't like Nevil much but Bella knew it perfectly well.

'I know you'll think I'm a wuss but I need to think about this.'

'Because?'

'Because I love my life here. If I turn Nevil down, I'd have to leave the agency.'

'There are other estate agencies.'

'Yes, but I do get away with things with Nevil — I mean workwise. He knows I sometimes do little makeovers to help sell houses, and although he tells me off, he lets me do it. I need time to make a plan really. I don't want to start all over again, like I did before, unless I absolutely have to.' She realised she sounded pathetic, as if she was asking Alice's permission to stay with Nevil, but what she said was true.

'So does he think you are going to marry him?'

Bella nodded. 'I said I needed time but, quite honestly, I'm sure he just thinks I'm being coy about it. But as he didn't really ask, I don't have to say yes or no.' And I could do worse, she added silently, knowing Alice wouldn't approve of compromise.

'Thinking about things is almost always a good idea.'

'That's what I felt,' said Bella, but she did feel a bit guilty. She should have told Nevil it was too soon for her but hadn't — for her own convenience. 'And what were you up to last night? I forgot to ask,' she said, changing the subject.

'Book group,' said Alice promptly.

'Oh. Did you like the book?'

Alice shook her head. 'Not awfully. Everyone else liked it but I thought it was rather dull and couldn't wait to get home. And then everyone started banging on about the 'five point two diet' or whatever it is. Apparently it's the cure for everything.'

Bella frowned slightly. There was undoubtedly something odd about Alice.

'Oh!' said Alice. 'I forgot to say. There was a phone call for you. Jane Langley.'

Bella was suddenly worried. 'Is she all right?'

'Oh yes, she sounded fine, but she said would you call round when you've got a moment.'

Bella retrieved her phone from where it was recharging on the dresser, and then went to her diary to check that day's appointments. 'I've got quite a lot on today. But I've got a couple of viewings tomorrow that aren't too far from her; I could call in afterwards. I'll ring her.' She frowned. 'You don't think Dominic will be there, do you? During the day? He'll be doing his lawyer thing in the office, surely.'

'Oh yes. Lawyers never bunk off early from the office,' Alice agreed.

'You're an expert on lawyers?'

Alice nodded. 'One of my many skills.'

* * *

After Bella had gone to work, Alice went back up to her study and checked her emails — again. She hadn't admitted to Bella that the reason she'd been so keen to get home from book group was so she could see if Michael had replied to her last email. And although it was quite unreasonable — she'd only sent it just before she left — she couldn't help feeling disappointed that he hadn't.

Part of her was loving her growing friendship with Michael. It was such fun to check her emails to see if there was one from him and, if there was, to analyse it for signs that he 'liked' her, as Bella would have said. But she was also torn between wanting to keep Michael secret and wanting to talk about him all the time. The previous night at her book group, when everyone was talking about diets, she had been terribly tempted to announce she had a relationship with a younger man. If she wasn't careful she'd be spotted walking along the street with her mobile phone pressed to her ear.

The sensible part of her told her she was being ridiculous and at her age she should know better. But Michael's emails appeared flatteringly often, and although she forced herself not to reply to them instantly and always kept her tone light, she did find she was thinking about him more and more.

While there had been no email last night, there was one this morning, which, she worked out, meant he must have logged on at midnight, after he'd got home from his business dinner.

She wasn't going to reply now. In fact, she was going to get into the garden and clear the end bed for some annuals before the promised rain set in. Then she might reply. It was a shame she'd rather gone off gardening recently.

* * *

Bella was on her way to the second viewing, under a darkening sky when she realised she didn't have the name of the client. She stopped in a lay-by and rang Tina, who ran the office.

'Hi, Teens. I don't seem to have a name of the client for the little three-bed up near the common. Can you help?'

'I'll have a look,' said Tina.

While she was looking, Bella watched the first spots of rain land on her windscreen. She felt sad for the house she was about to show. It was always hard to talk up a property when it was tipping it down outside.

Tina came back. 'Sorry, love, I can't seem to find it. I didn't make the appointment and I can't find out who did. I know Nevil was scheduled to do it . . . '

'Yes, he had to do something and asked if I'd go instead. He's not there, is he?'

'No. He's probably doing the thing that meant he couldn't do the viewing.'

Bella laughed. 'It's OK, I'll manage. I just don't want to look unprofessional.'

'You won't look that, Bella, trust me,' said Tina.

* * *

At least there was no one waiting for her, Bella thought, as she parked her car outside the house and then found the keys. The owners were out and she could nip in and familiarise herself with the property before the client arrived. She decided to start upstairs.

It wasn't very inspiring, she decided. Three fairly reasonably sized bedrooms and a family bathroom upstairs; possibly room for an en-suite in the master. There seemed to be access to a loft, but there was no time for her to see if it was boarded out or not.

Downstairs, the kitchen was definitely in need of a refurb — but that wasn't necessarily a bad thing. Prospective purchasers quite often wanted to put in their own kitchen and not, as someone once put it, pay for someone else's bling. There was just about room for a table and a door revealed a separate larder. That was a big tick.

But the sitting room had railway-carriage proportions and looked out on to a gloomy patio, and the dining room was so full of clutter it was hard to see if it was nice or not.

She had just spotted a useful downstairs cloakroom when the doorbell rang. She went to let her client in.

Bella stepped back, confused. Dominic stood on the doorstep shaking an umbrella.

'Oh!' she said. 'I was expecting someone else.'

'Who?' he asked, a dark eyebrow reaching towards his silver hair.

Bella sighed. 'I don't know. Er — come in. Let me show you round. We won't be able to see the garden, I'm afraid. The weather's getting worse.' She'd dealt with some difficult clients in her time, but they would seem easy compared to having to show Dominic round a house.

He put his umbrella in the corner of the

porch. 'We can look at it through the windows.'

'If we can see through the driving rain,' said Bella, trying to smile. She knew he was in the area, she knew he was looking for a house: she shouldn't have been surprised, really. 'Come through to the sitting room. It's not a bad size.'

'Hmm,' said Dominic, making his opinion quite clear.

'It has got rather a lot of furniture in it,' said Bella. 'If it didn't have these massive sofas — '

'It would still be very narrow.'

Bella opened a door. 'This is the dining room.' She rapped on the wall. 'You could possibly knock through?'

'Hmm,' said Dominic again.

Bella wanted to do a professional job for her own sake as much as Dominic's, but the house wasn't helping. 'I'm sorry you've got me instead of the boss.'

'It's all right. He promised me I'd be in very good hands when he told me.'

This was unusual. Why did Nevil bother to tell Dominic he couldn't do the viewing?

'He also referred to you as his fiancée.'

This was a shock. 'Agh! Did he?'

'You sound surprised.'

'It's not official,' Bella explained hurriedly, trying to gloss over her rather extreme reaction. 'We're not telling people yet, really.' So far, she'd only told Alice.

'And you're not wearing a ring.'

Bella looked at her left hand as if to check. 'No. Shall we see upstairs now?' She desperately wanted to get this viewing over with. The house was vile and being with Dominic made it difficult to breathe.

She stood in the doorway of the bedrooms while Dominic inspected them. 'Three doubles,' she announced.

'Only an estate agent would describe this room as a double.'

'You can get a double bed in there, with room to get in on both sides, and there's space for a small wardrobe,' she said irritably, forgetting Dominic was the client.

'So, do your parents like Nevil?'

Bella was instantly sent back to a summer day when the agency where she and Dominic had worked together organised a fun day in aid of charity. Her father and Dominic had ended up playing on the same cricket team and she and her mother had sat together watching. Her mother had turned, indicating Dominic, who was bowling. Bella had just said, 'Married.' Her mother had sighed. And while they had never said as much, she knew they didn't much care for Nevil. 'What's not to like?' she said flippantly.

They made their way downstairs. 'There is a little cloakroom, useful for storing buggies and things. Which kind of baby did you have? Girl or boy?'

'A little boy.'

'So is Celine going to come up and house-hunt too? Or will she leave it to you to find the right place?'

'We're not married any more.'

This was the last thing that Bella had expected. 'My goodness!'

'I would have thought you knew that.' He sounded sceptical. 'You and Celine were close at one stage, weren't you?'

Bella frowned. 'Not really. Obviously we've met but — '

'Oh, don't be disingenuous, Bella. It doesn't wash.' He sounded angry.

'I'm not. Celine and I only ever saw each other at company dos and I certainly didn't know you'd got divorced. Should I congratulate you or commiserate?'

He shrugged. 'Whichever.' He paused. 'Are you sure you haven't seen Celine since you left Owen and Owen?'

'Of course! Why on earth are you asking me?'

He shook his head. 'It doesn't matter. Now.'

As any pretence of behaving as estate agent and client had long gone, Bella said, 'Do you get to see your little boy much? It must be hard . . . '

'It is hard. But considering the circumstances, I get to see him quite often.'

'Good. Now do you want to brave the garden?'

'No thank you. I'm not going to buy this house.'

'So what precisely are you looking for?'

He shrugged again. 'This is the right area and about the right size. It's just the wrong house.'

'If you gave me just a bit more idea?' She realised she'd forgotten what he'd said, distracted from her usual professionalism. 'Do you want a new-build, period, lots of garden for your son to run around in or — ' She stopped. An expression of something almost like pain had crossed Dominic's face. 'Are you all right?'

'He's not my son.'

Bella was stunned. She didn't know what to say. How did you react to news like that? 'I — er — '

'It's complicated. I only found out when he was about a year old — when Celine asked for a divorce. Dylan and I had bonded. I loved him. Still do. But I'm not his father.'

'That's awful!' Bella whispered.

'Which is why, although I only have him one weekend a month, I consider myself lucky. Celine is married to his biological father now.'

'I don't know what to say.'

Dominic bit his lips, as if suppressing some reaction. 'I'd be grateful if you didn't say anything about it to anyone. It doesn't matter while I'm up here. He can be my son, which is how I think — thought of him.'

'If you don't mind me asking, why does Celine let you see him if you're not . . . related?'

He gave a mirthless laugh. 'I'd like to say it's because she's generous and good-hearted, but actually it's so she and her husband can have 'quality time' together.'

'I see.' As he didn't speak, she said, 'Shall we go? If there's nothing else you want to look at.'

He shook his head. 'Thank you for showing me round. Maybe if you check the details I gave your fiancé you might have an idea of what I'm looking for,' he said curtly. 'Goodbye!' he added and walked out of the front door and down the path.

It was only after she'd watched him drive away

that she noticed he'd left his umbrella in the porch. She picked it up, the front part of her brain thinking this was why she rarely carried one. Having curly hair she didn't mind if it got wet. But deeper in her consciousness, she was in turmoil.

10

Bella parked in the staff car park, grateful, not for the first time, that there was one, and dashed into the office. As Nevil's door was open and she could see him standing by the window and that he was alone, she went in.

Nevil came up to her and pushed his fingers through her damp curls. 'Hello, Curly.'

Bella's smile was so brief if you'd blinked you'd have missed it. 'What were you up to that you couldn't do that viewing in Little Hollow?'

'You didn't mind, did you, sweetie? It's just you're our very best girl, and Dominic Thane is a solicitor, new to the area, very useful contact.'

'Well, it was OK,' Bella said, 'but why on earth did you think he'd want that horrid little house?' She chose not to mention that she knew Dominic. Not yet anyway.

'Perfect location, perfect size — '

'Which is pretty much what he said, adding, 'Wrong house', which I thought was quite polite of him, considering.'

Nevil frowned. 'Considering what? That's a fairly normal response to a house that isn't quite right, I'd have thought. Bella, you didn't do anything to upset him, did you?'

'Of course not!' Bella was indignant. 'You know I'm always totally professional, otherwise why did you send me and not go yourself?'

'I was busy and you're always so good with

clients,' said Nevil calmly. 'No need to get all antsy about it. We'll find him something. There's that charming one by the river that was 'too flat' for your favourite clients.'

'I'm also sure we've got something on the books that would suit him but I want to know why you sent him to a complete no-hoper!'

Nevil's expression hardened. 'Bella, I shouldn't have to remind you that I am the head of this organisation and sometimes my duties include a bit more than matching houses to picky clients!'

Bella opened her mouth to respond, rewrote her spontaneous outburst in her head and then said, 'OK. I just wish you'd tell me what it is that's keeping you so busy these days.' She tried a conciliatory smile but retracted it. 'Conciliatory' wasn't going to work for her today.

'I can't tell you. As soon as I can, you'll be the first to know. Now, is there anything else? I have a lot to do.'

Bella shook her head. 'I'll leave you to it.' She got up.

'I'm sorry, Bells. Things are a bit tricky at the moment but I'll make it up to you as soon as possible. We can start planning the wedding!'

Bella responded to his smile and then left, wondering why he thought planning a wedding was the zenith of any woman's dreams, and then wondering why it wasn't the zenith of hers.

Back in the main office she went over to Tina Stanford's desk. She was the only one there at the moment, as the other two agents were out. Tina, who ran the organisation really, was a constant. A working mum, she kept her family and the office under firm control, and had a fondness for bright accessories. Today she was wearing a necklace that consisted of glass birds and fruit and flowers in jewel colours.

'Want a hot drink, Tina?'

'I think *you* want one! You check these property details for me while I get you one. I think you need hot chocolate.'

'What would we do without you, Tina?' Bella said gratefully.

'Photocopying, scanning and putting on the kettle,' said Tina dryly.

* * *

It was still raining when Bella drove home a bit later. And she still didn't know if she'd deliberately not told Nevil that she and Dominic knew each other, or if the opportunity just hadn't come up. And should she come clean now? But she knew she was kidding herself. Nothing would have been more natural than to say at some point, 'And by the way, we used to work together.'

It was only while she was under the shower later that she realised it was likely, considering Nevil had told Dominic they were engaged, that Dominic hadn't mentioned knowing her either.

But even if she wanted to, could she mention it now, without it looking as if she had deliberately not told him earlier? And if she did, it would involve no end of forensic investigation into how and where and how well they knew each other. Nevil did have a jealous side to him.

As she dried herself she decided her instinct not to tell him was for the best. What Nevil didn't know wouldn't worry him.

* * *

The sunshine the following day matched Bella's improved spirits. She had decided to stop worrying about Dominic and just get on with her life. The fact that her life was complicated was fine — everybody's life was, after all.

But in spite of a good day at work, which included her finally selling a house that had been on their books for months and months because it was so noisy (there were advantages to people being hard of hearing, she discovered), Bella was aware of being quite anxious at the prospect of meeting Dominic when she arrived at Jane Langley's.

As only Jane's ancient Corsa was in the drive, and the usual note about her being in the garden was on the door, she felt enormous relief. Bella kept meaning to mention that announcing to the world that she was out of the house and the door might well be unlocked was probably not a good idea, but now Dominic was living with Jane, at least during the week, that was his responsibility, not hers.

'Jane!' said Bella when she found her. 'How lovely to see you. How are you?' Bella hadn't called round since the awkward drinks, and so much had happened since, it seemed a long time ago.

Jane looked round from where she was tying a

delphinium to a stake, her shirtwaister dress blending in well with the blue of the flower. She tucked a wisp of hair back into her chignon and smiled.

'I'm very well, thank you! And do you know? I find I quite enjoy having someone else in the house.'

'Well, that's good!' said Bella, laughing.

'I was rather dreading it, but Dominic is very good — he's not in a lot and when he is, he cooks for me as often as I cook for him.'

'So I should hope!' Bella found she was not exactly pleased that Dominic had got on to such good terms with his great-aunt so soon.

'Let's go into the house. Needless to say, I made a cake.'

'So,' said Bella a little later, having sampled the cake, 'what can I do for you?'

Jane laughed. 'I missed your company, of course, but I really wanted to know if you could recommend a good builder. Dominic said he found some patches of damp when he went up to the top floor. We'd like to have it looked at.'

'Sure! I know some lovely firms. If you are going to have work done you'll need to get a couple of estimates at least.'

'Dominic said he'd sort all that out, if you can just give us some names of reliable people.'

Bella got out a pen and some paper and began writing things down.

'So how have you been, dear?' said Jane when Bella had handed her the names. 'Anything exciting to tell me?' She had an expectant look, and Bella realised that Dominic must have said something about her so-called engagement.

'Well, now you come to mention it . . . '

'Yes? Should I buy a hat?'

Bella relaxed and laughed. 'Not yet, that's for sure.'

'So you are engaged, but not officially, that's what Dominic said.'

'Dominic's right, but I wish he'd let me tell you myself.' She sighed.

'To be fair, he assumed I knew.'

'Well, it's very recent — in fact I'm not sure I am, really.' Jane looked at her quizzically. 'Nevil more or less announced that we were going to get married. He didn't actually ask me in so many words. I haven't said yes or no. But because I haven't said no, I suppose I've agreed to it.'

Jane frowned. 'You don't look every enthusiastic, my dear. Surely most young women are excited at the prospect of getting married.'

Bella shrugged. 'It's put me into a bit of a whirl.'

Jane nodded, obligingly not asking more questions, possibly picking up that this was not a cheerful topic of conversation for Bella. 'Did you know? I'm going to be eighty-five next week.'

'Really?' Bella was genuinely surprised. 'I suppose it's all the gardening that keeps you so fit, but I'd have put you in your early seventies.'

Jane had a timeless quality to her; she still wore the cotton dresses she would have adopted in her fifties and she had probably also had her chignon, white now, for a long time.

Jane smiled. 'Well, thank you, but I do have to

think about my position here, I think.'

'Dominic's been getting to you!' said Bella instantly.

'Really, he hasn't. But it is a big house and I can't manage the entire garden myself. I've let a large section go to grass. It would be better if this house had someone living in it who wanted a lot of garden — more garden than I can cope with.'

A thought came to Bella, but it would take so much tactful arranging that she mentally filed it under 'good ideas but just too difficult'. 'Well, don't move until you absolutely have to. And you could always get help with the garden.'

Jane nodded. 'I will when I find someone I can trust to do what I would have done myself. Aiden — your friend — is very good, but he's more of a weeder than a planter.'

Bella nodded, resolving to ask around to see if the right person could be found. 'So what are you going to do on your birthday?'

'The family are taking me to a hotel for lunch,' she said.

Bella regarded her friend thoughtfully. 'You don't look wildly enthusiastic about the prospect?'

Jane shook her head. 'They're all rather stuffy, my family. Some of them even call me 'Cousin Jane'. And I suspect them of wanting me to move so they can get my money before I actually die. Dominic can't come.'

'We are hopeless, aren't we? I'm not excited about my wedding and you're not looking forward to your birthday. Tell you what, if you're not sick of lunch after that, why don't you come

to me and Alice on Sunday? Alice is brillian
Sunday lunch and I know she'd love to m
you. Hotels are lovely but home is the best place for a roast, I always think. They can't seem to get the roast potatoes right in restaurants.'

Jane laughed. 'I agree with you there, but although that sounds very nice I think you should ask your godmother first! You can't invite strange people to lunch without asking her.'

Bella produced her phone. 'I'll text her. But I know she'd be delighted.' Bella was fairly sure about this. Alice liked doing Sunday lunch, but when it was just the two of them they didn't bother often. It would be lovely to have Jane over and spoil her a little. They could relax and focus on good food, and eat it companionably at the big kitchen table. Then, if the weather co-operated, they'd have tea in the garden.

Taking Alice's assent for granted, Bella looked up at Jane. 'I'll pick you up at about twelve thirty?'

'But you will ring and tell me if Alice even hints that it would all be too much, won't you? I'd hate to put her out.'

'Honestly, it won't be any trouble and I know she'd love to have you. I'll help her and clear up afterwards.' She smiled. 'You're worth washing up a few greasy pans for.'

Jane chuckled, satisfied at last.

11

Alice was pleased when she got Bella's text. Cooking a nice roast for a nice old lady was just the distraction she needed. It was a much more suitable occupation for her than obsessing over her phone and her email. But the fact that the text was from Bella and not Michael had caused a few moments' disappointment. Then again they hadn't really got into texting yet. They both preferred emails, which were longer and gave one more scope.

'Just as well I cleared that end bed then,' she said when Bella got home. 'I wouldn't like to have Jane Langley, famous gardener, to lunch with my own garden looking neglected.' She was aware that her garden was in fact a bit neglected. She used to spend hours in it but not lately. It just wasn't the focus of her life any more.

'You don't mind? Thank you so much,' said Bella, giving Alice a hug. 'I'll go to the organic butcher and get a nice piece of — what do you think?'

'Why don't you see what he's got? A leg of salt marsh lamb would be nice. I can still do Yorkshire puddings.' She smiled. 'I don't suppose you fancy coming to the garden centre with me? Or are you working this Saturday? It would be easier for me to decide what to put in that flowerbed if there are two of us.'

'No, I'm free. I'd love to come with you. And

I'll help you put the plants in. It's so kind of you to agree to have Jane.' She frowned suddenly. 'Do you think I should invite Nevil?'

'No,' said Alice, not pausing to think about it. 'Let's just have a girly lunch. Nevil doesn't care about gardens.'

'Fair enough. I'll tell him about it, and then he won't want to come.'

⋆ ⋆ ⋆

The garden centre was huge and only partially dedicated to plants and garden accessories. However, it had an excellent café and Bella and Alice always liked to have an excuse to go there.

'Let's have lunch first,' suggested Alice. 'I'll make better choices if I've eaten.'

Alice was enjoying her bowl of soup, discussing with Bella what sort of things she should put in her end bed, whether she should choose annuals for colour or herbs for a more long-lasting effect, when something caught her attention. It was Michael, sitting in the far corner of the room, and he was not alone.

She went hot and cold in rapid succession and then realised that it was a huge café and he was unlikely to spot her.

'What's the matter?' asked Bella. 'Broken a tooth on the wholemeal roll? You've gone a bit pale.'

Alice turned to Bella and shook her head. 'Don't turn round, whatever you do, but I've just spotted Michael.'

Bella's eyes widened. 'Oh my God! How can I

not look! Tell me where he is and I'll think of some way of getting a look at him.'

'Right over in the corner. But he's not alone.' Alice was deliberately sounding calm but Bella's hand shot across the table in sympathy.

'You mean he's with a woman?'

Alice swallowed. 'Worse. Two women.'

To her credit, Bella was discreet. She dropped her serviette and then bent down to pick it up, looking round the restaurant as she did so. 'Very far corner? Attractive man? With two very much younger women?'

'That's him. I think they might be his daughters.'

Bella nodded. 'OK. So what do you want to do?'

'I don't want to see him. I mean I don't want him to see me.' Alice was certain about this.

'Why not?'

Alice tried to find a rational explanation for her instinctive reaction. 'For a start, I'm not dressed right, I haven't got much make-up on and — well — it's far too early for us to introduce our families to each other.'

She didn't add that she was terrified of Michael's daughters who, she knew, although only in their twenties, had high-powered jobs. She didn't want to meet them until she was wearing supportive underwear and scientifically proven anti-wrinkle cream.

'OK, so let's not worry. We'll finish our lunch and then just go into the garden section, get what you want and leave. This place is so huge we'll be able to keep away from them.' Bella paused. 'You're actually looking great, Alice. You look happy and relaxed, as if you feel you don't need to try too hard.'

'Thank you, darling, but I haven't tried at all, which is why I don't want to see him, or his scary daughters.'

'They'll love you!' said Bella.

They ate quickly, Alice hoping to get what she needed for her garden before Michael and his party had finished lunch. 'Thank goodness it's self-service and we don't have to wait for the bill,' she said. 'Have you finished?'

Bella swallowed her last mouthful. 'I have now. Shall we go?'

Alice nodded.

She walked out of the café with her head turned away from Michael, hoping her back view was OK. Really, she told herself, she was far too old to ask 'does my bum look big in this' even though she was desperate to know.

Once they were in the garden part of the centre Alice felt better. Among all the Saturday hordes it was terribly unlikely they would see Michael and his girls again.

'I think I'll go for herbs,' she said aloud. 'I've got a bit fed up with doing bedding every year. Herbs last a lot longer and are less labour intensive.'

'Oh!' Bella seemed surprised. 'I've never heard you want to do something in the garden that was less hard work. You've always seemed up for the 'beautiful but difficult' option.'

Alice sighed. 'I know. I think I just need something else in my life, apart from gardening.'

Bella gave her a teasing look, but to Alice's relief, didn't say, 'Like a love interest.'

Alice was just leaning over to see if the lemon thyme at the back was in better fettle than the one at the front, when she heard Michael's voice. Bella had wandered off and she was on her own. Carefully, she withdrew her foot from the flowerbed and stood upright. Then she picked up the lemon thyme and walked off towards Bella.

To her relief she heard Michael discussing roses, which were far away from the herbs. She grabbed Bella's arm and hissed, 'Time to go home.'

Bella didn't flinch, allowing herself to be marched briskly between the aisles and straight to the checkout, not pausing to look at the tempting array of gifts and items no well-accessorised home should be without.

They were in the queue and Alice was hunting for her credit card when she heard her name.

'Alice! I thought it was you! But you were walking out of the café so quickly I didn't have time to check!'

'Michael,' she said weakly. 'Fancy meeting you here.' She stepped out of the queue.

He leaned in and kissed her cheek. 'How are you? And who's this? Don't tell me. Bella.' He put out his hand. 'I hope it won't make you nervous if I say that I've heard a lot about you.'

Bella laughed. 'Well, I am a bit nervous but it's obviously too late.' She shook his hand but, to Alice's relief, didn't say she'd heard a lot about him, too.

'So, Dad,' said one of the young women who

was hovering behind him. 'Are you going to introduce us to your new' — the slightest hesitation — 'friends?'

'Oh, of course, I'm so sorry. Alice, let me introduce you to my daughters, Hannah and Lucy.'

'Hello,' Alice said, but didn't shake hands. These women, who looked very alike, didn't seem very friendly, although why not, she couldn't imagine. 'And this is my god-daughter, Bella. She lives with me.'

'Hi,' said Bella. 'What Alice means is I rent a couple of rooms from her.'

'Well, as I said,' Alice went on, sounding very slightly hysterical, to her own ears at least. 'Fancy you being here. I thought you lived near Kemble.'

'It is one of the largest garden centres in the area, it's hardly surprising we'd come here,' said either Hannah or Lucy.

'Were you after anything particular?' said Bella. 'Alice is a bit of an expert if you need any advice.'

'I wouldn't say that, exactly,' said Alice, touched but embarrassed by Bella's praise. Bella must be about the same age as Michael's daughters but she couldn't be more different.

'Lucy was looking for some roses. She and Phillip — her husband — have just moved into a new house and there's nothing much in the garden,' said Michael.

'I think I can manage to choose a few rose bushes without help, thanks, Dad,' said Lucy, who turned out to be the crosser-looking one.

It was a shame, thought Alice, she'd be so pretty if only she didn't look so bad-tempered.

'So, remind me,' said Hannah, 'how did you and Dad meet each other? I don't think you told us, Dad.' She shot her father an accusing look.

'No, you didn't say anything about meeting a woman called Alice,' said Lucy.

'We met on a train,' said Alice. 'We don't know each other very well.' She looked carefully and saw a flicker of relief cross the faces of Michael's daughters.

'No, but we have met up since, and I'd love for us to get together again soon,' said Michael, either not noticing or ignoring his daughters' chilliness.

'Well, I'm doing lunch for a friend of Bella's — it's for her eighty-fifth birthday,' said Alice. 'Perhaps — ' She stopped herself. She had been about to invite Michael to lunch, but had realised it would look as if she was inviting the daughters too. But she couldn't leave them out, really. She made a decision. She'd invite them all and trust that only Michael would accept. 'Perhaps you'd like to come along? Although you're probably busy.' She looked at Michael, hoping he would guess she only really wanted to invite him. The daughters knew there would be a very old lady present as a chaperone, so they shouldn't feel too protective.

'Are we invited?' said Lucy, looking at her sister. 'And can I bring Phillip?'

'Darling,' said Michael. 'We can't impose — '

Alice forced a hospitable smile. 'Of course you can!' she said. 'That's the joy of Sunday lunch, it will always stretch to a few more.' She looked at Hannah. 'Have you got a partner you'd like to bring?' She'd lumbered herself with one grumpy young woman and her husband; she might as well go the whole hog.

'Well, yes, I have got a partner, but I don't want to bring him. He's away anyhow.' Hannah gave everyone the clear impression that her partner would die before he'd have lunch with a load of strangers.

Alice swallowed, determined to look utterly relaxed at the prospect of having six people she hardly knew to lunch. 'Of course,' she said. 'It'll be delightful. Michael, you've got my address. We'll see you all tomorrow? At about one? Now I must pay for this lot.'

* * *

Bella followed Alice as she walked to the car, pushing her trolley full of plants. Alice seemed perfectly calm but Bella wasn't so sure she really was.

'Is this OK, Alice? It's turned into a party!' Bella asked when they'd loaded the back of the car with plants and Bella had got rid of the trolley.

Alice turned to her god-daughter. 'It should be fine, darling. Have you got the meat?'

Bella shook her head. 'I rang to ask if the butcher could save me a leg of lamb. I'd better go and see how big it is. If it's on the small side I'll get two.'

They drove home and Bella left Alice to take

her plants into the garden before setting off for the butcher. She was wondering how Alice could ever get to Michael past his Rottweiler daughters, who were not even willing for their father to have lunch with a potential woman-friend without them being there. Although, she conceded, there was an age difference. She might feel the same if it was her father. However, she was sure if the woman was like Alice she'd stop worrying pretty quickly.

The butcher also sold a variety of organic local products — cream, meringues, soft fruit, and Bella added these to the items on the counter while her second leg of lamb was being brought through from the back. Alice was usually a very relaxed hostess who provided wonderful meals without apparently doing anything except open the oven and produce golden-brown offerings that smelt delicious. Bella had a feeling it would all be a lot harder work tomorrow.

12

'It'll be fine!' said Bella as she and Alice ate toast together at half past eight the following morning. 'You do amazing roasts. Michael will instantly want to marry you.'

Alice rested her head on her hand. 'Don't say that! Those girls will think I'm trying to snare him.'

'I was only joking — and don't bother about them. They practically invited themselves, after all. They probably just wanted a free lunch.'

Alice looked up, trying to smile. 'No such thing.'

Bella, still determinedly upbeat and supportive, said, 'Not for us, anyway! Maybe we should charge them. I wonder what you'd pay for a really nice Sunday lunch in a pub . . . '

Alice smiled obligingly. 'I hope Jane Langley won't mind all the extra people. This was supposed to be her special birthday lunch.'

'She'll be delighted, I'm sure.' Actually, Bella wasn't sure the two glossy young women who'd invited themselves were going to be Jane's companions of choice, but Michael was delightful.

'I'd better go and wrap Jane's present and then I'll be your right-hand woman.'

When the present was wrapped, Bella went round with the hoover, checked the flowers and generally tidied, waiting to be summoned to the kitchen for chopping and peeling duties. As she worked she thought about Michael. Alice had said that his daughters were in their twenties. Would that put Alice off, having to deal with young women? She had always been great when Bella was a child — she just treated children in the same way she treated adults, and Bella had loved that. And when Bella had gone to her in a state, after having had to leave her parents' house needing comfort and a home, Alice had been a haven of wisdom and supportiveness. It was always going to be a temporary arrangement, but somehow she'd never felt the need to move on.

But would the daughters see how nice Alice was? And was Michael remotely serious? She would hate it if Alice fell for him and he didn't feel the same. Given her reaction to seeing him unexpectedly at the garden centre, Bella thought Alice probably cared a bit more than she'd like people to know.

* * *

Alice was just debating with Bella about the need for a third pudding and whether two sorts of potatoes was overkill when Bella's phone went. She pulled it out of her pocket. 'It's Jane,' she said to Alice. 'I hope she's not going to cancel when you've gone to all this trouble. Hello!'

'Bella? I'm just ringing to say that Dominic is here. He'll run me over so you don't have to pick me up.'

Even hearing his name was a shock. 'Oh well, if he doesn't mind.'

There was an awkward pause. 'Can I be terribly rude?' Jane went on. 'Can I invite him to lunch?' Bella's mouth went dry and she couldn't answer. 'Do say no if it's not convenient, but I'd feel bad leaving him here to fend for himself . . . '

'But does he want to come? It's just that I don't think I'm his favourite person. Beans on toast at yours might be more to his liking.'

It was Jane's turn to hesitate. 'Well, to be honest, I was aware that you and Dominic seemed a bit awkward when we had drinks but when I mentioned I was coming here' — Bella could hear her embarrassment — 'he asked if he could tag along. I was a bit surprised, but when I questioned him he insisted.' She paused. 'Maybe he's heard how good Alice's Sunday lunches are?'

Surely, not even Nevil, who'd experienced a few of them, would have added 'and her godmother does great roasts' into the conversation when he'd told Dominic about their unofficial engagement? Bella couldn't work out how this might have happened. But as they were bound to run into each other sooner or later, it might as well be sooner. And maybe it would be easier if it happened at Alice's, and she was expecting it.

'Well — I'm sure that would be fine.'

'Thank you so much! And the thing with a joint is there's always enough for one more.'

'So they say,' said Bella, and as she'd bought the lamb, she knew that it was true.

* * *

'I must say having you here to help is making me feel so much calmer,' said Alice as Bella went into the kitchen with her news. She slammed something back into the oven. 'It wouldn't do for two of us to be panicking. I need you to talk me out of making another pudding. I do have some lovely raspberries left over from the trifle, I could easily knock up a raspberry and chocolate — ' She stopped. 'Oh. Something bad happened?'

'Yes!' Bella had intended to sound relaxed about adding an extra guest — extra to the other extras — to Alice's lunch party but her voice betrayed her feelings. 'Well, I expect it's OK really. Dominic is coming too.'

'Dominic? *The* Dominic?'

'That's the one.'

Alice didn't speak for a few moments. 'Well, I must confess I'm longing to get a look at him.' She laughed. 'And you know what? I think it's time for a gin and tonic.' She went to the fridge and got out a couple of cans of tonic and some ice cubes. 'I was taught how to make these by an ex-boyfriend.' She poured gin over the ice cubes. 'He said it's called gin and tonic, not tonic and gin so that has to be the largest ingredient. Mine aren't quite as strong as his were.'

Bella frowned. 'Do you think it's a good idea to get drunk before all these people come for Sunday lunch?'

'Essential, darling. Now find the lemons.'

They agreed that lunch would now have to take place in the dining room and Bella set the table before rushing into the garden with a pair of secateurs. She just needed a few sprigs of something to gussy up the flowers in the dining room, and she really wanted some fresh air. If only she could stay out there until lunch was over and everyone had gone home. The prospect of Dominic and Michael's overprotective daughters was not inviting. But she owed it to Jane and Alice to do her bit with a sunny smile.

Not long after this, the kitchen full of the smells of roasting lamb, garlic and rosemary, Alice and Bella heard the crunch of gravel and looked out of the window.

'Nice car!' said Bella, hiding her relief it wasn't Dominic and Jane. 'Is it Michael's?'

'Yes,' said Alice peering out of the window beside her. 'And there are those terrifying young women and one of their — which one?'

'Lucy,' said Bella.

'And Lucy's City boy husband.'

'Don't worry, it's all going to be fine,' said Bella, giving her godmother an affectionate squeeze.

'You'll be just as jittery when Dominic and Jane turn up,' said Alice.

They just had time to share an agonised look and a reluctant chuckle before the doorbell rang.

'Do come in, everyone,' said Alice. 'Michael, how nice to see you.'

'We're rather a crowd, I'm afraid,' he said, putting a bottle into her hand.

'That's all right,' said Alice. 'You're not the only ones coming.' She smiled at the young man who followed the others into the house.

'This is Phillip,' said Michael. 'Lucy's husband.'

Phillip kissed Alice's cheek. 'Hi.' He had a deep, well-bred voice and a lot of confidence: the air of someone who knew he had loads of charm and was prepared to be generous with it.

'This is Bella,' said Alice, and Phillip kissed her cheek too.

'Come on through to the sitting room. It's a shame it's not warm enough to sit in the garden but we can look at it. It might warm up later.' Alice shooed everyone down the hall.

'Sounds like a lot of fun,' Bella overheard Lucy mutter, which made her wonder why on earth they had come if they didn't want to be there.

The sitting room did look lovely, thought Bella. It was a large, well-proportioned room with French windows opening on to the garden. The furniture was comfortable and stylish, although none of it matched. The room had never been designed, it had just developed organically and the effect was charming.

As Bella watched the group finding places to sit on the sofas, she thought again it would have been a lot less stressful if it had just been her, Alice and Jane there to enjoy it.

'Right, drinks,' said Alice. 'Who wants what? Gin and tonic? Wine? Sherry?' She and Bella had loaded a tray with enough different drinks to open either a small cocktail lounge or a juice bar.

'Who drinks sherry?' asked Hannah, unable to hide her disdain.

'Quite a lot of people actually,' said Phillip. 'It's getting quite popular with the younger crowd. Although it is served chilled, usually.'

Bella smiled at Phillip. He was probably just showing off his greater knowledge to his sister-in-law, but she was grateful anyway.

'You could have ice in the sherry, and Alice's G and Ts are amazing,' said Bella. 'If you're not driving, that is.'

Just then a kitchen timer buzzed in Alice's pocket and Bella spotted a look of panic cross her face for a second.

'You go and see to that,' said Bella. 'I'll carry on here. What would you like, Lucy?'

Before Lucy had a chance to answer the front-door bell went again.

'I'll do drinks,' said Michael, 'they're well within my skill set — unless you'd rather I got the door?'

Bella would have loved to let him get the door, but she knew it was her responsibility. 'Drinks would be brilliant. Thank you!'

No wonder Alice likes him, Bella thought as she went down the hall. She opened the door and there was Jane, in her best silk dress and pearls, and behind her was Dominic, giving off, Bella felt, a lethal combination of sex and power. But while he wasn't looking exactly friendly, he wasn't looking hostile either. It was a start. If only her legs hadn't just turned to jelly. She pulled herself together and greeted her friend.

'Happy birthday, Jane. Do come in.'

'I hope you didn't mind me inviting Dominic,' Jane said a little hesitantly.

'It's fine, as I said on the phone.' Bella kissed her. 'Alice would have been horrified to think he'd been left at home, hungry.'

'I wouldn't have been hungry, but it would have been bread and cheese,' said Dominic, and to Bella's surprise he smiled properly.

'Come in, both of you,' said Bella, after a second of eye contact with Dominic that sent her heart racing.

She herded them into the sitting room and then realised she'd have to do the introductions. She made an instant decision not to describe Michael, but just give his name.

'I'm in charge of drinks,' said Michael, when she'd done the rounds. 'What can I get you? There's some delicious sherry, as well as almost anything else you can think of.'

While Michael sorted out refreshments Bella remembered that somewhere in the house there was a gin and tonic needing her attention. A good slurp would be helpful.

Alice appeared and Bella performed more introductions. 'Well,' said Alice, when everyone had kissed or shaken hands, 'I hope no one is vegetarian and hasn't told me.'

Bella knew it was a light-hearted, throw-away remark, but Lucy said, 'I do eat meat but not wheat.'

'Well, I'm sure that's OK,' said Alice. 'You just have to avoid the Yorkshire puddings. Now I'm afraid I have to abandon you again for a few minutes. Lunch won't be long.'

There were several moments of silence that felt like hours.

'I can see Alice has a lovely garden,' said Jane. 'Could I look at it?'

'Maybe we shouldn't do that until after lunch,' said Dominic.

'I think Alice would like to give you the tour,' Bella agreed. 'She'd be able to tell you what everything is. I can only recognise about three sorts of flower.'

'Gardening is so for old people,' said Hannah.

'Really?' said Michael.

'I think I'd really be into gardening, if I had more time and my own home,' said Bella.

'So why don't you have your own home?' asked Lucy. 'Is it the horrendous property prices? Although I suppose being an estate agent you'd get the pick.'

'Estate agents have to buy houses in just the same way as everyone else,' said Bella. 'But I really like living here with Alice. There's plenty of room so we don't get on top of each other.'

'It does seem a lovely big house,' said Michael.

Seeing him glancing round made Bella suddenly worry in case he was after Alice for her real estate. Was he noting the period details: the fireplace, the coving, the ceiling rose and the tall shutters? Although perhaps he was just interested in architecture.

'It is,' said Bella, 'but, of course, houses like this cost a fortune to keep up. There's always something that needs fixing.'

'It would be worth it though,' said Phillip, looking around more blatantly than Michael had. 'A house like this would give you status.'

'I think more people should share property,' said Jane. 'It's ridiculous us old people living in huge houses. On the other hand, I don't want to move either. Sharing is the solution.'

'You're absolutely right, Jane,' said Bella, glad, for private reasons, to hear this.

'But you are sharing your property,' said Dominic. 'With me,' he added for the benefit of the others.

Hannah frowned, surprised. 'You're sharing? Why?'

Dominic turned to Hannah, giving her his full attention. 'I'm working in the area now and haven't decided on what sort of property I want.'

'Otherwise Bella would find him one,' said Jane. 'She's a brilliant estate agent.'

Bella blushed. The property she'd shown him hadn't been that brilliant, although it had been Nevil's pick, not hers.

'It's not often you hear anyone say anything nice about estate agents,' said Phillip. 'They're mostly hate figures.'

'Hate is putting it a bit strongly,' said Bella, smiling to make it clear she hadn't taken offence, although she had. 'People just don't understand all that the job entails, that's all. They'd be far more sympathetic if they knew what was involved.'

Hannah didn't seem to care about the reputation of estate agents; she was still focused on Dominic. 'You seem too independent not to have a place of your own.'

Watching her, Bella wondered if Hannah fancied him and suffered a pang of jealousy, the sharper because it was entirely unjustified.

He acknowledged Hannah's comment with a polite nod.

Bella searched around for something to say to cover the awkward silence. Then to her enormous relief Alice came back in. 'Bella, if you can just give me a hand in the kitchen. Michael, would you be a dear and get everyone sitting down? Jane's place is obvious as it has her birthday present there, but otherwise people can sit anywhere.'

'Oh, dauphinois potatoes!' said Michael, when at last all the food was on the table. 'My favourite!'

'They're a heart attack on a plate,' snapped Lucy. 'Don't have any, Dad.'

'Two sorts of potatoes?' said Jane. 'I'm very impressed.'

'Well, I've got a huge cooker as well as a Rayburn, so it's not hard,' said Alice. 'Now, carving. Dominic and I are sharing it to make things quicker. Are you all right with that knife? It's nice and sharp.'

'We had an electric one as a wedding present,' said Lucy. 'It's really good.'

Bella was beginning to be seriously impressed with Michael. He poured the wine, found soft drinks, made sure everyone had something, all without saying a word. She sent him a smile of gratitude but he was looking at Alice — a look that made Bella understand why his daughters were so concerned. If she was any judge, he was very interested in Alice. Maybe she should worry in case he was just after a great cook who had a very lovely house — although looking at him now it seemed unlikely.

'Has everyone got everything?' said Alice,

checking plates for omissions. 'Wine?'

'It all looks absolutely terrific,' said Michael, sounding like a hungry schoolboy faced with pizza after a term of school meals.

'I think so too,' said Jane. 'Can I propose a toast to the cook?'

Alice laughed. 'Just a quick one, then, I don't want it all getting cold.'

There were some moments of silence broken by the clatter and scrape of knives and forks. Then several people began speaking at once.

'I have to say,' said Phillip, 'this is the best bit of lamb I have ever tasted. I wish you could cook as well as this, Lucy.'

Alice hesitated only a second. 'Don't worry, Lucy, it took me years to perfect my roasts. It's not something that comes immediately. Phillip will be saying that about yours very soon.'

Phillip considered. 'I don't know about that. My mother must be older than you, Alice, and her potatoes are never brown and her gravy is rubbish.'

No one knew how to respond to this.

13

At last the sun came out, lunch was finally over and Alice offered to show Jane the garden. Michael tagged along having done more than his share of dirty-plate ferrying. Phillip, Lucy and Hannah went into Bella's sitting room to watch some sporting event on television, and Bella was left in the kitchen, putting the last few items in the dishwasher and giving everything a final wipe down.

Dominic came in and took the cloth from her hand.

'Come on. It's done now. Show me Alice's garden.'

She wanted to protest that if he'd wanted to see it he could have accompanied Alice and the others, but felt it would be a bit rude.

'OK, as long as you know I'm not an expert.'

'It's an excuse to get you out of the kitchen. You've been here long enough.'

They went through the French windows together and as the doors were a bit narrow they bumped into each other. Bella flinched. Being near him was enough to make her nerves jangle and actual physical contact sent her into a flurry. It was, it dawned on her with a horrible realisation, because she still fancied him as much as she ever had.

She felt she should apologise for being such a fool a few days ago. 'I'm sorry — ' she began, just as he said the same thing.

'So,' said Dominic, looking unexpectedly quizzical. 'What are you sorry for? I think it's me who's in the wrong.'

She gave a nervous laugh, irritating herself as she did so. 'I was going to say sorry for Nevil sending you to that ghastly house.'

'Ah — well, I think he thought he had to come up with something to view the moment he took my call. You were out of the office,' he added, 'and the kind and helpful woman who answered the phone thought I should speak to Nevil. And Nevil certainly agreed with her.'

She led Dominic to the little summer house, right at the top of the garden. It would take a while for the others to get there and she needed time to think what to say. 'Nevil is brilliant at the business decisions, the broad-brush stuff, but he isn't quite as good as matching clients to the right properties.'

Dominic nodded. 'And Nevil is your fiancé.'

The way he said it implied she was sticking up for him for not being very good at his job. It put her on the defensive. 'Yes, but he is good. He got to own a franchise for an estate agency when he was very young. He's got some project on — ' Too late, she realised she probably shouldn't have said this, especially as she had no idea what he was working on.

'So what's that?'

'It's confidential,' she said, to cover up the fact she didn't know. 'Sorry, I shouldn't have mentioned it.' And wouldn't have, if you being near me didn't turn me into an idiot, she added silently.

'I see.'

'But I promise you, I'll personally see that your house needs are met. If you tell me in detail what you like and don't like — '

'No need to sound apologetic. I was going to apologise to you.'

'Really?'

He didn't reply immediately. 'I think maybe — maybe I misjudged you.'

Bella was just about to ask him how he'd done this when the sound of approaching voices meant that she'd lost her opportunity. She didn't want to discuss it in front of Alice and Michael.

'Come along,' said Alice. 'Time for cake.'

Alice had made a beautiful coffee cake and put a few silver candles on it. She and Bella had agreed you didn't need to be too specific as to the number. Jane gamely blew them out and Alice cut the cake into slices.

'I didn't know I had room for anything else until I tried the cake,' said Michael a few minutes later, looking at Alice.

'It is excellent,' agreed Jane. 'Thank you so much.'

'Bella said you were always making cakes for other people, and it's nice to have one on your birthday,' said Alice.

'You've all been so kind and spoiling,' said Jane. 'Thank you so much.'

* * *

Alice was asleep on the sofa, a three-year-old episode of *Escape to the Country* playing on the television. The last crumb of cake and drip of tea had been wiped away. All was quiet. Bella felt it was time to ring Nevil.

'Hey, you!' he said softly by way of answer. 'What have you been up to?'

'Alice had some friends for Sunday lunch.' She paused. 'If I'd known it was going to be more than just me and an old lady I'd have made you come.'

'And who was the old lady?'

'Friend of Alice's.' The lie came tripping out unaided. While Nevil approved of her friendship with Jane, any mention of her would produce a little lecture about getting her to put her house on the market.

'And who else came?'

'More friends of Alice's. They were only there for the food.'

'Well, Alice is a fabulous cook.'

'So, what did you do today?' asked Bella.

'Me? Oh, I just caught up with some work.'

'You? On a Sunday? That's not like you.' Nevil prided himself — aloud — on his work/life balance.

'I like to start the week with a clear desk,' he said smoothly. 'And by the way, sweetie, would you mind coming in a bit early tomorrow? I want to run some things by you before the morning meeting?'

'Oh, OK.' Perhaps he was going to tell her what he'd been doing recently that involved confidential phone calls and working on Sundays.

They chatted on for a few minutes and then

Bella ended the call. She was slightly surprised, but not unhappy, that he hadn't suggested meeting up for a drink later. As far as he was concerned, they were an engaged couple. Was it really normal to go through a whole weekend without seeing each other? she wondered. Maybe it was.

* * *

Alice opened her eyes. Bella was standing over her with a cup of tea. 'Oh, lovely, thank you so much.'

'Do you want supper? A little scrambled egg? Toast?'

Alice swung her legs off the sofa. 'It's all right. I'm not an invalid. But nor am I remotely hungry. What about you?'

'I'm not hungry either.'

Alice exhaled. 'That was a shattering experience.'

Bella chuckled and sat down in an armchair. 'Was it? For you? It all went so well! They were amazed at your cooking.'

'I know that,' said Alice, feeling less thrilled by this than she should. 'But I couldn't do it again. Oh — not Jane, I could have her every Sunday very happily, but the others.'

'I thought Michael was lovely!'

'Yes, but the girls! And Phillip! I'm not up for this, Bella. I'm going back to being a happy single woman and member of a book group.'

Alice's words were light but she meant them seriously. She foresaw choppy waters ahead with

Michael's daughters. And could she face spending every Sunday wrestling with enormous joints, huge greasy dishes and mountains of potatoes, her reward being mere grunts and groans of satisfaction. It wasn't what she wanted and it was only fair to tell Michael as soon as she could that theirs could only be a very casual friendship.

She took herself up to the bathroom satisfied she'd made the right choice.

Michael rang her after she'd fallen asleep. She'd taken her phone up to bed with her for some reason and she answered it without thinking. 'Hello?' she said sleepily.

'Oh, love, I woke you!' said Michael.

'No, no, it's fine. I don't mind. I'll go back to sleep again. What is the time?'

'It was far too late to call. I'm so sorry. That is terribly inconsiderate of me.'

Alice did usually have fairly uncharitable thoughts about people who rang after a certain time. 'Sorry, what is the time?'

'Half past nine,' he said.

'Ah, not all that late really.'

'You were exhausted.'

She sat up in bed. 'Well, I'm not now.'

'You feel up for a chat?'

Alice settled herself more comfortably. 'Oh yes.'

Later, when they'd finally disconnected, she told herself there was plenty of time to tell Michael it was over when she knew exactly what was going on between them. At the moment it was just lovely light-hearted banter between two people who had a lot in common.

14

Bella drove to work in the morning full of enthusiasm for the day ahead. The sun was shining, the hedgerows were full of wild flowers, and she'd survived a difficult Sunday with no blood shed. Everything was going to be just fine.

Too late she remembered that Nevil had asked her to go in early but as she was always very prompt for the Monday-morning meeting she hoped she'd be able to skate over this without him noticing. Maybe she was going to find out what he had been so mysterious about recently. The trouble was, she didn't really want to know. While her passion was finding the right homes for the right people, Nevil was much more interested in making money. And sometimes he seemed a bit ruthless about getting it.

At Alice's insistence, Bella had brought the leftover cake from yesterday. She cut it up and put it on the tray with the mugs of tea and coffee she and Tina had prepared. Then she went into Nevil's office. He was on the phone so she waved gaily and went out again. That was her coming to see him early, as far as she was concerned.

* * *

'So,' said Nevil, opening the meeting, which was really an informal rundown of what was going on. 'Who's got what to report?'

Edward, who was Nevil's second-in-command, said, 'Well, there's a big farmhouse in a state of dilapidation about to come on the market. I'm going to do a valuation today.'

'What sort of money are you thinking?' asked Bella.

'Hard to say, and it might be a money pit, but I'm thinking probably the four hundred mark.'

'How big?' asked Nevil.

'Five beds, plenty of garden — '

'Oh, I know who'd like that!' said Bella. 'Can I show it to the Beesdales first?'

'Remind me who they are?' said Edward.

'They lost out to sealed bids a few months ago,' said Bella. 'I've been trying to find them something ever since, but they haven't got much money and need a lot of space.'

'If you need a lot of space you have to be prepared to pay for it,' said Nevil, reminding Bella that he hadn't been as upset about them being outbid as she had.

'Well, they're cash buyers,' she said, 'so they should be able to get a bit of a bargain.'

'I'll let you know how the valuation goes, shall I?' said Edward.

'Yes please!' said Bella.

'Or maybe tell me? Edward?' said Nevil, smiling.

'Oh yes, of course, Nevil,' said Edward, discomforted.

'OK, Bella, what have you sold since we last met?' Nevil said this light-heartedly but Bella felt a bit affronted. It wasn't possible to sell something every single week and he knew that.

'Well,' she said, feeling smug. 'I've got a buyer

for the three-bed on Hammond's Way.'

'Really, that one right on the roundabout?' said Nevil.

Bella nodded. 'Yup. To a couple who need space, don't have much money and who — vital point this — are quite hard of hearing!'

'Oh, genius, Bells,' said Tina.

'Luck more like,' said Nevil, 'but well done.'

'I do believe there is a house for everyone,' said Bella, 'and it's perfect for them. They just didn't notice the road noise, even when I drew it to their attention.'

'Oh,' said Tina, 'I nearly forgot, Bella. Your Mrs Agnew rang. Can you get back to her?'

'She's not my Mrs Agnew,' said Bella.

'Oh yes she is!' said the others in chorus. 'Only you have the patience!'

* * *

'Bella,' said Mrs Agnew when Bella called. 'You're never going to believe this but we want to see that house over by the river again.'

Bella ran through all the properties she had shown them. 'The one you rejected because the bedroom overlooked the front of the house? In spite of the lovely meadow views? Badger Cottage?'

'That's the one. Though there are other things wrong with it, it's the best you've shown us.'

'There are other estate agents you know, with other houses on their books.'

'Of course we know that, and we do sometimes go and look at houses that are on with other agents, but they're never any good.'

'To be fair, the ones I show you are never any good either!' said Bella.

'But we do want another look at one you've already shown us. Which does prove you're better than the other agents . . .'

Bella laughed. 'I'll ring you when I've set up the viewing.'

* * *

Bella got out of the car and thought, yet again, what a pretty property Badger Cottage was. Double-fronted with dormers in the roof, it even had roses growing round the doors. It had a square front garden with a path down the middle to a little white gate. Surely this time her fussiest clients, the Agnews, would realise how perfect it was. She spotted the Agnews, parked in the layby a little way down the road. They were always early and, seeing her, they got out of their car and walked towards her. They greeted each other warmly.

'So why do you think it might suit you better this time?' said Bella as they went up the path to the front door.

'We're getting a bit desperate, to be honest. We've sold our house and we don't want to have to rent,' explained Mr Agnew.

'And finding somewhere to rent wouldn't be easy either,' said his wife. 'We are so very fussy.'

Bella smiled, acknowledging the truth of this, but determined that they should find somewhere they loved before too much longer. 'Discriminating,' she corrected. 'Anyway, let's go inside. It really is a charming house. One of the nicest I've shown you, I think.' She found the keys to the house and let them in.

They were much more enthusiastic this time. Mr Agnew tapped the upstairs walls. 'You see if we knocked this down and put it up this way, we could have a lovely big bedroom overlooking the back garden.'

'So you could,' said Bella, impressed. They had obviously thought about it quite carefully. But, reluctant to get excited about possibly having found them a house at last if they were just going to turn it down again, she decided to remind them of why it was unsuitable last time. 'Now didn't you think the garden was too small?'

'Yes,' agreed Mrs Agnew, 'and I agonised about it, but as we back on to fields, we think it might be all right.'

'I'm so glad to hear it,' said Bella.

She left the Agnews to it. On a second viewing people knew what they wanted to look at, and it was best if she kept out of the way unless wanted. They took a long time, which gave her reason to be optimistic as she leant on the bonnet of her car checking emails on her phone.

'Well?' said Bella as the Agnews emerged from the house. They were smiling. It had to be good news.

'We're still not sure,' said Mrs Agnew.

Just for a second Bella felt utter exasperation. She thrust it aside. 'Is there anything I can do to help?'

'I don't suppose so. Unless you can make the

garden bigger.' Mrs Agnew was apologetic. 'Is there anyone else interested in it, do you know?'

'I don't think so, but I will check. But don't hang around too long if you do want it. It is very desirable. It's the location, you see.'

'It is a lovely spot,' said Mr Agnew, 'although you can hear the motorway.'

Bella listened hard. In the very far background, currently drowned out by a wren singing its heart out, she could hear a very faint hum. 'To be fair, it's not loud.'

'No,' agreed Mrs Agnew. 'And you can't hear it at all in the house.'

'So . . . ' Bella hardly liked to ask. 'Do you want to put in an offer?'

'Um — no, not just yet,' said Mrs Agnew. 'There are a few things we need to check out.'

Bella hid her frustration behind a laugh. 'Of course. It's such a big decision, you can't rush into it.' Although lots of people did, she knew perfectly well — just not the Agnews.

15

When she had seen them off, Bella sat in her car for a few moments. She couldn't help thinking of all the lovely properties she had shown the Agnews over the months they had been house-hunting. Some of them hadn't been all that lovely, she admitted, but one or two would have been perfect had it not been for some detail that wouldn't bother anyone else. The house that was quite near a recreation ground, for instance — most people would have appreciated more green space close by, but Mrs Agnew didn't like the sound of children playing.

As Dominic was never far from her thoughts — wondering what he thought of her, what he was doing, when she might see him again — she immediately wondered if he might like it. That house might very well suit him down to the ground, with the swings just a short walk away.

Impulsively she scrolled through the numbers on her phone until she found his. It was business, after all. Perfectly reasonable for an estate agent to ring a potential client if they had a suitable property.

'Hi, Dominic,' she said in her best 'work' voice when he answered. 'I've got a property that might be perfect for you. I wondered if you'd like to view it?'

'If you think it's suitable, then yes, I would. Could I do it now, do you think?'

'That is extremely short notice,' said Bella, not sure if she was thrilled or dismayed by this response. 'I'd have to pop back to the office and pick up the keys, but the vendor is abroad at the moment and very keen to sell so it should be fine.'

'It's just I've got the day off. It would be a good opportunity to look at houses.'

'Yes,' agreed Bella, glancing in the rear-view mirror to see what her hair looked like. Not too wild, thank goodness.

'I've got Dylan with me,' Dominic went on. 'He's the reason for the day off.'

'Brilliant. I think he'd like this house, too.'

Dominic sounded amused. 'Oh, why? The newly installed kitchen-diner with views over the garden?'

Bella giggled, feeling giddy suddenly. 'Well, no actually, because there isn't one. But there is a play area really close.'

'It sounds perfect.'

'I'll make a call and then go and pick up the keys. I'll ring you when I've got the details with a postcode, and then you can put it into your satnav. You have got satnav?' If he hadn't she'd have to meet him somewhere so they could go in convoy. It was a bit hard to find.

'I have. All mod cons.'

'Honestly, you sound like an estate agent!' she said, and disconnected.

Back at the office, Bella took the time to rummage in her desk drawer for her emergency make-up kit. This consisted only of a stub of kohl pencil and some dried-up mascara, but it did make a difference. It was important not to look as if she'd put on fresh make-up for him. This wasn't a date; it was a business meeting. She had to look professional, not pretty. She was wearing her nicest cotton dress, and the lettuce-green cardigan that went round her shoulders didn't look too like part of a twin set. She'd done her toes the night before too, which was good. They set off her sandals nicely. She felt smart but knew she didn't look as if she'd made an effort especially for him.

She picked up the keys and a set of details and set off. How would Dylan react to her, she wondered. And would he look like Dominic at all? What a shock it must have been to discover the little boy whose nappies you'd been changing wasn't yours after all.

* * *

Dominic arrived shortly after she'd parked her car. She got out. 'I promise you faithfully this is a zillion times better than the last property I showed you.' She gestured to the pretty front garden and the path that led up to a small front door. 'Although it is smaller,' she added as she unlocked the door.

'I'm very glad to hear it. This is Dylan, by the way.'

'Hi Dylan, I'm Bella. I'm showing your — er — Dominic this house in case he might like to buy it.'

Dylan, who was clinging to Dominic's neck like a baby orang-utan, managed an anxious nod. He was terribly like his mother, Bella realised, with blond hair and blue eyes, which would have probably stopped Dominic ever questioning that he was Dylan's father.

'OK,' said Bella, retreating into estate-agent mode to overcome the awkwardness she felt at meeting Dominic's stepson. It was weird really. Before he was born, this little sweetheart had caused Bella so much heartache. If she'd known then he wasn't Dominic's son, she might never have left her hometown.

'This is the hallway: not enormous but there's a handy utility for buggies etc.' She indicated a room to the right that had a washing machine, loo and washbasin.

'So it doesn't need a huge amount doing to it then?' asked Dominic.

'Not a huge amount, no. It has got lovely period features and a good-sized garden. The huge kitchen and dining room you might well want would have to be added, although there is space for it.'

They went through to the kitchen, which currently was more 'galley' than 'eat in'. It was in need of an upgrade, but Bella didn't mention it. He could see that perfectly well for himself.

'Let's go through to the garden. It's lovely. Even Mrs Agnew — fussiest client ever — liked the garden.'

Dominic put Dylan down and the little boy ran across the expanse of lawn towards the untidy but fully stocked border at the end, obviously relishing the chance to move.

Bella took off after him. 'There's a pond at the end, Dylan. We don't want you falling into it.

Could happen to anyone,' she added, seeing the little boy look affronted at the idea he could be so silly. He was a very mature two-year-old, she realised as she took him by the hand. 'But over here is a rather cool rockery. You can climb on it if you like. It's quite safe.'

Dylan looked up at her and grinned, before releasing himself and setting off up the stones. He really was a darling, she decided.

Dominic walked up the lawn to join them. 'They are secure,' said Bella, watching Dylan. 'The Agnews had a wriggle at those stones when they viewed it, to see if they'd be hard to get out. They don't go much on rockeries. Not sure I do either.' She paused for long enough for him to have a good look round and see how Dylan appreciated the space. 'So, what do you think?'

'All this garden might be a bit much for me actually. I don't have a lot of time, and zero skill,' said Dominic.

'Oh,' said Bella, knowing then he wasn't going to buy it. 'Although your Aunt Jane would give you all the advice you need.'

'I know but I still don't have time. Even if I 'got a man in'.'

Bella nodded, a bit disappointed. She hated to be wrong, and she'd been so sure this house would be right for Dominic. 'Any point in going upstairs? Three good-sized bedrooms and a boxroom.'

'En-suite?'

'It's a period property. You could probably knock through to the boxroom though and create one.'

He shook his head. 'Let's inspect this play area you told me about. That might make us a bit more interested.'

Bella smiled, knowing he'd made up his mind. She didn't think there was anything intrinsically wrong with the house, but for some reason it hadn't worked for him. Maybe one with a smaller garden and in need of less work would be better.

'Why don't you two go ahead?' she said. 'I'll lock up and join you in a mo'?'

After she'd locked up, she called Tina to see if there was anything that required her urgent attention back at the office. 'I won't be long but I don't want to rush back unless I have to,' she explained, hoping Tina wouldn't ask why.

'I think you're OK,' said Tina after a few moments. 'There are some property details you need to check, but I typed them so they're perfect.'

'Of course they are!' said Bella, feeling suddenly light-hearted. It was a beautiful day and she was about to spend half an hour or so with a man who — in spite of her best efforts — she was still attracted to.

She'd worked so hard on forgetting him, distracting herself, going out with Nevil, and now here she was, back where she started.

Dominic was pushing Dylan on the baby swing, and Bella couldn't resist getting on the bigger one and pushing herself off. Too late she realised her skirt would blow up and show her thighs, but she decided not to care.

She was slowing herself down when the sound

of 'Greensleeves' broke into the afternoon sunshine. She jumped off. 'Hooray! Ice cream!'

Dominic laughed. 'Why don't you carry on pushing Dylan while I go and get the first round in?'

'How many ice creams do you think we're going to eat?'

Dominic shrugged. 'If you're a lightweight when it comes to ice cream, Dylan and I will just have to plough on without you.'

Bella smiled. 'What does he call you, by the way?'

'Dom, mostly, although he does revert to Daddy sometimes.' His expression was a little tight. 'But our relationship hasn't really changed. I'm just like an absent father to him, I think. His real father is OK.'

'That's good.'

'It is. It would be unbearable if he was a brute instead of a computer programmer.'

Bella laughed. 'Given a choice of those two, I'd prefer the computer geek too. And when you finally get round to the ice creams I'd like a cone but no flake please.'

'Whatever you like,' he said, and set off towards the van.

Bella took over swinging duties without really noticing. She was fighting her feelings. She couldn't let herself fall in love again. It had been too much hard work getting over it last time. She couldn't go through that again.

The ice-cream van's cheery chimes had obviously alerted other families, because Bella saw two front doors open and mothers and children emerge. The door of a very pleasant villa — twenties, four-bed Bella thought —revealed an older woman, possibly a grandmother, as well as a mother and a springing toddler. The grandmother went to the van while the mother came towards the swings, her little boy skipping by her side.

'You might need to come off the swing now, Dylan,' said Bella when they arrived. 'That other little boy needs a turn.'

Dylan smiled shyly at the other boy as Bella helped him off the swing, and she thought how good and sweet they were being. Probably due to kick off at any moment, she thought a second later, not letting herself feel too gooey.

'It's Dylan, isn't it?' said the mother, looking curiously at Bella.

'That's right. Do you know him?'

'Yes. He goes to the same nursery as Nathan.' She indicated the child she was helping on to the swing. 'They're closed today, which is why I brought him up to see Mum, who's getting ice creams.'

Bella smiled. 'Well, it's a lovely day for it.' She could see Dominic coming towards them with the ices and felt suddenly awkward, as if she'd stepped over a line. She was just the estate agent. Why was she pushing her client's stepson on a swing? Heaven forbid if it looked as if she and Dominic were a couple. 'We're having ice cream too.'

The woman looked up. 'Oh, that's Dominic.'

Bella smiled and nodded, knowing the woman was desperate to know who she was.

'I'm a friend of Celine,' the woman went on. She looked expectantly at Bella.

Accepting she wasn't going to get away with remaining anonymous, Bella said, 'I'm an estate agent. I've just shown Dominic and Dylan a house. Sadly, he didn't like it.'

'Oh? The one that's been on the market a while? What's it like?'

'Nice. Period features, very good garden, needs a bit of work.'

The woman nodded. 'I remember looking at it online. I thought it was rather overpriced.'

People always thought this. 'Are you planning to move into this area, then?'

'Not really. Although it would be nice to be nearer Mum, it would be a ghastly commute for my husband. Ah,' she went on, 'here are our ices. And yours. And I see Dominic's remembered not to let Dylan have a flake. Celine's very strict about him not having chocolate.'

Before Bella could do more than think about snatching the second ice cream with the flake from Dominic, announcing that she'd changed her mind, Dominic had handed her the flakeless cone.

'Here you are, Bella. One cone without flake, and here's yours, Dyl. Special treat for you!'

'Hello, Dominic,' said Nathan's mummy. 'I'm Wendy. We've met picking up the boys at nursery?'

'Oh yes,' said Dominic vaguely.

'I'm not sure if you're aware,' the woman went on, 'but Dylan's not allowed chocolate?'

'A small amount won't hurt him,' said Dominic.

Wendy laughed, taking her own son's ice cream from her mother and handing it to him. 'I hope it doesn't! Celine never lets him have any at all.'

'He doesn't have an allergy,' said Dominic firmly. 'I know Celine doesn't like him having too much sugar. And neither do I — not that it's anything to do with me. But in my experience he doesn't actually eat more than one bite. Then he flings it on the ground, pretending it's a spear. Like that.'

Bella laughed, trying to alleviate the slightly awkward atmosphere, and then, wanting to get away, ate her ice cream quickly enough to give herself a headache. She said, 'I've got some wet wipes in the car. Shall we go and find them? Have a clean-up?'

'Yes, let's,' said Dominic. 'I also have baby wipes.'

They were both aware that Celine's officious friend was sure to tell her about the chocolate flake before Dominic even had a chance to get the child home, but she might not mention that he hadn't eaten it. Once clear of the swings, Dominic let Dylan run ahead. Bella was glad; it meant she could say what she was thinking.

'It was good of you to take Dylan today,' said Bella. 'I assume it's a nursery day usually?'

'Yes,' said Dominic. 'I was able to take the time off at short notice. Neither of his parents was in that position.'

'Does he have grandparents?'

'Yes, but while they love him and would have had him, he would have spent most of the day sitting on the sofa eating crisps and watching telly. Not ideal for a two-year-old.

'Celine is very lucky to have two dads for him,' she said after a few moments. Dominic must love Dylan very much to take a day off work for him.

'She doesn't see it like that. She thinks I'm very lucky to have access to him at all. Which I am.'

Bella felt that Celine was taking advantage of Dominic's love for Dylan while at the same time making him feel grateful for any contact he could get. She knew she couldn't say that.

'Well, Dylan's a very lucky boy, to have you for a stepfather — or whatever you are,' said Bella.

'Well, as I said, I think I'm the lucky one.'

The easy light-heartedness that had prevailed before the arrival of Celine's friend had gone completely. Now Bella felt awkward and a bit sad as she watched Dominic deal with Dylan's chocolatey hands and face. When he had strapped Dylan into the car seat, she said, 'Well, I'll leave you guys to it. It was nice meeting you, Dylan.' Dylan nodded solemnly. 'And thank you very much for the ice cream, Dominic.'

'Thank you for showing us the house. I'm sorry it didn't quite work for me. Although Dylan loved it.'

Bella shrugged. 'If a property isn't right, it isn't right. Better luck next time.'

As she got into her car she realised that Celine had managed to ruin the afternoon, even though she hadn't actually been there.

16

Alice was at the kitchen table the following day, stringing beans, when her mobile phone went. Before she met Michael she wouldn't have dreamt of having it beside her at all times; now she had to have it handy. She saw that it was Michael calling her and forced herself to let it ring a few times before picking up.

'Alice.'

'Michael.' She hoped he couldn't hear her slightly increased heartbeat over the phone.

'I'm trying to work out how to thank you for lunch.'

'Michael! You sent flowers, which were lovely. I told you. That's thanks enough. It was only Sunday lunch, not a banquet for fifty.' Now Alice felt embarrassed.

He laughed. 'It's easy enough to send flowers. I want to do something special.'

Alice became suspicious. 'Why, exactly?' Then she worried that she'd sounded rude.

'OK, I'll come to the point.' He paused.

She waited as long as she could. 'Well, go on. Please come to the point.'

'It is a bit awkward.'

'Now I'm worried.'

'The thing is, the girls are rather concerned — they are a bit overprotective. You see I've never gone out with anyone remotely seriously since the divorce.'

She gulped. 'Are we going out seriously?'

'I'm very serious about you, Alice.'

She found this intensely sexy, and terrifying at the same time. She swallowed and moistened her dry mouth. 'Oh.' For some reason this was a bit of a shock. It shouldn't have been, really, but hearing him say it, in so many words, gave her a jolt.

'I don't want to rush you,' Michael went on, obviously unaware of her reaction, 'but I think it would be good if the girls could get to know you better.'

'Really?' She felt hot suddenly. This was a dreadful idea.

'Don't sound so worried!' He laughed gently at her. 'I meant having a treat together, on neutral territory, like a spa.' Alice suppressed a groan, but obviously not well enough. 'What? Don't you like spas?'

She took a breath and tried to explain. 'Spas are lovely but — I don't know if you've been to one lately? — they involve lying around not wearing very much. I don't want to do that with your daughters. They are young and lovely. I wouldn't feel comfortable.' She'd managed not to say 'old and fat', which was a triumph.

He didn't answer immediately. 'I see. I think I understand. I'll think of something else.' He paused. 'Personally I'd love to be lying around with you while you're not wearing very much.'

Alice laughed. 'Idiot! It's not all it's cracked up to be, I promise you.'

'I don't want to get into an argument about it, but I'm sure it would be lovely. So, what would you like to do instead of a spa?'

'I don't know! I don't think you should try to force me and your daughters together. It would be better if it all happened more naturally.'

'It would but I'm not sure how long I can wait.' He sounded a bit serious suddenly. 'I'll have a think and get back to you.'

The runner beans had been steamed and eaten (with butter and black pepper, her favourite supper), but not cleared away, when he was back on the phone. 'I've got the very thing! Are you free next Monday?'

'Think so. What is it?'

'A baking course! And just near you. I know you're all going to love it!'

* * *

'OK, get into groups of four,' said the chef in charge of the course on the following Monday. He was, by anyone's standards, very good-looking, and all through the instructions Alice was aware that every woman in the room wanted to do well for him. Most of the other people were young and one or two, to Alice's absolute horror, were there because they were getting married and wanted to impress their new husbands. She had glanced around to see if anyone else was appalled by this statement but no one else seemed to be.

They were in the kitchen of the local college, purpose-built to teach cooking to a professional standard. At first Alice was a bit daunted by the acres of stainless steel and huge ovens, but she

soon forgot any doubts when she started listening to the chef and became engrossed. She had thought she knew a bit about baking, but had already learned so much more.

'Don't worry if you're not with your best friend this time,' he went on, 'I'm going to change the groups around so everyone will work with everyone.'

This was a relief. Alice went to a group of three others who included a keen young man. Michael's daughters had shot off in the opposite direction, no keener to work with Alice than she was with them. Really, Michael's optimism that this would be the ideal bonding session was completely misguided, if rather sweet.

Alice concentrated on the young chef, whose enthusiasm was such that even a non-cook would be excited by the magic of yeast, of how different flours worked and the mystery of sourdough. She made notes and tried to focus, sure that from across the room Michael's daughters were giving her evils.

But once she got into the baking, stretching, pulling and shaping of the dough, she forgot why she was there and let the soothing feel of the dough do its work. It might not have been the bonding exercise Michael had planned but it was something she did really enjoy.

Deep inside her heart she felt that she should end it with Michael before she fell even more in love with him, but it would be a horrible wrench, even now, after such a short time. She'd never thought she'd feel like this about anyone at her age. It was lovely, but his daughters would make

everything so difficult, and she wasn't sure she could cope.

When everyone's plaited rolls had come out of the oven they were lined up for inspection. Alice was quite happy with hers, but as the cute chef went along the line making comments, she became aware of a sense of competition. Michael's daughters were in the second group to be judged and there was a certain amount of teeth-sucking and head-shaking as their efforts were assessed. The chef was a good teacher and very kind, but he was used to professional kitchens and so didn't pull many punches. She was sure she heard the words 'teacher's pet' from one of Michael's daughters as the chef complimented Alice on her beautiful rolls.

'OK, currant buns next, find new groups to be in, please!' called the chef and everyone shuffled around.

Alice liked making buns. It reminded her of when she first went to work, and the little shop next door sold 'double butter, triple fruit'. As the office junior, it had been her job to buy them.

'So, how did you learn so much about cooking?' asked Darren, another young man with cheffy aspirations watching Alice sprinkle on her currants with a casual hand.

Alice smiled and tried to look enigmatic. She didn't want to tell him it was from a past boyfriend, with whom she'd had a short, very passionate relationship that had been as much about food as about lust. The love of food had lasted, although the passion had not.

'OK, guys,' said their teacher a little later.

'You've all done really well, even though baking is obviously new to some of you. Now, I want you to get together into your final groups for this last item. It's rum babas, newly back in fashion and quite right too. They take a while so let's get going!'

Inevitably Alice found herself with both Lucy and Hannah. Then Darren rolled up. 'I wanted to be with you again, Alice. I reckon I could learn a lot from you,' he said.

Before Alice could feel flattered, Hannah broke in. 'Yes. Older people do know about baking and stuff.' Alice stiffened, slightly tempted to give details of how she'd acquired her 'older person' knowledge, aware that it would 'gross them out'. She smiled instead. She was here to bond with Michael's daughters, and she owed it to him to make a bit of an effort to do so.

'Not that you're old,' said Hannah, quickly, possibly slightly embarrassed by the rudeness of her previous statement. 'It's just . . . '

'I'm older than you,' Alice agreed.

'And older than Da — ' began Lucy before Hannah dug her sister hard in the ribs.

'Shall we get on?' interrupted Darren. He had all the energy of a potential MasterChef and twice the ambition.

'So why do we have to keep the salt and the yeast separate?' asked Lucy, looking at her notes and scratching her head.

'Because the salt stops the yeast working,' said Alice. 'He did tell us. Really you'd get on better if you listened, instead of picking out dough from under your fingernails.' Too late she realised she shouldn't have said this. It was understandable — they just weren't paying attention — but fatal if she wanted to keep Michael in her life.

'Yeah!' said Darren. 'Now measure out the milk.'

Somehow, in spite of the bickering and the lack of focus, their babas came together. While everyone was waiting for them to prove, the chef gave a demonstration of how to make strudel dough. As this was something Alice had always wanted to try, she ignored Hannah and Lucy and concentrated hard.

'I can't believe it's so thin!' said Darren. 'You really could read a newspaper through it!'

When the time came, Hannah (annoyingly) proved an adept piper and piped the batter into the baba moulds very neatly. When they were baked (Darren squatted by the cooker, peering into it, to make sure they didn't overbake) they added the syrup and later, the cream and fruit.

'They look really good, don't they!' said Hannah, surprised.

'Yes, you've got a way with a piping bag,' said Alice, her sense of fairness overcoming her reluctance to praise her.

When the chef came round to taste them he took a huge bite and chewed thoughtfully. 'That's a good light baba, just the right amount of rum in the syrup. Well done. I think yours are the best.'

They were each awarded a rolling pin and wooden spoon.

'That was really cool!' said Lucy.

'Yes, well done, everyone,' said Alice, genuinely pleased. 'It all came together at the end.'

'It so did!' agreed Hannah. 'Well done Dad for a cool idea.'

'I like winning,' added Lucy. Alice looked at her and realised she was being sent a message: they'd cooked with her at the end because they wanted to be the best; they didn't care about Alice personally at all. 'Now let's get all this stuff home. Phillip is going to be so thrilled. He doesn't think I can cook at all!'

17

A couple of days later Bella was not having a very good time at work. She was wearing the wrong clothes and her feet were freezing in their new sandals. She'd intended to go home at lunchtime to change although she'd have had to start from scratch and put on trousers (socks with sandals not being a look she favoured), but she hadn't had time. And although she'd rung the Agnews days ago to tell them that currently there wasn't anyone else interested in Badger Cottage, she still hadn't heard back from them. She was also totally distracted by thoughts of Dominic. She tried to convince herself he was only a client, but she didn't really manage it.

Their time at the swings together had been lovely, even if it had been cut short. And Dylan was a poppet. Seeing them together had been heart-melting. But not, she realised, good for her resolutions.

It was still only four o'clock, and with not much else to do except paperwork, Bella faced another hour at the office with cold feet.

Fortunately, before she could get too gloomy, her fiancé swept by her desk and said, 'Fancy an outing?'

Bella looked up. 'I do! But now? It's not home-time yet.'

He grimaced at her childish expression. 'Yup. I'm the boss and I give you permission.'

Bella made a face at her colleagues, who reciprocated with 'get you' expressions, fetched her things and joined Nevil in his car. She pulled on her cardigan. 'So where are we going on our outing, and does it include a nice little café?'

'I think that could be arranged.'

'It's a shame it's raining. We could have gone to a lovely tea room and sat in the garden.' She knew just the place.

'You're a simple soul really, aren't you Bella?'

He managed to make this sound as if she was a bit thick, but she persisted in her cheeriness. She knew he didn't mean it really. 'This is so much fun!' she said, stirring up enthusiasm. He was being spontaneous and jolly, and she was away from her desk. Of course she was happy! She brushed aside thoughts of ice cream and swings with Dominic and Dylan.

'So where are we going?' she said, when Nevil had offered no information and they'd been driving a good twenty minutes.

'It's a surprise.'

'A good surprise?'

'Very good indeed.' He paused for a few moments and then said, 'Oh, OK, I can't do surprises. I have to tell you. We're going to look at a house.'

'But we're estate agents, Nevil,' said Bella, teasing. 'Looking at houses is not a surprise. It's what we do. It's actually work.'

'But this house is special. It's going to be our house.'

Bella felt a rush of something she only recognised as fear a little later. Her 'sort of' engagement to Nevil was OK — as long as she didn't give it too much thought. He hadn't mentioned it again, and she was reasonably happy with how things were at the moment. But suddenly the thought of them having a house together, sharing it, being a couple, was making it too real. She wasn't sure she was ready yet. If only she could get wretched Dominic out of her mind, she'd be able to focus on Nevil.

'It's quite a long way from town, isn't it?' said Bella, more for something to say than anything else. 'How far are we going?'

'It is quite far. But it's worth it. You'll see.'

Bella tried to think what sort of house she might be about to be shown. If she fell in love with it, would that make her feel better about Nevil? Would she find herself marrying him for a house? It did happen, she knew. She also knew of couples who were miserable with each other, but stayed together for the sake of the house, which neither could face leaving. Not good.

Eventually, Nevil turned up a track that had the marks of heavy machinery on it. A little way along, the track opened out into a building site. And what a building site! It seemed big enough to justify its own church, school, pub and shop. She'd never seen so much mud in one place before.

'Goodness me!' she said, fighting the horror she felt at the sight of the bulldozers, diggers and small cranes which were dotted around.

'It looks nothing now, but you wait until you see the show house and the plans!' Nevil's excitement was palpable.

Bella tried harder. 'I can't wait! But I wish I had my wellies.' She always had them in the boot of her car and she silently reproached Nevil for not suggesting them. He knew what he was coming to, after all. She stepped gingerly out of the car, trying to avoid a large puddle.

'You'll be all right. Follow me!'

In his much sturdier footwear, Nevil strode ahead to where Bella could see a large house, presumably the show home.

She caught up with him, slipping in the mud. 'Nevil! We could never afford to live here!' But what she didn't add was, 'And why would we ever want to?'

'Come and see. Prepare to be amazed.' He ushered her through the front door into a nearly completed house.

She knew he preferred contemporary properties — his own flat, though small, was very cutting edge, and Bella quite liked it. But this was so vast it was more like a public space than a home.

'This is the hallway,' he announced and Bella realised how annoying estate agents must be, stating the bloomin' obvious. Of course it was the hallway.

'It's massive!'

'It's all travertine marble and there's room for an eight-foot Christmas tree there. It's part of the spec,' Nevil announced. He was like a man showing off his new sports car to his mates, assuming they'd be as impressed as he was.

'It's extremely spacious,' Bella agreed, trying to suppress her inner gloom.

'Underfloor heating, naturally. Come on through to the kitchen. I think you'll like.'

The kitchen could have hosted a party for twenty people who didn't speak to each other. It was vast. The surfaces were marble, the floor was marble and all the door fronts were some highly polished surface that looked like marble. It reminded Bella of an ice rink. There was an island near the cooking area with two sinks, and a range the size of a double bed. It was attractive, but it seemed to Bella to be big enough for mass catering on a grand scale. Bella felt she'd rather live in a swimming pool and yet Nevil seemed completely seduced by the size and grandeur of it.

'Here.' Nevil produced a brochure giving details of the range. 'You can cook anything on that. And look at that bad-boy cooker hood. Bosch.'

Bella inspected the cooker hood which to Nevil seemed to be the kitchen equivalent of a Ferrari. She glanced down at the brochure. 'It says it's the perfect choice for the modern family kitchen.'

'It's the top of the range.'

Bella hid a smile at his unintended pun. He always had to have puns explained to him anyway, and now he was on a mission to show her a dream home, he wouldn't appreciate her going off topic.

Nevil pulled open a door. Inside was a fridge-freezer that could have accommodated a whole bullock and champagne for a medium-sized wedding.

Bella, wishing she had her old rollerblades to speed her progress, went across to the other side of the room. Here a dining table for twelve was set as if for a very smart dinner party.

'This is the biggest kitchen I've ever seen,' she said.

'I knew you'd like it!' said Nevil excitedly. 'Look, a built-in coffee-maker, wine-fridge, cheese-larder — everything you could ever need really.' He pulled her to him and gave her a hug, assuming she'd be as enthusiastic about it all as he was.

'Amazing.' She knew she didn't sound amazed, she sounded shell-shocked. Fortunately Nevil didn't notice the difference.

'Come and see the main reception room, although, as you'd expect, there's more than one.' He was off again.

Bella wondered briefly if giving ballet lessons in her own home would justify a room so large. It had been arranged with massive leather sofas and a television with a screen that wouldn't have disgraced a small cinema. The phrase 'masses of taste and all of it bad' floated into Bella's head. She opened a door and found herself in a slightly smaller room.

This had the advantage of looking out into what would become a garden. She went to the French windows, trying to imagine Alice's mature lawns and trees instead of the skid marks of heavy machinery and mud. She turned back into the room. Her imagination had failed.

'Fireplaces, I see. Do they work?' she asked.

Nevil was striding about, obviously having

mentally moved in already. Bella had seen this with clients — it was almost always a sign that they'd fallen in love and would make an offer. 'Probably not but they're hardly necessary, with underfloor heating throughout.'

Bella opened her mouth to say that open fires were about a lot more than heating, but didn't. She knew Nevil didn't really get the magic of real logs and flames.

'Let me take you upstairs,' said Nevil. He took her hand and led her up the wooden staircase. 'This will all be carpeted of course. There are five bedrooms, three en suite, and the master has a dressing room as well. Come and see.'

Bella wanted to say it looked like a picture in *Hello!* magazine, before the celebrity couple got expensively divorced, but she didn't. There was a bed that would sleep five easily and an enormous dressing table. She imagined wrestling the sheets on to the huge bed, and moved quickly into the en-suite, which was the size of Alice's main bathroom, easily. A glimpse of the taps, inset with crystals, and she hurried out again. If she'd been with Alice, they'd have giggled at the ghastly flamboyance of it all. It was such a dreadful shame that Nevil's dream home was more like a nightmare for her.

Nevil, possibly picking up on some of her horror, said, 'If you don't want sparkly taps, you don't have to have them! At this stage we can design it just how we want it.'

'We couldn't change the basic dimensions, and it all seems a bit — well, big.'

'Oh, don't be silly! How can a house be too

big? I've seen you drool over bloody great mansions before now!'

'But they were old. They didn't seem quite so enormous somehow.' There were other things she could have said about this house, quite a lot of them, but she didn't want to upset Nevil. He was in house-heaven.

'Silly girl! And with a new-build we won't have the endless maintenance a big old house would land us with.'

She couldn't argue with that so said, for the second time, hoping that this time he'd listen, 'But, Nevil, we could never afford this.'

He looked pleased and knowing.

'Nevil, how much is it?'

'Not telling.'

'OK, I'll guess. I'd say one point two.'

He shook his head. 'Way more. One and three-quarter million is the asking price.'

Bella raised an eyebrow. 'It's on an estate.'

'Of four very exclusive houses. Who wants to live out in the sticks, isolated and on your own?'

'People with that sort of money, which is not us.' She smiled. 'It's been fun to see it, it really has, but shall we find some tea?' Really a stiff drink would have been more useful. How could Nevil think they could afford it? Even with a huge discount from the builder, which he implied he could get, it was way, way out of their league. Thank goodness.

'Come back down to the kitchen. Look how beautifully the stairs and bannisters and things are made? That's craftsmanship!'

'Which is why we can't afford it,' she said

when they were back in the ice rink.

Nevil shook his head. 'We wouldn't be paying the full price, Bells. We'd be getting a deal. A really good deal.'

'It could be half-price and we couldn't afford it, Nevil. You know that.'

He smiled. 'I know nothing of the kind. I have dreams, dreams and plans, sweetheart. This is the sort of lifestyle we deserve.'

'Not if we can't afford it,' said Bella.

Nevil made an impatient noise. 'I wish you'd stop worrying about the money! It's not going to be a problem!'

'How isn't it? I don't understand.'

Nevil shook his head. 'You've just got to trust me on this.'

'But Nevil — ' Bella started but she was interrupted.

'Really!' he went on, less vehemently. 'I'll look after the money side. You just think how you'd like your dream house to be.'

Bella really wanted to say that this was as far from her dream home as it possibly could be, but she knew it would hurt Nevil's feelings terribly. She just said, 'It is quite far away from work though. Three-quarters of an hour, I reckon.'

'That's not far. Anyway, why does that matter?'

'It's also quite far away from our family and friends.' Bella didn't only mean in distance. She couldn't imagine having the sort of cosy dinner parties she sometimes gave for the people in the office, when they sat in Alice's kitchen, eating, drinking and laughing. Compared to this gadget-filled palace, Alice's felt like a glorified pantry.

She walked across to the window and looked at the site again. 'How big is the plot, Nevil?'

'Big enough for a bit of a lawn in thc front, and at the back — you know, a patio area, barbeque area, space for a hot tub. The usual sort of entertainment spaces you'd expect with a house like this.'

'But not many actual flowerbeds?' she said, shuddering at the mere thought of a hot tub.

'We don't have time for gardening, sweetheart. We're busy people.'

'No one should ever be too busy to grow roses,' she said.

He ruffled her hair. 'Who invented that load of crap?'

'I did.'

He ruffled her hair again, and she tried not to show her irritation. 'No wonder it's crap then.' He paused. 'Tell you what, let's go back to mine. I'll take you out to dinner later. There's a new resto in Cirencester — '

'Nevil! I can't go to a restaurant. I need my car and my shoes are covered in mud.' They might well never be the same again, but she kept this to herself.

'OK, fair enough. We'll go and get your car and then go to mine? Maybe you could pop home and pick up some underwear for the morning?' He gave her the sort of look which made his meaning clear.

Bella felt cornered, but nodded all the same. With luck Alice would still be out, and she wouldn't have to sense her disapproval. It wasn't that Alice was prudish, but she didn't think Nevil was right for Bella. And maybe he wasn't perfect. But she couldn't forget how Nevil had picked her up when she was heartbroken and restored her self-esteem. She owed him some loyalty for that. And she'd be able to talk him out of wanting to live in this monstrous house. She just needed a bit of time. He might be a bit patronising sometimes but she was sure he did love her. He wouldn't want her to live somewhere she'd be unhappy.

In the end they decided not to go out. Bella really didn't want to, and Nevil wanted to catch up on a bit of work, so while he tapped away on his computer and made phone calls, she rummaged in his fridge and cupboards and found pasta sauce ingredients. Nevil's kitchen was small and functional and only just had room for a table-for-two, and yet she preferred it to the enormous room he seemed to think was any woman's dream.

That thought hit home. Whether she owed him loyalty or not, the fact was that they were utterly different and maybe it really was time for them to part. Yet Bella shrank from the fallout it would cause. She knew Nevil's ego would never permit her to stay at the agency he managed if she dumped him. She might find it difficult to go on working with him; he'd find it impossible, his pride would be too damaged. She'd have to leave the job and colleagues she loved. But what about the Agnews? She had to get them settled first — no one else would care about them in the way she did and they were such a challenge! Tomorrow she would press them about Badger Cottage and then, if they decided to buy, she would think about it all in more depth and make a decision. Nevil hadn't mentioned their engagement again, which was good — maybe he was going off the idea of them getting married? But there was that house. No, he obviously felt they had a future together. It was a mess.

As she scraped away at the Parmesan cheese to go on top of the pasta, she realised she was no better than the women who stayed with the wrong man because of the lovely house. She was staying to preserve the status quo. She thought about it as she gathered up the saucepans to wash. She would have to leave her job, but would she have to completely relocate like last time? Was the small town big enough for both of them? Was it fair on Nevil for her to stay? She had a lot of thinking to do.

18

Alice was in Waitrose early. She wanted to make Michael something they'd learned to cook, as a thank you. She just needed to decide what. Rum babas? Focaccia? Or her own favourite, cheese bread?

She was in the bakery aisle inspecting a packet of spelt flour as someone had once told her it was less fattening, when she became aware of the sound of sniffing. She looked up. It was Michael's youngest, Lucy.

She glided out of the aisle with alacrity, irritated at having her shopping interrupted, certain that she didn't want to have to say hello to one of her least favourite, people. The sniffing was probably an allergy — Lucy was just the sort of person to have allergies — but why did she have to have them in her Waitrose? There was a perfectly good one in Cirencester where she could sniff away to her heart's content. Did the girl have no idea of boundaries?

Annoyed that she'd allowed herself to be driven away from the specialist flours, Alice went back.

Lucy was still sniffing, but in a way that was more like a sob. Well, Alice wasn't going to ask what was wrong! As if! Besides, she was the last person Lucy would want making sympathetic noises. If the situations had been reversed — heaven forbid — Alice would throw herself under the nearest trolley rather than allow Lucy to offer fake concern. Lucy was sure to feel the same about her.

Besides, she was a little cow, utterly self-absorbed and completely unworthy of having a lovely man like Michael as a father. She must take after her mother.

And yet, a few moments later, without knowing how she'd got there, Alice found herself next to the unworthy little cow holding out a tissue produced from her handbag. It had a picture of Rodin's *The Kiss* on it.

Lucy snatched it, blew her nose loudly and sobbed some more. 'Oh God! It's so awful!' she howled.

Alice handed her another tissue and heard the words 'Would you like to go for a coffee?' come out of her mouth.

'Ugh! I can't imagine anything worse!'

As Alice felt very much the same, she prepared to move away but Lucy went on, 'Coffee makes me sick at the moment.'

A suspicion about what might be causing the tears popped into Alice's head. 'Tea then?'

Lucy nodded and just for a moment Alice saw a very distressed young woman, and not a spoilt brat having a tantrum. 'Actually, Alice, you might be able to help.' She gave her a nervous smile.

Wary, and trying not to feel flattered, Alice guided both Lucy and the trolleys to the coffee shop. They found a table in a corner. 'You sit down. Do you want ordinary tea or something else? Peppermint? Ginger?'

'Peppermint. Please,' Lucy added. Now she was no longer sobbing, her social skills were beginning to return.

Alice came back a few minutes later with the drinks and a plate of toasted teacakes. In her opinion, few things in life were so ghastly that a toasted teacake wouldn't help.

Lucy sipped at her tea with her lips pursed, as if it might be medicine in disguise. Then she took a second, more confident sip. She regarded the teacakes suspiciously.

Alice drank her tea, considering Lucy. She watched as a hand came out and took a piece of teacake. It was like watching a feral cat deciding to accept food.

The first piece of teacake went down and Lucy helped herself to a second.

Alice regarded her. 'Are you pregnant?'

Lucy looked up, aghast. 'How do you know? I can't possibly show yet! I've been so sick I've lost half a stone!'

'Well, while I've never been pregnant myself, when my best friend was pregnant she went right off coffee, alcohol and, oddly, rice. She also developed a passion for sweet things. How are you with rice?'

'OK, but I can't face flesh — meat or fish. Dad wanted us to go on a cookery course, but I had to convince him that baking was better.' Lucy sighed. 'No one is supposed to know I'm pregnant, and you could tell so easily!' She looked as if she might start crying again.

'Don't worry. No one else would notice. It's just me because of my friend.' Alice wasn't actually sure this was true, but she couldn't bear any more tears. She'd run out of tissues for one thing. 'So, what had so upset you in the bakery aisle? Presumably no one had said, 'Got a bun in the oven, I see.''

Lucy almost smiled. 'No. Worse than that.'

'What then? Was it: 'Who ate all the pies, porker?''

The smile was better developed now. 'No one said anything to me — it's just the whole ghastly situation.'

Alice's heart sank. 'Oh?' She trusted Lucy would elaborate. As long as she didn't want Alice to escort her to a special clinic she could cope, but if it was that, she'd send for Lucy's sister.

'It's so bloody unfair! Why me?'

It became apparent this wasn't a rhetorical question. Alice took a breath. 'Well, if you don't take precautions . . . '

Lucy regarded her as if she was mad. 'What are you talking about?'

Alice shook her head. She took a different tack. 'Did you want to get pregnant?'

Lucy gave Alice a look that made her feel very stupid. 'Of course!'

'Oh. And Phillip knows?'

'Of course!' Lucy said again, as if Alice was an idiot.

'Your Dad?' Alice felt if she was going to be treated as if she'd completely lost her brain, she might as well get all the stupid questions out of the way. Otherwise she might die before she found out why the wretched girl was so upset.

'Yes!'

'So why the big drama?'

Lucy frowned. 'Phillip's bloody f — grandmother.' Then she looked horrified. 'Sorry. Shouldn't have sworn.'

Alice nodded. 'It's all right, you stopped before you said anything really bad. Besides, you don't get to be as old as I am without hearing that word from time to time.' She didn't add that she even used it herself, from time to time.

'You're not that old — it's just — '

'OK, that's enough about my age. Now tell me what the problem with Phillip's grandmother is?'

'I've to open up her house and cook a meal for the entire family.'

'Oh?'

Lucy nodded, obviously glad of an opportunity to get something off her chest. 'Yes. The house is about to be sold and the grandmother wants a last family gathering before it is. It's her dying wish. Not that she is dying, more's the pity.'

'But why do you have to do it? You're not that keen on cooking, are you?'

'I hate bloody cooking!'

'So — if the whole family is involved — why ask you to cook?'

'Good question! Basically, it's bloody Phillip!'

Alice took a few seconds to take this in. Phillip, knowing his wife was pregnant, that she hated 'bloody cooking' and was probably dreadful at it, was making Lucy cook for his grandmother. It took male insensitivity to levels bordering on insanity. 'He's making you do this?' Alice had to check she hadn't got it wrong.

Lucy nodded, gathering up the teacake crumbs with her finger.

'Well, you must say no. Play the pregnancy card. Get some takeaway menus. Put your foot down, Lucy.'

Lucy shook her head. 'I can't. It's really important that I do this.'

'Why?'

'Because . . . It's hard to explain.' Lucy looked at Alice pleadingly as if she didn't want to go into details.

Alice stared relentlessly back. 'There has to be a very good reason to put you through cooking a meal for a family — '

'In a house no one's lived in for — like ever!' added Lucy.

' — when there are other family members involved who could possibly do it quite easily,' finished Alice.

'Oh God!' wailed Lucy, rubbing her forehead. 'It's all so difficult!'

'Then don't do it,' said Alice firmly, the solution simple. 'Just say no.'

'Everybody in Phillip's family thinks I'm silly and uneducated and can't do anything useful. Basically they hate me. This is my chance to prove I'm not useless.' She paused. 'Phillip got a lot of stick when he married me and I want to prove to them he didn't make a mistake.'

Alice nodded. 'And his grandmother thinks all that too?'

'His grandmother . . . ' Lucy took a deep breath. There was obviously much worse to come. 'She thinks I'm common.'

Alice knew she mustn't laugh, however much she wanted to. 'Really? Do people say things like that these days?'

Lucy nodded. She seemed pleased with Alice's reaction. 'She is the snobbiest person on the planet, and thinks Phillip was a fool to marry someone like me just because I'm 'quite pretty in a vulgar way'.'

'Good Lord,' said Alice. 'She sounds like someone out of Oscar Wilde.'

'Who's he?'

'Never mind. It doesn't matter. I still need to know why you're cooking for this anachronism when you probably don't have to. You are pregnant.'

'I know I'm bloody pregnant!' wailed Lucy. 'But apparently it's vulgar to suffer from morning sickness or 'make a fuss'. God, she probably doesn't even approve of pain relief in childbirth!'

'Well, she's not going to be there when you have it, so you don't have to worry about that. But just tell me, I'm still not getting it, why do you have to cook?'

'So she doesn't cut Phillip out of the will.'

Alice shook her head in disbelief. 'This isn't Oscar Wilde, it's Dickensian!'

Lucy frowned. 'I have heard of Dickens. I'm not that uneducated.'

'I still don't think Phillip should put you through this.'

'Nor do I!' Lucy looked defiant. Then her expression changed. 'But I don't want to let him down. He's always stuck up for me and I want to make him proud.' She looked at Alice. 'You're good at cooking. You might be able to help me? Give me a few tips?'

Alice nodded. 'I certainly know a few good cheats. When is this banquet?'

'Tonight.'

'Oh, short notice. So what are you planning on cooking?'

Lucy's expression became despairing. 'I have no idea. Fish and meat both make me sick at the moment.'

'You want ready meals then, something someone else has already cooked. Has Phillip told you of any particular likes or dislikes?'

'Not really except she's very old-fashioned so no 'foreign muck', and there must be pudding.'

'OK, we can do this. I'll whizz round and get a few things for you, then I'll tell you how to do it.'

Lucy's bottom lip trembled.

'Now what?'

'You couldn't actually come with me, could you? To the spooky old house that no one's been in forever?'

Alice sighed. 'I'll get the food first and think about it. But . . . ' She paused to give her words extra weight. 'If I do come, you have got to swear you will absolutely not tell your father!'

'OK, but why not? Why don't you want Dad to know?'

Alice took a breath to explain, and realised she didn't really know. Or if she did, she didn't want to describe her complex reasons to his daughter. She didn't want Michael to think she was doing it so he would like her more, and so make herself look too keen. 'It's complicated.'

She needn't have worried; Lucy wasn't that interested. 'OK. But I can tell Phillip?'

'If you absolutely have to. Now I'll get on. How many are you cooking for?'

'Six. Me and Phillip, his grandmother, his two brothers and his sister.'

'So you're the only non-blood relative?'

Lucy nodded. 'I'm the only one who's pregnant too, but there it is.'

Alice went to find her trolley.

Back in the aisles, she abandoned the ready-meal idea. There weren't enough packets of any one thing that wasn't obviously 'foreign muck', and so she decided it was easy enough to make a simple chicken casserole. Then she added some ready-rolled puff pastry to her shopping to turn it into chicken pie. No one could object to chicken pie, she decided. Feeling happily convinced that the grandmother would die of disapproval, she loaded up with pre-made mashed potato and ready-prepared veg. Then she bought the makings of a trifle, which would take two minutes to prepare, be delicious and was as old-fashioned as you like.

'OK,' Alice said, back at Lucy's table. 'I'm done. Let's go.'

'I've just looked at my list,' said Lucy. 'We need whisky. A single malt.'

'I'll find it. Which one?'

'Glen-something.'

Alice sighed. 'Loads of them are called Glen-something. You'd better ring Phillip. It would be fatal to get the wrong one.' Probably not fatal, she amended while Lucy was on the phone, but definitely not good for Lucy.

They loaded up Alice's car and set off in convoy.

19

'Are you sure this is the place?' Alice had parked her car behind Lucy's in front of a house that looked like the set for a modern version of *Sleeping Beauty*.

'Yes. I did say no one's been here for years.'

'And Phillip's grandmother wants to sleep here? I can't believe it!'

Lucy shrugged. 'It's her house and it's going to be sold and she feels sentimental about it, even though it'll be damp and horrible. But actually the real reason is she's too mean to go into a hotel.'

'She might have to,' said Alice grimly. 'Have you got the key? Let's go in. If we can get past the laurels, that is.'

Alice had been joking, but actually it was a bit of a struggle. What had once been bushes had turned into trees and they had to duck under to climb the steps to the front door.

Lucy's key was stiff and it took them a while to get the front door open.

They both coughed as dust and stale air hit them.

'I'm sure this isn't healthy for pregnant women,' said Lucy.

'I'm sure it's fine,' said Alice glibly, not at all sure. She wasn't sure it was good for elderly ladies either but this one was probably built of stern stuff and wouldn't be affected by a bit of dust. 'We'll open some windows and get some fresh air in.'

'If you can open the windows,' said Lucy gloomily.

Alice ignored this pessimism, but felt Lucy might well be right.

'It's what Bella would call 'ripe for restoration',' Alice said as they entered the sitting room, which she felt should really be called a parlour. It looked like the set of a period drama, only with dust.

'Definitely in need of a makeover,' agreed Lucy. 'But I like the period details.'

Alice glanced at her, surprised. She hadn't expected this from Lucy.

The room was fairly small and Victorian in period and style. The mantelpiece had ornaments reflected in a carved mirror. Below, by the fireplace, was a neat little 'companion set' — poker, shovel and brush — all hanging on a stand and looking fairly unused. The fireplace itself was concealed behind a needlepoint fire screen.

'Yes. If it was clean and less cluttered it could be a very pretty room. And I bet you could knock through to the next room if you wanted.' She tapped on the wall. It sounded solid. 'You might need to support the ceiling, though.'

'We'd better find the kitchen,' said Lucy. 'Which will have an old range and a spit over an open fire. I don't think the maids in mop caps and frilly aprons will still be there though.'

Alice followed her out of the room, feeling more inclined to like her as well as feeling desperately sorry for her. A sense of humour seemed to be emerging from the gloom and hysterics.

'Well, it does have an electric cooker,' said Alice. 'Probably pre-war though.'

'I expect you're right.'

They looked at the cooker, which had one square solid plate at the back and two smaller ones at the front. Lucy turned a switch and held her hand expectantly over the solid metal plate. 'It doesn't work,' she said after a few moments. 'Which either means we have to get hold of a camping stove or call the whole thing off.'

'I'm all for calling it off,' said Alice, 'although we have got quite a lot of food. But I expect the electricity has been turned off at the mains. I just hope they're not in a dark cupboard which we won't be able to find.'

They tracked the fuse box down to a cupboard full of old, cracking mackintoshes that smelt strongly of perishing rubber and threatened to break when they moved them. Alice pulled down a lever.

'Let's hope that's the right one. Turn on a light, Lucy.'

'Are you sure it won't electrocute me?'

'Reasonably.'

Lucy found a beautiful old brass light fitting and flicked the switch. High above them, almost entirely concealed by a dark-red lampshade, a bulb glowed.

'That's a start!' said Alice. 'Let's go and investigate the kitchen again. What time are you expecting them?'

'About six.'

'It's only twelve now so we needn't panic. Shall we go upstairs first? If it's totally uninhabitable for your grandmother-in-law we'd better give Phillip plenty of time to find her a suitable hotel.'

'Cool,' said Lucy. 'I want a nosy anyway.'

'So do I,' said Alice, following the girl up the stairs.

The bedrooms were as Victorian as the sitting room had been, only in here dark patches of damp had lifted the rather charming floral paper.

'I think the roof must leak,' said Alice. 'Phillip's grandmother certainly can't sleep here.'

Lucy nodded. 'Do you think Phillip will say he'll find a hotel and we can have dinner there as well?'

'That would be good,' said Alice.

But Phillip obviously didn't have the authority to make the decision. 'I'll get back to you,' was his reply when Lucy called him.

'Well, let's have a good look round while we're here,' said Lucy. 'If it's all going to be grim we might as well get some fun out of it.'

There were two more bedrooms, also damp, with old-fashioned paisley eiderdowns on the narrow single beds. They then found and admired the bathroom, with a genuine roll-top bath with ball and claw feet. Next door, in a room of its own, was a 'Crapper' lavatory, with a proper overhead flush with a chain and a ceramic handle that said 'Pull' on it.

'You know, I miss those,' said Alice. 'These water-saving ones are all very planet-friendly, but they don't give you that satisfying swoosh of water.'

'This house is a museum. But I like it,' said Lucy.

Phillip came back to Lucy quite quickly. She'd put it on speakerphone so she wouldn't have to relate it all to Alice. 'Sorry, hon, we've got to go through with it. She's agreed to sleep in a hotel but she wants dinner in her own house. It's why she's come down, after all: to have a last meal in the house where she was so happy with Grandfather.'

'OK,' said Lucy, 'but the cooker might not work. If it doesn't, it's a hotel, OK?'

Alice couldn't actually hear Phillip sighing but she knew he was. 'OK, darling, but please try!' he said out loud. 'This is so important to everyone!'

'Yeah, sure. So important they want me to do it when they know I can't cook.' Then a few moments later she said, 'OK, I'll do my best. I really love this house, even if it does leak and smell of mice.'

Alice was not optimistic about being able to cook in the kitchen. It wouldn't be easy even if everything worked, and that was by no means certain.

'Phillip's grandmother must think everything's fine or she wouldn't ask you to cook in it,' Alice said, peering into the oven. At least it wasn't full of long-forgotten roasting tins.

'Well, I'm sure she's quite nasty enough to ask something that's blatantly impossible, but she does think her house is liveable in. She told

Phillip there was nothing at all wrong with it.'

'OK, let's see if this works.' Alice turned a knob. Instantly the overhead light went off. It didn't make a huge difference, given that it hardly provided any light, but it didn't look good from an electrical point of view. 'If Phillip's grandmother decides not to sell, and you and Phillip end up inheriting this house, Lucy, you must promise me you'll have it rewired.'

'God, yes!'

'I'll go and see if I can work out what's wrong.'

Alice went to burrow in the coats again, and emerged a bit later having flicked more switches.

'OK, I'm not an expert on electricity but that might work.'

Again the light went out the moment the cooker went on.

'All right, it's either cooker or lights. We can cope with that. But will the cooker actually get hot enough to cook on?' she said.

Both she and Lucy held their hands over the plate, as if trying to cure themselves of frostbite. Eventually Alice bravely flicked the plate with her finger. 'Actually, that's quite hot.'

'But how can you cook in the pitch dark?' asked Lucy, half scowling, half curious.

'Wait here,' said Alice.

She returned a few minutes later and Lucy burst out laughing.

'Why? What's so funny?' said Alice, straight-faced.

'You're wearing a head torch!' shrieked Lucy. 'It's bloody hilarious!'

Alice kept her mouth prim. 'I don't know why

you should think that. It's a perfectly sensible solution to our problem.'

'Sure but why do you even *have* a head torch?' said Lucy, when she had stopped laughing enough to speak.

Alice allowed herself to be amused. 'It is a bit mad, but Bella gave me an emergency kit to keep in the car one Christmas. It had things like chocolate and brandy and stuff which all went immediately. But the head torch and the first-aid kit are still there.'

'I knew you were the right person to ask for help,' said Lucy.

'Let's face it, I was the only person you could ask. I don't suppose you were going to trawl through the Waitrose customers looking for helpful women of a certain age, were you?'

'I suppose not. But I am really glad we met up there.'

'I'm sure,' said Alice and realised that she was too. 'Now we'd better get this meal going.'

20

The day after Nevil showed her the house she had so hated, and which demonstrated so clearly that he just didn't have a clue about her taste, Bella went into the office full of resolution. She wasn't going to wait any longer. She was going to get the Agnews to decide about Badger Cottage, one way or another. Having admired Tina's particularly pretty jewel-spangled sandals, she told her the plan.

'You mean it's time they pissed or got off the pot?' Tina asked, having waggled her feet in recognition of Bella's praise.

Bella nodded. 'Obviously, they are clients and I wouldn't dream of saying that, but yes, that is exactly what I mean.' The phone was answered. 'Mr Agnew? It's your favourite estate agent — '

'Bella!' Mr Agnew sounded delighted. 'I was just about to call you. We want to look at Badger Cottage again!'

'Oh, hooray!' said Bella. 'I am so pleased. And let's hope this time you realise how absolutely perfect it is for you.'

'Well, we think it is. Of course it's taken a lot of thought, but then I made a model of how the upstairs could be and my wife's been won over. And we've done a few other checks.'

What the hell these might be, Bella couldn't imagine. Surely they hadn't tried to do their own searches? 'That's brilliant news,' she said, still enthusiastic. 'When would you like to have another viewing?'

'Well, we'd really like to see it as soon as possible. I don't suppose this afternoon . . . ?'

'Perfect!' said Bella. 'No time like the present. When can you be there by?'

* * *

Bella had to work very hard in the next two hours to give herself time to show them the house, but she felt so excited at the prospect of making a sale that she didn't mind. She thought about telling Nevil she was showing Badger Cottage to the Agnews again, but decided against it. His negative comments about them being time-wasters and totally incapable of making up their minds would rankle. And if they turned it down yet again (which was perfectly likely) he would gloat. On this thought, she became determined to get them to commit this time. There was no reason why it wasn't the perfect house for them.

Badger Cottage was doing its absolute best to get sold, Bella decided. For some reason to do with wind direction, the motorway was silent. The sun shone; the resident wren sang long and loud. A row of peonies had appeared in the border in front of the house and roses bloomed everywhere.

She unlocked the door. No previously undiscovered patch of damp had appeared, and no sinister smells made her estate agent's nostrils twitch. The house was 'move-in' fresh. Bella felt that if they turned it down this time she might really have to consider giving up on them.

As she stepped out of the front door she saw the Agnews' car arrive. She felt a glimmer of satisfaction at having arrived before them for once.

'You don't need me to show it to you,' she said, stepping back from the front door so they could enter. 'You know it as well as I do now, probably better.'

They laughed and Bella was further encouraged. They wouldn't be so cheery if they were just going to shake their heads and say the garden really was too small, or the light came through the front windows at the wrong angle. On this summer afternoon it was a perfect spot.

Bella went and sat on the grass under a tree on the verge. After a quick check of her emails, she thought about Nevil. Why was he convinced he could get that massively expensive house at a price they could afford? Was it anything to do with the fact he'd become so secretive recently? He never used to shut his door, liking to hear what was going on in the main office. Now he seemed to close it whenever his phone rang. He was always shooting out to go to unspecified meetings that weren't written in the diary, and when he came back, he'd never say where he'd been. Bella had been vaguely aware of all this without taking much notice. However, since the visit to that house she'd realised he'd been behaving quite oddly.

She chided herself for being unusually dense and admitted it was because she'd been distracted by thoughts of Dominic. I must stop it, she told herself sharply. I must pay attention to what's going on with Nevil. But then she realised just telling yourself that you mustn't think about someone meant you were thinking about them. In the end she played *Angry Birds* as a distraction.

* * *

'Well?' She tried not to sound too eager as the Agnews emerged from the house a little while later. They were holding hands.

'We think we'd like to put in an offer.'

'Ah!' Bella felt quite tearful all of a sudden. 'That's wonderful! What made you finally decide?'

Mrs Agnew was rueful. 'Well, I was aware that I couldn't get what I really wanted on our budget and that I did have to compromise.'

'Besides,' went on Mr Agnew, 'we'd be just as fussy renters as buyers, and we realised that while this isn't our dream home — '

'No one lives in their dream home. Everyone has to compromise.' Bella was smiling but she did sound quite firm.

'Exactly,' said Mr Agnew. 'But it's still a charming little house that we could easily sell if our dream home came up — '

'At a price you could afford,' prompted Bella.

'That's it,' Mr Agnew agreed.

'And this is one of the prettiest houses on our books.'

'Very sweet,' agreed Mrs Agnew.

'Well, I couldn't be more delighted,' said Bella. 'Sadly I don't have the vendor's details on my phone' — she'd felt putting them in would jinx the whole thing — 'but I'll go back now and get in touch.' She paused. 'So how much do you want to offer?'

Mr Agnew suggested a figure that wasn't insulting, but was less than the full asking price. 'Do you think that's about right?' he said afterwards.

'I think that's perfect,' said Bella. 'Room for manoeuvre, but not rude. Will you move a bit on that if you have to?'

'Yes we will, but obviously we do want to do work on it and don't have a massive budget.'

Bella knew exactly how massive their budget was and it wasn't, really. 'Fine. So, will you wait here? Or go into town and get a cuppa?'

'Definitely. A cup of tea to celebrate finding our home at last.' said Mrs Agnew. 'Could we meet you at that little café on the corner? You know — on the junction between the High Street and Queen Street?' She laughed. 'We've been house-hunting so long we know all the best places to get tea and cake.'

'Of course,' said Bella. 'I'll go back now and get in touch with the vendor when I've got the paperwork in front of me.'

* * *

She swept into the office on a tide of euphoria. 'Yes!' she said, punching the air. 'I have sold a house to officially the fussiest couple in the history of house-selling!'

There was a lot of exclaiming: 'Yeah!' and 'Well done' and 'Good for you, Bells', and the noise drew Nevil out of his office.

'What's all the fuss?' he asked. 'It had better be good. I was having an important phone call.'

Her euphoria faded. 'Badger Cottage! The Agnews are finally putting in an offer, after seeing it goodness knows how many times.' Nevil's expression froze. 'That's good, isn't it?' Bella prompted him, wanting him to acknowledge her achievement.

'I'm sorry, Bells. Can you come in here a moment?'

Bella went through to his office, annoyed he couldn't just be pleased that the Agnews were finally suited.

'I'm afraid it's not for sale. It's off the market.'

'What is?' Bella was confused. 'What property are you talking about?'

'Badger Cottage.'

Bella shook her head. 'I think you're getting muddled. I rang the vendors to make sure I could show it to the Agnews — this morning. It was on the market then. In fact, they were pleased to think they might be finally selling.'

'And they have sold, but not to the Agnews.'

Bella realised her mouth had fallen open in disbelief and closed it. 'Are you saying that I have to go back to the Agnews, who've been looking for so long, and tell them that the house they have finally — finally! — decided to buy is not available?'

''Fraid so.'

He did seem embarrassed, but Bella was in no mood to sympathise. She swept out of his door and into the main office. She picked up her bag and her keys from her desk and marched to the door. Then she stopped, turned round and stepped back in. 'Sorry, guys, the celebration has been cancelled.'

Her gloom gathering, she got in her car and set off, wondering what on earth she could say to the Agnews to lessen their inevitable disappointment. It was so awful! Just as they'd finally made up their minds.

* * *

The Agnews were sitting at the table with a laptop open in front of them.

'Hi,' she said.

They looked up and seemed strangely embarrassed.

'Shall I order some tea?' Bella asked, although the table was strewn with evidence that they'd had tea. 'I want some even if you don't.'

Mrs Agnew smiled weakly, looking ashen. 'Tea would be good. I'm afraid we've got some bad news for you.'

Bella bit her lip. 'Ah. I'll have cake too then.' She realised they were going to pull out. What excuse could they possibly give this time? It was just as well, as they couldn't buy Badger Cottage even if they wanted to. When at last her tea was in front of her, Bella took a sip. 'OK, so what's your bad news? Can I guess?'

'You probably can. I'm afraid we can't buy

Badger Cottage. We don't want to make an offer.' Mr Agnew looked mortified.

If it hadn't been for Nevil's revelation about the house no longer being on the market, Bella would have been extremely irritated. As it was, she was relieved. How much worse would it have been for her to have to tell them that the house had been taken off the market in the couple of hours since they'd last seen it?

'Can I ask why?' she asked. 'You seemed so certain this time.'

'I know,' said Mrs Agnew, 'and we're terribly sorry . . . '

'Yes?' Bella prompted.

Mrs Agnew looked at her husband for support.

He took over the explanations. 'You remember I said we were doing more checks?'

Bella nodded.

'Well, we did and' — he turned the laptop towards her — 'this is the result.' He moved the cursor about the screen and then said, 'Watch this.'

It was quite hard to see, but it seemed to be a film of the outside of Badger Cottage.

'It's our security camera,' explained Mrs Agnew. 'We record the creatures that come to the garden at night. We had to check there was wildlife at Badger Cottage.'

'It's right in the country, there's bound to be wildlife,' said Bella.

'That's what we thought,' went on Mrs Agnew. 'But we didn't quite expect this.'

'And don't worry, we put the camera on the

verge, not on the property,' said Mr Agnew.

Bella wasn't bothered by possible illegalities. She peered at the screen. She could see two men who seemed to be digging in a ditch just outside the garden.

'Here,' said Mrs Agnew. 'You can zoom in if you like.'

The picture was even more grainy, but Bella now recognised one of the men. It was Nevil. Her heart seemed to stop beating for a moment. What on earth was going on?

'I'm afraid we can't buy the cottage now. Not if this sort of thing is likely to happen right outside,' explained Mrs Agnew apologetically. 'We were expecting wildlife, not people. I'd never be able to sleep a wink there now.'

'I quite understand,' said Bella, who no longer cared if they bought the cottage or not. She was frantically trying to work out what the hell Nevil was up to and why.

'Do you know when you took this bit of film?' she asked, deliberately keeping as calm as she could, although her brain was racing.

'The date is on there,' said Mr Agnew.

'Oh yes. Sorry, I didn't notice,' said Bella. 'Have you uploaded this recording somewhere? Is it possible for you to send it to me? A link?'

'Certainly,' said Mr Agnew. 'I've got your email address.'

'Actually,' said Bella quickly. 'Can I give you my private address?'

'You don't want anyone from the office to see it?' asked Mrs Agnew.

'I'm not sure. Maybe not,' said Bella,

desperately trying to work out what she'd seen in the video. There might well be a perfectly innocent explanation as to why Nevil and someone else should be digging in a ditch at the dead of night, but Bella couldn't immediately imagine what it might be. 'I'll have to try and work it out.'

'What do you think is going on?' asked Mrs Agnew, having kindly refilled Bella's cup.

Bella shook her head. 'I have no idea,' she said, although privately she was fairly sure it was something to do with the other buyers.

'It is very odd,' said Mrs Agnew. 'We've been filming wildlife for years like this and we've never come across a person before.'

'I'm sure,' agreed Bella, wondering how soon she could leave to try and sort out this mess.

'We are a bit fed up,' said Mr Agnew. 'We thought we'd really found our home.'

Bella turned her mind to her clients with an effort. 'I promise you, I will find you a home. And soon.' Really, she could kill Nevil for putting her in this position. Not only did he sell the house under her nose, in a manner of speaking, he also took a starring role in a very bizarre piece of film. It was a mystery and not one she was enjoying.

Suddenly she realised that the Agnews didn't know it was Nevil in the picture and that it was his fault they couldn't buy Badger Cottage even if they could get over the men-in-the-ditch thing, which obviously they couldn't. She didn't blame them. It was one thing to see Mr Brock the Badger fossicking about in the undergrowth, but his human counterpart was quite different.

'You've already worked so hard for us,' said Mrs Agnew.

'And I will succeed.'

Even as she left them to their tea and their laptop, her idea that the Agnews and Jane Langley could join forces returned. Jane was finding her house and garden too much for her but didn't want to move. The Agnews wanted to live in a small stately home but didn't have anything like the budget. Could she convince them both that living together might be the answer?

* * *

Bella found the link to the video while she was still in her car. She replayed it over and over but still couldn't work out what the men were doing. Was it something harmless? If so, what? And what if it wasn't harmless? She still couldn't work out what they were up to. She headed off back to the office, determined to get some answers out of Nevil, if only to who had bought Badger Cottage.

She walked into his office without knocking. 'So? What happened?'

He looked up from some papers, which he turned over quickly before he answered. She couldn't decide if he looked apologetic or defiant. She hardened her gaze.

'I am so sorry, sweets,' he said.

'Not as sorry as I was. Imagine having to tell people who've been house-hunting forever, who have finally found something they like, that it's no longer on the market?' He didn't need to know she hadn't had to do this, that they'd pulled out for different reasons. After all, the reason was his fault too.

Nevil shrugged. 'Shit happens.'

'No! Not to me! I check things, Nevil. I don't show people round houses that are not for sale.'

He put his head on one side. 'Well, you do sometimes, Bells.'

'It's not funny! I'm not going to let you get away with this. I know you're the boss, but you put me in a horrible position.'

'I know I did, but there wasn't time to warn you.'

Bella put her hand on her hip and scratched her head. 'Why wasn't there? I mean, house sales usually take a few days even if everything is being rushed. With Badger Cottage it was for sale in the early afternoon and off the market before teatime! Fastest sale ever!'

'It was quick,' he acknowledged. 'And obviously we haven't gone through all the processes, but the deal was done.' He glared up at her.

Bella sighed with frustration. 'For goodness' sake!'

Nevil shrugged. 'I am the head of this firm. I'm allowed to sell property too, you know.'

'Don't pull rank, Nevil.'

Their eyes locked for several seconds. Bella contemplated walking out now, forever. She was so angry. He'd behaved completely unprofessionally and he didn't even care. He treated her with less respect than the office wastepaper basket. What the hell had she ever seen in him?

Nevil blinked first. 'Let's do dinner. Let me take you out and — '

'Explain what the hell is going on?'

He nodded. 'Something like that.' He paused. 'It's all good news, Bells. Really it is.' He gave her his best winning smile. 'Pax?'

Bella relented, mostly because if she didn't, she might never find out what was happening.

Dinner with him was not an enticing prospect but she needed to find out what he was up to, and if possible discover what on earth he was doing digging a hole with A. N. Other in the middle of the night. He needed to keep her in the picture, tell her things, not let her try and sell houses that had been sold already. As far as he was concerned they were engaged, and yet he didn't seem to trust her with quite basic information. They had to sort things out.

21

Bella decided to dress up for her dinner with Nevil. She wanted to look in control and professional, so he wouldn't be tempted to ruffle her hair and treat her with amused contempt. This was serious.

She hadn't yet decided how to deal with the matter of the video — it was hard when she didn't know what it really revealed. Although there was nothing she could think of that wasn't dodgy in some way. Or why do it at the dead of night? If only she could ask someone for advice. But until she knew a bit more she didn't really know *what* to ask anyone. She didn't want to go off at half-cock and look an idiot.

Really she just needed to find out about Badger Cottage, and not warn Nevil she knew he was up to something until she knew exactly what he was up to.

It was while she was in the shower that she remembered a half-heard conversation between Tina and one of the others in the office about a sale Peter had been about to close, only to find the property was no longer for sale.

Bella had been deeply involved in something at the time and had just put it down to Peter not checking out the situation properly, but now she wondered if in fact the same thing had happened to him. The trouble was, she couldn't ask him now, about a month later, without him asking why she wanted to know. She didn't want to involve anyone else until she knew more. The whole thing was like a jigsaw puzzle with too many pieces unconnected. She needed a few more bits so she could see the picture.

She put on her new pencil skirt with the high, tight waistband that made her look slim and elegant and feel like Audrey Hepburn. She added a chiffon blouse and pearls round her neck and in her ears. By the time she'd battled her curls into a chignon — only possible because her hair needed washing and even then it required a lot of product — she felt different: a force to be reckoned with and not Nevil's tubby little curly top. She almost wore dark glasses to go with the 'early James Bond spy' style, but restrained herself. It wasn't the expected look for a cosy dinner with her fiancé, but this was different. She walked to the car, carrying her stilt heels, wearing her loafers. She'd left a note for Alice telling her she'd be out for the evening.

As she drove, she contemplated breaking off her strange engagement — she could use the awful house as the reason — but again dismissed the idea. If she left Nevil she'd have to leave the agency, and her curiosity wouldn't let her do that until she'd found out what he was up to.

* * *

'Darling! You look amazing!' said Nevil, sounding surprised and kissing her ear. 'Loving the new look! A lot more sophisticated. Though maybe you should have run the straighteners over your hair before you put it up?'

Bella didn't actually own any straighteners, and wasn't going to get any to please Nevil. How did he even know about straighteners anyway?

'Glad you approve,' she said, ignoring his caveat. She moved past him into the sitting room. If she'd really loved him she'd have been hurt that he seemed to prefer her looking like this to her more natural, everyday self.

He seemed to sense something more had changed about her than just her clothes.

'Drink? I've got a bottle of fizz.'

'No thank you. I'd rather have something soft.'

'Aren't you staying, then?' He looked surprised and hurt and Bella felt a pang. If he'd been a different sort of person she probably could have broken up with him and stayed in the job she loved. But if he'd been a different sort of person maybe she wouldn't have stopped loving him.

She forced a smile and shook her head. 'Better not. I've got so much to do tomorrow. And aren't we going out to eat? I'll drive if you want to drink?' Although socially it would be much easier for her if they went to a restaurant, she realised it would also be much harder for her to get him to explain about Badger Cottage.

'I've cooked,' said Nevil. 'I thought it would be easier. We need to talk.'

Just for a moment Bella wondered if he was going to break up with her. How perfect would that be? He would say, 'It's not you, it's me,' in a firm but kindly way and then add, 'Of course you can stay on at Rutherfords. I'd hate to lose you. But I'm not ready to commit just yet.' She could be hurt and upset but not storm out of the firm, because she was professional. She could carry on with the job, burying her supposedly broken heart behind a brave smile. But she knew this was just a fantasy. Nevil would never question a decision, and if he'd decided he wanted to marry her that was that. No, she would have to be the one to break it off; she just had to wait for the time to be right.

'Sounds a bit ominous.' She was preparing the ground so it didn't look too suspicious if she burst into tears later.

Nevil held up a protesting hand. 'Nothing bad, I promise you. In fact, I put the champers in the fridge so we could celebrate. Are you sure you won't have a glass?'

Bella pushed aside her disappointment. It had been a bit of a vain hope anyway. If Nevil was planning to break up with her, he wouldn't have invited her to dinner. Why waste the money on a woman you had no use for? 'OK then.' But she wasn't going to be talked into more and have to stay the night. 'In a minute you must tell me what we're celebrating, but first, I do want to talk to you about Badger Cottage. You put me in a very embarrassing situation today.' He didn't know exactly how he'd done this, but he did know he'd sold Badger Cottage under her nose.

'Oh, sweets, I absolutely want to tell you about that. Totally.' He took a little while taking the wire and foil off the bottle and then eased out the cork. 'There — a perfect 'angel's fart',' he said, referring to the sound of the cork leaving the bottle. He poured wine into two glasses he had ready.

He was trying to distract her, and her suspicion was growing. He was up to something and he wanted her approval otherwise why the champagne? Was it something to do with their wedding? Or was the celebration for a business reason?

'Here's to you, darling,' he said, clinking his glass against hers.

'Cheers!' she said in reply. She took a sip. 'So, about Badger Cottage?'

He laughed and Bella knew he was embarrassed. 'Can't you wait until we've eaten for the business chat?'

Bella shrugged. 'I don't know. It depends how long it will take to explain. It is very odd, you know, taking a house off the market without even telling the owners.'

'It's not all quite as it seems, babycakes.'

'Babycakes? When have you ever called me babycakes!'

'Just now.' A glimmer of the humour she had once liked about him appeared for a second. Then something suppressed it — nerves, she thought.

'So? What's going on?' she said firmly. She perched on the arm of the sofa.

Nevil adjusted the framed photograph of himself in cricket whites receiving a cup.

'I'd sold it to someone else while you were showing it to the Agnews.'

She inclined her head. 'Oh? And did you get a good price?'

'Price isn't everything.'

'It is to the vendors. They usually want the highest price unless there are other things to take into consideration.'

'Absolutely — other things to take into consideration.' He was definitely a bit on edge. 'Look, I've got to go and look in the oven. You watch the news or something.' He left the room before she could reply.

She couldn't face watching television so she picked up a copy of *Cotswold Life*. She ignored the property pages and went to the column at the back. It was a quirky slant on life by a very funny writer and it always made her laugh. She needed light relief just now. Every word Nevil said made her more and more certain he was up to something dreadful. She wondered how he'd gift-wrap what he told her so she wouldn't just walk out on him halfway through the pie and mash that was his signature dish.

It seemed to take for ever before she and Nevil were sitting opposite each other at his dining table, a large meat pie between them. Nevil took a spoon and dug into the pastry. He handed Bella a rugby player's portion.

'Help yourself to veg, darling.'

'That's a big helping for someone who's supposedly watching her weight,' she said, ladling on some peas, wishing she could have just held her tongue and not prolonged the agony.

'Everyone's allowed a treat sometimes,' said Nevil with an indulgent smile. 'And we're celebrating.'

'Are we?'

'Oh yes. Yes, definitely.'

He might have been certain all was going well, but he was being very unspecific. Surely the words 'we're celebrating' should be followed with the reason? Would he never get to the point?

There then followed more of Nevil's delaying tactics. They involved more discussion about wine, and whether she could stay, and why not. To end it Bella had eventually allowed him to put wine into her glass just to stop the argument.

When she could bear it no longer she said, 'OK, tell me all. Why are we celebrating? And what's going on with Badger Cottage?'

He didn't speak for a bit. 'It's not straightforward.'

'I had got that. And I didn't think it would be.' He seemed to find her gaze disconcerting and couldn't look her in the eye. It was looking worse and worse. If it was something simple he'd have told her by now. Was it so bad that the whole firm could be implicated? She took a sip of her wine.

'OK, Bells, I'll be frank with you. I want something better out of life. You know? I don't want to just be an ordinary guy with a two-bed semi, maybe upgrading to a three-bed when the kids come along. I don't want it for me and I don't want it for you.'

Bella nodded, not in agreement but to encourage him to get to the point.

'And I have a colleague who can help. He helps me; I help him.'

Was that the man in the film, she wondered, digging the hole with Nevil? 'Who is he?'

Nevil shook his head. 'Can't tell you, highly confidential.'

Frustrated and irritated, Bella was tempted to press him for the name but managed to restrain herself. She didn't want to sidetrack Nevil into an argument about 'needing to know'. He might do that tapping-the-side-of-his-nose thing and then she might throw something. 'OK, so how does he help you?'

'He shares information and — other things — in exchange for . . . what I can do for him.'

'Which is?'

'Bella! I'm a bloody estate agent! How do you think I help him?'

'You get him properties at below the market value?' This was an educated guess but she felt she might be right.

He shrugged. 'In a way.'

She couldn't believe he'd actually admitted it. He must only be telling her because he thought they were engaged and he could depend on her discretion. Was he really admitting to taking backhanders? Surely she must have got it wrong. Not even Nevil, at his worst, would be that unscrupulous.

'But that's cheating the vendors out of their money.' She spoke mildly, but inside she was horrified.

'No! No I don't! The vendors actually get more money!'

Bella knew he must be lying but she wanted to hear Nevil's argument. 'How?'

'It would all be totally over your head, sweetie, and I don't want to bore you to death.' He added some more wine to her almost untouched glass. 'Suffice it to say that it's because of all this that we can afford that amazing house. I know you had some doubts about the fine detail but you know that was the show home. We don't need to have crystal-studded taps if you don't like them.'

'No.'

'But you 'lurved' the cooker, right? What's not to love, eh? Huge! With every add-on you can think of.'

She thought about the huge black cooker, the size of a small car, and suppressed a shudder. She knew Nevil was deliberately trying to divert her attention so she'd forget what they were supposed to be discussing. But then she began to wonder if it wasn't better if she didn't know the details until she was in a position to do something about it. The more she thought about it the worse it became and she couldn't risk being implicated.

She took a sip from her very full wine glass. 'Nevil — '

'Babes, I know you're very straight. You like to play things by the book, right down the line, but we're never going to move on if we're not a bit flexible with the rules.'

Bella realised she had to say something, although really she wanted Nevil to bluster on and reveal exactly what was going on. 'I don't like to think of people being diddled.'

Had she been a bit sharper she'd have brought a tape recorder from work, or activated her phone to do it. Yet somehow that would have felt like spying. She didn't know if she could have brought herself to do that.

'But they're not! That's the beautiful part!' He was waving his hands in excitement. 'It's all fine! Honestly, Bells, it's all fine! I wouldn't step over the line. Surely you know that?'

She put her knife and fork together. She couldn't force down another mouthful. She knew he wasn't telling her the truth, or if he was, it was only his version of the truth, but she didn't want to call him on it yet. She suddenly felt she had to leave. She got up from the table, as if to go to the bathroom.

Just then, the theme tune from *Rocky* — Nevil's ring tone — sounded. He leapt up. 'I'll have to take that, honey.'

Bella nodded and left the room but then crept back to the kitchen door so she could listen to what Nevil was saying. So far it wasn't terribly revealing.

'Ya, ya, uhuh.' But his tone was low and confidential. Then there was a long silence interspersed with tiny noises.

Bella made a decision. She walked boldly into the kitchen and she indicated that she had to leave, ignoring his frowns. Eventually he said into the phone, 'Can you hang on a moment?'

Before he could speak Bella said, 'Darling, you're busy and I can't really stay. Catch you tomorrow, OK?'

Then she left the room, changing her heels for her loafers in the porch. Before Nevil could do or say anything she was in the car and driving away.

22

Alice parked the car and sat in it for a few moments without moving. She was tired and felt flat. Yesterday, cooking with Lucy had been challenging and fun. Today, sorting jumble with a group of volunteers, none of whom were particular friends, had been less so. Her mind had not been on the job and kept harking back to the previous day.

It wasn't that she'd wanted to be at the dinner party with Phillip and his family, but she had desperately wanted to be a fly on the wall.

Now, as she gathered her bits of shopping she found she was still speculating about it. Was the grandmother really such a dragon? Or was she a sweet old lady who had always been misunderstood by her family? Would she be genuinely happy to have her family around her to eat a last meal in her beloved home? Although, given how long it had been neglected, maybe it wasn't as loved as all that.

Finding herself mildly amused by her thoughts, Alice pursued them as she put her bags on the kitchen table and sorted out her groceries. Had the Dragon (she was definitely a dragon, she decided) regarded Lucy over her pince-nez and said, 'This is almost edible. How unexpected!' and had the rest of the family said, 'Not half bad, Luce. Who'd have thought it, with you preggers and all.'

And had Lucy gracefully accepted the compliments (as Alice had instructed) or admitted to someone — Phillip or maybe Hannah — that she'd had help?

Any family member who knew her would know she'd have had to have help to produce that meal, simple though it was. Alice chuckled when she imagined Hannah's horror if Lucy had confessed to her from whom she'd had the assistance.

Alice finished putting away the tins of tomatoes, chickpeas and other store-cupboard staples and reached for the bottle of wine that stood on the counter, stoppered but otherwise ready to pour. Then she changed her mind and retrieved the whisky from the cupboard. Wine wouldn't cut it today.

She took her drink into the sitting room, although she knew she should be finding herself something to eat. She felt both flat and somehow agitated. She opened the French windows and stepped out into the garden, relishing the warm scented air that surrounded her.

She wandered to the table and chairs where she and Bella sometimes had breakfast at weekends and sat down. She knew that, even without Michael, she had everything a woman at her time of life could want: health, security, friends; and yet even with Michael — a wonderful potential romance — she still wasn't content.

A couple of sips into her whisky she realised what was bothering her. She'd really enjoyed helping Lucy in those very difficult circumstances. (Had Lucy told anyone about the head torch and their other problem-solving ploys?) Now she realised life didn't offer her many new challenges, and somehow the old challenges (the garden, her book group, a bit of voluntary work) didn't seem enough.

She blamed Michael. Meeting him had given her a glimpse of something more and the excitement of the emails, the texts, the girlish thrill of a new relationship had made her aware that other aspects of her life were a bit lacking.

Would she feel like this if she'd had children? Possibly not, although she'd have grandchildren by now and everyone loved those. (How people went on about them!) On the other hand, she'd never felt confident around babies and small children. Young adults, though, were different. She loved spending time with Bella, and yesterday, getting Lucy to brace up and face the challenge, had been stimulating. She'd ended up liking Lucy, something she'd never thought she'd do. But the girl's spikiness and determination to do something difficult out of loyalty to her husband had been endearing.

Another sip of whisky and Alice found herself wondering why she had been so adamant that she didn't want Michael to know she'd helped Lucy. Really it was because she didn't want him to think she was doing things to ingratiate herself. But that was mad, really. He'd gone to a lot of trouble to bring her and his daughters together for a baking day: he deserved to know he'd succeeded. But there was still Hannah. She'd be harder to become friends with, and even with Lucy onside, she might well put up enough opposition to stop Michael and Alice becoming a proper couple.

Alice hugged herself, suddenly chilly. In spite of the fragrance of the evening, she decided to go in. The summer night was making her feel sentimental.

Just as she was about to do this, she saw a figure at the gate and put her glass down. She could see it was male, but the distance meant she didn't recognise him. He waved.

'Alice? Is that you?'

It was Michael. Any flicker of unease at seeing a man by her gate at this hour vanished. She smiled and stood up.

'Of course it's me,' she called. 'Who else would it be? Come in. The gate isn't locked.'

Her heart soared as she watched him stride across the lawn towards her. She didn't speak again; she just stood there. When he arrived he took her into his arms.

At first they had just hugged and then his lips found hers and they were kissing in a way that Alice hadn't been kissed for years. For some seconds she worried that she'd forgotten how to do it. Then she stopped thinking at all.

She had always found the garden at night sensual and romantic, and now the scent of the honeysuckle and jasmine made everything even more intoxicating.

When they stopped for breath she said, 'That was a bit of a surprise.'

'I'm sorry, I had to come, the moment I found out what you'd done for Lucy.' He kissed her again, just briefly.

'You weren't supposed to find out.' She stood in the circle of his arms feeling girlish and protected.

'Phillip let it slip. Apparently it was a triumph. Suddenly my little Lucy stopped being the idiot girl Phillip had been so stupid as to marry and became the heroine of the hour, not to mention bearer of the first great-grandchild.' He paused. 'She told everyone about the head torch.'

Alice smiled. 'It was silly, but it did make Lucy laugh. She needed a laugh just then.'

'You were an utter heroine.' He kissed her again.

A shuddering sigh went through Alice. She hadn't felt like this for aeons and it was so wonderful. Then a bird, suddenly alarmed, returned her to her senses. They really couldn't stay there all night, kissing, however wonderful it was.

'Have you eaten?' she said.

'No, actually. I came straight here from the office. I took the car in today, so I could leave immediately and not wait for the train.'

'That's a long day! Come into the house. Let me make you something to eat.'

'I don't want to put you to any trouble.'

She laughed. 'You won't be. I haven't eaten either and it'll be something made with eggs.'

* * *

It was just gone ten when they heard Bella's car. Alice got up from the sofa quickly, straightening her clothes. She didn't want Bella to know she and Michael had been kissing. She reached the hall just as Bella came through the door.

'Hello!' said Alice, aware she sounded a bit odd. 'How nice to see you. Michael's here.'

Bella's eyes widened a little and she said, 'Then I won't interrupt. I'll just slip upstairs.'

'Don't run away,' said Michael, joining Alice. 'It would be nice to chat.'

'And aren't you back rather early, if you've been having a romantic dinner with your fiancé?'

Bella shrugged. 'Not that romantic. It was pie and mash.'

'We're just about to have a brandy,' said Alice after a quick look at Michael. 'Why don't you join us?'

'Oh no, I wouldn't want to — '

'We'd like that,' said Michael. 'I've just refused brandy, so you could keep Alice company.' He glanced down at her. 'It would stop her feeling bad about it.'

Bella wrinkled her brow. 'Actually, now you've suggested it, I think that brandy is a good idea.'

Alice began gathering signs of their supper guiltily. After they'd eaten their scrambled eggs, she and Michael had moved on to the sofa with very indecent haste. She realised this feeling of being caught out enhanced the magic somehow. There was no reason why she and Michael shouldn't do as they liked but 'making out' wasn't what was usually expected of respectable middle-aged people.

'As I said, I wanted to have a chat,' said Michael, while Alice found glasses.

'Oh?' Bella sat down, looking expectant.

'Yes,' said Alice, putting the glasses and the bottle down on the table. 'Michael is taking me away for the weekend. I wonder if you'll be OK looking after things here? There are some plants I won't get put in before I go and they'll need watering.'

Bella smiled, as if relieved to be asked to do something simple, and Alice wondered how her dinner with Nevil had gone. It wasn't only her god-daughter's slightly different clothes that made her speculate, it was her demeanour. Bella seemed worried.

'Of course I'll do that,' she said. 'And a weekend away. How lovely! Are you going somewhere in Devon, or Cornwall? I can just picture it. Lovely walks by the sea, cream teas, open fires if it's remotely chilly. It sounds like absolute bliss!' No one spoke, so Bella went on. 'So, where are you going?' She picked up her drink and looked at Alice and Michael expectantly.

'We're not going to the West Country actually,' said Michael.

'Oh?' The brandy gave Bella continental ideas. 'Paris then? Rome? Florence? A lovely city break? Maybe Venice? I've always wanted to go to Venice.'

'It sounds to me as if you need a break yourself,' said Alice.

Bella smiled again: to Alice's eyes, rather sadly. 'It would be lovely' She paused. 'So, where are you going then?'

Alice looked at Michael and then back at Bella. 'Marrakesh,' she said.

'Oh my!' said Bella. 'That sounds amazing!'

'It is a long weekend,' said Michael. 'And the joy of it is, it's not a long-haul flight but it is a long-haul destination, if you see what I mean.'

'Totally!' said Bella. 'Oh, Alice! How amazing! And — how surprising!'

'I owe Alice,' said Michael, 'and I don't think a cosy weekend in Devon — however lovely that sounds — would quite repay the debt.'

'Alice! What did you do? Give him a kidney or something?' Bella laughed and sipped her drink. To Alice's acute ears she sounded a bit brittle.

Michael laughed too. 'Well, nearly. She helped my daughter out in a very difficult situation.'

'Oh, how?'

Alice smiled. She hadn't had an opportunity to tell Bella about rescuing Lucy from her plight. 'To be honest, it wasn't all that much, but Michael and Lucy were very grateful for what was only quite a small favour, and one which was great fun.'

'So tell me?' Bella was now desperately curious.

'Lucy had to cook dinner for a very demanding grandmother-in-law,' began Alice.

'And she can't cook and currently can't even face food. She's pregnant,' said Michael.

'And Michael wasn't supposed to know about it,' said Alice.

'What? That Lucy was pregnant?'

'No!' said Alice. 'That I helped Lucy sort things out.'

'Why not?' asked Bella.

'I asked that too,' said Michael, 'but I didn't

get a satisfactory explanation.'

Alice and Bella exchanged looks and Alice realised Bella understood. Alice didn't want Michael to think she was helping his daughter for his sake. It was for different reasons.

'So . . . ' Bella asked.

'I met up with Lucy in Waitrose, by chance,' Alice explained. 'We'd got to know each other a bit at the bakery course, if you remember?' Alice also remembered, but couldn't possibly say, describing Lucy and her sister as little cows.

Bella nodded encouragingly, possibly wondering about Alice's change of view.

'She told me the situation and I offered to help. Nothing more than that. I like Lucy,' Alice added.

Michael laughed. 'Which, considering what a spiky little thing she can be — even when she hasn't got her hormones to blame it on — is quite something.'

Michael got up from the table and put his hand on Alice's shoulder. 'So, you'll come to my house by two tomorrow?'

Alice turned and looked at him. 'That should be plenty of time to get to the airport.'

'And you're sure you don't want me to pick you up?'

'Certainly not. You'd be going in the opposite direction to Heathrow.'

'OK then.' He kissed her cheek but wouldn't let her get up. 'You stay there. I'll see you tomorrow.'

Alice and Bella didn't speak until they'd heard Michael let himself out of the front door.

'Get you!' said Bella, sounding envious. 'Now tell me everything!'

Alice shrugged. 'He's taking me to Marrakesh.' She tried to sound matter-of-fact but couldn't stop herself grinning with excitement.

'I know that! And it's wonderful! But why do you now like Lucy when you really didn't before?'

Alice sat down and refilled the glasses. 'She has spirit. And although I absolutely swore her to secrecy — she was not to tell Michael about me helping — she told Phillip, who told Michael.'

'And you didn't want Michael to know because you didn't want him . . . '

Alice sighed deeply. 'You got it. I didn't want him to think I was trying to catch him by sucking up to his daughters. I think Lucy worked that out and respected it. But she also felt I deserved the credit for helping her out.'

'So why did you help her out?'

'Because that grandmother is from hell. She's a bully and a snob and you know I can't stand either of those.'

'And you and Michael are in love?'

Alice nodded, biting her lip to hold in her joy. 'I didn't mean it to happen but really, one doesn't have as much control over these things as one would like.'

Bella laughed fondly, their roles entirely reversed. Bella was now the elder, happy that her younger friend had found love. 'That is exactly right.'

23

When Bella was getting ready for work the next morning, Alice had anything remotely 'summery' in her wardrobe spread out on her bed.

'If you've got your passport and your credit card,' said Bella, who had brought her up a cup of tea, 'you don't need to worry. You can just buy anything you need.'

'That's just the kind of thing I say to people,' said Alice, accepting the mug. 'Why is it that sort of advice is so hard to take?'

Bella shrugged and then glanced at her watch. 'I have to go in a minute. You'll sort it out, and have a lovely, lovely time!'

When they'd finished embracing and saying goodbye Bella felt all over again as if she was the older friend, sending the giddy girl off on an adventure. She only just managed not to say, 'Do be careful!'

Bella was glad to have Alice's trip to think about — something positive and happy when her own life seemed such a muddle. Seeing Alice and Michael together, obviously very much in love, had really highlighted what a poor imitation of it was shared by her and Nevil. If they'd had that slightly insane giddiness in the beginning, Bella could hardly remember it. And although she did think Nevil loved her, it was only because she was the type he needed to progress through life. She was capable and could cook. She was well spoken and had good social skills. She would never embarrass him, and Nevil could take her anywhere and be confident she would enhance his image.

But Bella needed more than that. Nevil wanting to marry her because she ticked all the boxes wasn't enough. She wanted to be loved for other, less specific reasons. Michael loved Alice because she was Alice, not for her cooking or her house or even because she was nice to his daughter. While she couldn't know for sure, Bella felt their body language told her this. Bella desired that for herself.

If only she could finish with Nevil now and stop pretending! But how could she find out what he was up to if she didn't have access to the files and records at the agency? The internet was amazing, but although she'd had a look around on her laptop last night, she was no further on with her investigations.

She wished again that she had someone she could consult: Tina, or one of the other agents, perhaps? But if Nevil wasn't doing anything wrong, it would be wrong of her to involve anyone else who worked for him. He might even be able to sue her for defamation of character or something.

Although Dominic was never far from her mind, it was only when thinking about being sued that it occurred to her he might be able to help.

She ran a quick check to make sure she wasn't using this as an excuse to get in touch with him, and realised he could be just the person — a solicitor who was experienced in property law

— and felt cheered. She'd do a bit more research herself and then ask him. Simply realising she didn't have to deal with this entirely on her own raised her spirits, and she returned to the job in hand.

It was lovely to focus on what she knew she could do for a little while, and stop trying to be a private detective, and she decided that if she could get the Agnews settled she could leave the agency if she had to; they wouldn't be cast adrift on the raft of other people's lack of interest. She had a fairly off-the-wall solution and it involved Jane Langley.

Knowing she was an early riser, Bella rang Jane before she left the house. She needed to speak to her about this personally, and decided to get a meeting in the diary. She could arrange the rest of her work round it.

Jane indicated she'd be delighted to see her and promised there'd be rock cakes. They fixed a time and Bella set off for work.

Although she was a little late she was surprised to see Nevil in the main office. He seemed full of surplus energy and excitement, like a collie at an agility class, waiting for the command to leap over or under or through something.

'Hi, darling,' he said, obviously forgetting his own rule of not letting the office know Bella was his girlfriend — although of course everyone did.

'Nevil.' Bella tried to hide her dismay behind a smile. 'Can I help you?' Too late she realised she sounded as if she was talking to a client, not a lover.

'Oh yes. Can you do a viewing? Now?'

'Erm — can it wait until I've got myself sorted? I have only just got through the door.'

Nevil glanced at his watch, possibly drawing attention to the fact she was late. 'Not really. They've come down from London and have houses to see. We can't afford to hang around.'

'Can't you do it? I mean if it's urgent,' she added, remembering he was her boss.

'Waiting for a phone call,' he said.

No change there, then, thought Bella, thinking of the phone call that had interrupted them the previous evening, ignoring the fact that she'd been so grateful for it.

'At your convenience, obviously,' he went on, 'but we are here to sell houses.' His smile was a toxic combination of sarcastic and patronising.

Inside Bella wanted to scream. Last night he'd seemed to want to ingratiate himself with her. This morning he was playing the boss with a vengeance.

Any doubts she'd had about breaking off their relationship vanished. The moment the Agnews and Jane Langley were sorted and she'd got to the bottom of his shenanigans, she'd be out of there before Nevil could even see her leave. 'Which house?'

'You know? The one we had all that work done to and is now a little gem? Lots of interest already?'

'Oh yes, Mrs Macey's.' She looked at him, ignoring the 'we' that indicated he had something to do with the makeover, and trying to keep her expression bland. 'It is still for sale, is it?'

He rolled his eyes. 'Of course it is!'

'Then I shall get on to it instantly!' She aimed for a smile. She couldn't really afford to fall out with him yet, and in her heart of hearts she would have hated him to show anyone round what she considered to be one of 'her' houses.

Bella went to fetch the paperwork. Thinking about Mrs Macey's home, charming but rather tucked into the hillside, made her realise a possible reason for Badger Cottage being snapped up behind everyone's backs. It was next to a large field and, if the right permissions were granted, could be a site for a valuable little development. Was the developer of Nevil's dream home — the one worth well over a million, and that he could get for a bargain price — the purchaser? Was this quick sale to help him?

Suddenly it was obvious. Nevil was in cahoots with a property developer, and was planning to get very rich on the proceeds. She felt sick suddenly. It was so shocking. And she'd definitely need help. Dominic was the only solicitor she could confide in. Before she could change her mind she sent him a quick email, with the link to the film of Nevil and someone digging in the dark outside Badger Cottage, and then asking if they could meet, explaining she needed his advice. She could think exactly what to say to him later.

By the time she went back into the main office Nevil had disappeared behind his closed door and her colleagues looked at her sympathetically as she made her way outside.

She loved her job; she loved finding the right houses for the right people: it was like being a matchmaker! Why did Nevil have to be so greedy? Why did he have to mess everything up? Then she felt a pang of guilt. If he did really love her though, she'd have to be a bit tactful when she broke up with him. And then find another estate agent. That was the downer, starting again, again . . .

She set off for Mrs Macey's, wondering if what Nevil was doing was in fact illegal or merely immoral. She needed Dominic to tell her and hoped he'd get back to her soon. This whole business was really worrying.

Bella loved showing people round Mrs Macey's cottage. She always arrived early for viewings so she could water the geraniums if necessary, and sometimes pick some flowers from the garden and put an arrangement in the sitting room. She always opened the windows to make sure there was no smell of damp. As she did these things today she wondered if she was also being dishonest. There was no damp-proof course, the cottage did need a lot of work to bring it up to modern standards, so should she just let it look like what it was: old, small and darkish? Was what she did to make it look lovely a bit underhand? She thought about it and then decided no. Her ministrations were only hints about how the cottage could be with a little investment of time and money.

'Oh my goodness, look at that view!' exclaimed the woman who had just got out of her car. 'It's amazing!'

Bella smiled. If people fell in love with the view she was halfway there.

The woman was joined by her husband. They were a couple in late middle age who, judging by their car and their clothes, were affluent and had taste. Bella just hoped they weren't looking for a second home.

'Hello!' Bella said, holding out her hand. 'You must be Mr and Mrs Truelove? I'm Bella Castle. Now come on in . . . '

When Bella finally drove away, having told the Trueloves that they must get a full structural survey and everything else negative she could think of, she knew they were determined to buy it. She felt pleased for the grumpy Mrs Macey. She was going to be thrilled — and if 'thrilled' wasn't in her vocabulary of emotions, she would have to admit that the small amount of money she'd spent on dolling it up had been worthwhile. Bella glanced at her watch. She had time to get through most of her 'to do list' before going to see Jane Langley. She just hoped Jane would be open to the idea — however unconventional it seemed. And to her relief, Nevil was nowhere to be seen when she got back to the office. She couldn't face him at the moment. She was so horrified about what she suspected he was up to.

* * *

Jane and Bella were sitting in their favourite spot in the garden, with a tray of tea on the rickety table, when Jane said, 'Well, dear, lovely as it is to see you, I sense you have a purpose beyond rock cakes.'

Bella nodded. 'Yes I have. And I'll come straight out with it. You know you've been worrying about the work that needs doing on the house, where you'll find the money, will you have to move, everything like that?'

Jane did seem a bit taken aback by this list of concerns but she nodded. 'Ye-es.'

'Well, I might have found the solution.' Although Bella had intended to just say it without preamble, she found she'd stalled.

'Which is? Apart from buying lottery tickets?'

'That you sell part of your house. I mean divide it properly, possibly into a sort of maisonette flat, so you have most of the downstairs but the others — and I'm coming to them, I promise! — the others have a good ground-floor reception room and share the garden too.'

Jane didn't reply, but hadn't fainted with horror either, so Bella went boldly on. 'Of course it would have to be with the right people, but I think I might know them.'

There was a long and agonising silence. At last Jane Langley sighed and then spoke. 'Oh. Well, of course I had thought about this as an option, but I could never work out how it could be arranged. But your idea of a maisonette, so whoever I shared with had a decent sitting room and bedrooms, sounds encouraging. And then there's the garden! I wouldn't have to have a fence. I'd be happy to share it with the right people, but I'd want to be able to see it.'

Bella allowed herself to breathe. 'You don't need to worry about the technical stuff — I know someone who could sort all that out for you — and Dominic could do the legal part. What you need to find out is, could you bear to share your house and live with this couple? Although you would be self-contained.'

Jane nodded. 'I think I could, although it would be vital to find the right people, especially with regard to the garden.'

'Absolutely.' Bella waited. Something she'd learnt as an estate agent was when to speak and when to stay silent. So many of them — Nevil for one — never grasped this.

'Tell me a little bit about them.'

Bella resisted the temptation to say, 'Oh, you'll love them,' although she was fairly sure Jane would. She knew how annoying it could be when people made this assumption. 'Well, they're late middle-aged but young at heart. They absolutely love the countryside, and the woman is a very keen gardener.'

Jane looked wary. 'What sort of gardener?'

'It is quite hard for me to say,' said Bella honestly, 'not actually having seen hers, but going on the gardens I've shown them — and there have been a few — I think their tastes are more to Alice's and your sort of garden: lush and a bit wild, not ordered rows of bedding plants.'

'Well, I'd have to check, of course, but I couldn't share my garden with someone who was devoted to massed ranks of scarlet geraniums interspersed with dark blue lobelia.'

'Actually, I'm rather fond of scarlet geraniums,' said Bella, thinking of Mrs Macey's pots. 'Or should that be pelargoniums?' Something Alice had once told her flitted into her head.

'Technically, yes, and so am I fond of them — in their place. Lobelia too — you can get it in such a wonderfully intense blue — but not in rows.'

'No.' Bella paused again. 'I have to say, while they have been desperately fussy clients, I do really like them. And if Alice was thinking of dividing her home and chose to sell half to them, I wouldn't hesitate to encourage her.'

'It would be a very sensible solution, for me if not for Alice.'

'And you might like the company?'

Jane nodded. 'The family would certainly like me to have someone else here — when Dominic goes, I mean.'

'Is Dominic thinking of going?' The words were out before she could censor her thoughts.

'Well, you know, it was never going to be permanent.'

'Of course not.'

'And between you and me, I think things are tricky with his ex-wife.'

This news was like a stab in the solar plexus. Surely now they were safely divorced she shouldn't still be causing Dominic trouble? Bella bit her lip and nodded, hoping Jane would read the gesture as sympathy not despair.

'So your people might be ideal.'

Bella brought herself to the matter in hand. 'Can I bring them to see you?'

Jane nodded. 'Of course.'

It couldn't have been easy for her, Bella realised, she was confronting a massive change in her life, but she was facing up to it, and Bella was humbled.

'I'll arrange it. And if you have even the smallest doubt about them we'll say no more about it. You must be completely happy. And so must Dominic.'

'Absolutely.'

'You will promise you won't accept these people if you're not sure?'

'Yes! Now when can I meet them?'

As Bella moved away so she could ring the Agnews to suggest they came to meet Jane the following day at teatime, she realised she had unwittingly made them seem more appealing because she hadn't pushed them on her. She was almost holding her breath waiting for them to answer.

They might say 'no' immediately, she knew, but although they'd always been so insistent on having a detached property, she had a feeling they might at least consider the idea, if only to get to see a lovely house. And fortunately she was right. They were intrigued and keen to see it. Naturally they didn't make any promises, but Bella knew more than to expect that.

When the arrangement had been made and directions given, she felt both relieved and anxious. Supposing the two parties she was so keen to help didn't get on?

'Well, if it's all right with you, they could come over tomorrow?'

'For tea? That would be nice.'

Bella was cautiously optimistic. Her plan might yet come together. 'I'll bring them so you won't be alone and there won't be any awkwardness.'

'Dominic will be here too, I think.'

'Oh, brilliant.'

Superficially she was pleased because having Dominic there would give Jane confidence. But Bella couldn't pretend the reason for her pleasure was because of this at all. She wanted to see him because, she now — finally — admitted, she was as in love with him as she ever had been. She couldn't keep up the pretence of being in love with Nevil any longer. Even if Dominic wasn't free or had no interest in her, her feelings for him meant she'd rather be single than with anyone other than him. And if he was there tomorrow, they might get a chance to talk about Nevil and his goings-on.

24

Duty made Bella go back to the office, although she felt like sloping off home after the meeting with Jane. But as it had only just gone five when she left her house, she decided to make sure there were no loose ends she should tie up before the weekend.

Nevil was in the main office again, apparently waiting for her. 'So, where have you been all day?'

He was still nervy and reminded Bella of an enthusiastic dog, but this time something less benign than a seesawing collie. Maybe his phone call hadn't come, or maybe it hadn't been good news.

'Well, there was the viewing at Mrs Macey's? I left all sorts of notes on your desk about that — they're making a very generous offer, in spite of everything I said about it needing so much work, including a damp-proof course.'

'Bella, I know you're good at your job — you wouldn't be here otherwise — but do you have to emphasise the negative all the time?'

As Bella felt she was a lot better at the job than he was she ignored that and went on: 'I explained that all the flags on the ground floor would have to be taken up for a damp-proofing membrane to be put in' — she looked up at him, smiling blandly — 'and they're still buying it.' She paused. 'You were out when I got back and

I've been busy ever since.'

Nevil shrugged apologetically. 'Sorry, I'm a bit on edge. Fancy some tea?'

Bella was awash with tea but he didn't often offer to make it so she said, 'Oh, yes please!'

'Tina?' Nevil said, indicating he expected her to get it.

So he wasn't offering to make it after all. No change there then. She'd have refused if she'd realised.

'So — what's Alice up to these days?' said Nevil, when Tina had brought in the tray.

It was unlike him to ask about Alice — something must be wrong. 'Oh — well, actually she's going away for a long weekend.'

'Really? Where? Somewhere nice where they do special deals for pensioners?'

'Nevil! That's not very kind!'

'It's only the truth. She is a pensioner.' Alice had had a small gathering for her sixtieth, and Nevil had been there.

'Well, maybe, but she's not off to Budleigh Salterton or Bournemouth or wherever.'

'Pardon me for showing an interest. So where are whatever group she's going with going?'

'Marrakesh. And she's going with a man.'

Nevil looked shocked.

'Yes. A younger man.' Too late she realised that this told Nevil she would be alone in the house that weekend. Although there was no real reason for it, Nevil didn't like staying over with Bella if Alice was there. What excuse could she possibly make not to invite him?

He looked abashed. 'Hey! You have an

'empty'! We could party all weekend! If only I didn't have to be somewhere.'

'Oh.' Bella wasn't sure her disappointed expression quite hit the mark. 'Where? And pleasure or business?'

'Business! I wouldn't leave you alone all weekend if it wasn't important!' He looked outraged. 'No, I've got to be with some people — can't really go into detail — but it's an all-boy thing and definitely counts as work.'

'You are allowed to have weekends off, Nevil,' said Bella gently, 'if you're not in the office, that is.' She always enjoyed working on Saturdays, as the office was so busy, but Nevil wasn't keen, so something was up.

'Oh, babes, I know that! I just feel mean not seeing you on the weekend, but I promise all this is going to pay off — big time.'

Bella smiled and then took a heartening breath. She was going to ask him about Badger Cottage — again. And this time she'd get an answer. 'Nevil, I really want to ask you — '

His phone went and he snatched it up and clasped it to his chest. 'Sorry, babes, this is confidential.'

Angrily, Bella snatched up the dirty mugs and left his office. Really, the amount of confidential phone calls he was getting was ridiculous! Even if she hadn't had a film of him digging in the middle of the night, she'd have been suspicious. He never used to have confidential phone calls.

She was psyching herself up to go back into his office to get her answers, when the phone on her desk rang. At just after five thirty the main estate agency line had been put through to her office. She picked it up.

'Bella Castle.'

'Hi. I'm terribly sorry to ring so late on a Friday night,' said a man's voice.

'It's OK, it's only just gone five thirty. I'm still here.'

'But it is late to ask if me and my family could look at a house,' the man went on, sounding stressed.

'No, we can make an appointment — Oh, you mean you want to see something now?'

'We are in a bit of a hurry. We've sold so we're cash buyers but we have to move on Monday and we've nowhere to go.'

'Oh dear.'

'And the baby is due on Wednesday. Not that they ever come when they're due . . . '

Bella made a decision. 'OK, I'm happy to show you a property but it's unlikely the vendor will be too thrilled at having a viewing at this hour.'

'Well, it's for one on that new estate?'

'Oh, OK. That might be doable.'

* * *

Half an hour later, Nevil still hadn't emerged from his office, and Bella had assembled all she needed for a viewing. Getting the contract to sell these new-builds had been down to Nevil but, having secured that, he hadn't done a lot about actually selling them, apart from putting an ad in the paper. Still, this couple had seen the ad and were now very keen. Bella wrote Nevil a quick note explaining what she was doing and left the building, keys in hand.

As Bella parked her car, she saw a family on the steps of one of the three-beds and realised they were her clients. She'd been hoping for just the parents, but here was a very pregnant woman holding a very large baby and a harassed young man with a toddler clinging on to his leg. No wonder they were in a hurry to buy.

'Perhaps I could hold the baby?' asked Bella later, when she realised that the couple were finding it difficult to think with their infants so close. Mrs Archer was trying to open the fitted wardrobes to see how big they were and had already hit the baby on the head twice.

'He's very easy-going,' Mrs Archer said.

Bella had seen this for herself. He'd hardly murmured when the wardrobe door had hit him. She held out her arms and then staggered as he was thrust into them. He weighed a ton. 'He's a big boy. How old is he?'

'Ten months,' said his mother crisply. 'And yes, I am going to have my hands full. Which is why we need somewhere to live!'

Bella shifted the enormous baby in her arms. 'There are three double bedrooms. And it's very well arranged for families downstairs.'

'They aren't exactly massive, are they? The bedrooms?' Mrs Archer went on.

'You can fit a double bed in them,' said Bella, feeling defensive. 'And these houses are priced to sell. You could put bunk beds in one of the rooms easily.'

Mrs Archer nodded and went to inspect the bathroom.

'Could you explain the heating system?' asked her husband, who still had a small child attached to him.

Bella did her best, but she was aware she was just repeating what she'd been told and didn't really understand the finer points. 'There is a leaflet though,' she finished.

The downstairs was better than the upstairs, everyone agreed. 'It's lovely to have a big kitchen-diner when you've got children, they tell me,' said Bella. 'And the view over the garden means you can keep an eye on the little ones while they play.' She realised she sounded unbearably twee and decided to shut up. This family would either like this house and buy it, or not.

Half an hour later she locked the door behind them with relief. Not only had she got the viewing done without any damage to the property or the children, but they had decided to buy!

'That's very good news,' she said, watching them being strapped into the car and wondering if she ever wanted children herself. 'I'll arrange the paperwork so, with luck, you'll be able to sign fairly soon.'

'As quick as you can,' said Mr Archer. 'We're staying with Dawn's mother until we can move.'

Bella nodded. 'I completely understand. I'll make sure it gets done immediately.'

Everyone had gone home by the time she got back to the office. She let herself in, having decided to pass on the sale of the house to her colleague who would be there all day that Saturday.

She had just opened the photocopier so she could copy the leaflet about the boiler and send it to Mr Archer, when she saw there was a set of plans there.

She picked them up. It was so easy to take the copy and leave the master in the machine. She did her copy and then decided she should find a home for the plans.

Looking at them she realised they were for a property they'd sold some time ago. She remembered it clearly. It had gone to sealed bids and Bella's clients — a large untidy family who'd been looking for a while — had lost out to someone Nevil was dealing with.

She opened them out and saw they'd been drawn on. Next to the old farmhouse, lines had been drawn that took in the neighbouring properties. Studying them more closely she realised the whole area was up for demolition. A huge supermarket was about to take their place.

Did the area really need another supermarket? When she'd shown the family round, one of the prize points had been how close it was to Tesco. And now they and others were going to be deprived of housing that was much needed.

She was tired and dejected and decided to go home. Nevil was behind this, she knew.

25

Alice was trying to pack. All the virtues Michael was so sure she had — the reasons he had declared made him fall in love with her — seemed to have deserted her.

She was a welter of indecision. What would the weather be like in Marrakesh? Would it be a dry heat or would it be humid? She didn't want to take too much stuff, it would make her look silly and indecisive, but nor did she want to be without some vital something.

'OK,' she said aloud. 'Take out everything that doesn't match anything else.'

This done it was easier, and she began to create outfits out of various items. Then she added a black maxi dress in fine cotton jersey, a handful of scarves and decided she was packed. The bubble of excitement that had been suppressed by her packing worries popped up again. But in this bubble the wonderful anticipation of going somewhere new with an exciting man she was girlishly in love with was dampened by the prospect of having sex for the first time in years.

On the one hand the thought was thrilling and magical and made her catch her breath with desire. But would everything still work? Would she still know what to do? And supposing he recoiled at the sight of her no-longer-young body? Well, if he did, he did, she decided, and while it would be very sad — heartbreaking even — there was nothing she could do now that would prevent it happening if it was going to.

With that sensible and down-to-earth thought, she disappeared into the bathroom armed with scissors, wax and hair dye to do her very best. When she'd done what she could, she checked her watch and rang the local beauticians to see if they could fit her in for a pedicure. There was something about having brightly painted toenails that would cheer her up if things didn't go well.

At last, her spirits still yo-yoing from blissful anticipation to deepest gloom about how he would flinch from her nakedness, it was time to set off for Michael's house. On balance, she decided, she was happy. And very excited.

Michael was satisfyingly pleased to see her. He hugged her long and hard and Alice's fears faded.

'Is this all you're taking?' he said, seeing her case, when he'd put her down after kissing her.

'It's only a long weekend,' she said, smoothing her clothes.

'Yes, but what a long weekend it's going to be!' said Michael, putting his arm round her and squeezing her to his side.

'I know. I didn't want to pack too much but however little you pack you often only wear half of it.'

He laughed. 'The trick is to know which half! Right, shall we get going?'

Then they were on their way to the airport in Michael's car.

* * *

Nevil had made his excuses about the weekend, but maybe he would want to do something on Friday night. Just as she was wondering what, if anything, she should do about it, he called her.

'So sorry, sweetie, did I say? I've got to shoot off down to Sussex the moment I've finished up this paperwork.'

Bella longed to ask for details, the plans she'd found in the photocopier sharp in her mind, but was fairly sure she wouldn't get any so she just said, 'I'll see you on Monday then.'

'You're very understanding,' he said, obviously relieved.

'I am understanding. You could try explaining things to me sometime. I might well grasp it all quite well.'

'Bella!' he said reproachfully. 'What do you mean?'

'Never mind, Nevil. You do what you have to do and have a good weekend.'

'You're a honey,' he said.

'I know,' she agreed. 'Bye now.'

It was late and having made herself a sandwich she went upstairs to run herself a bath. Seeing her godmother's bits and pieces round the house, Bella couldn't help thinking about Alice and wondering how she was getting on. It was nice to have someone else to think about. Her own life seemed such a mess at the moment. She hadn't heard from Dominic. Had he received her email? Or was it just that he couldn't help her? She went to bed, tired and somewhat down-hearted.

* * *

Bella was aware it was a beautiful summer Saturday the moment she awoke. She was pleased. It meant that most of the meeting between the Agnews and Jane could take place in the garden, which really was the best bit about the house. It was also the bit that worried Jane most. Since Bella had suggested that she sleep downstairs, Jane had mostly ignored the upstairs. But it was here that the major work needed doing. The Agnews would have to be tolerant about living with workmen for a few weeks if they wanted to move in immediately. If indeed they wanted to move in at all. And if Jane wanted them to.

It was rather a radical way to solve two sorts of problems, Bella realised. Usually the owner of the big house would decide to divide it up and then look for buyers — buyers who were up for living in a shared house, and who hadn't put 'detached' at the top of their list of requirements.

What she was suggesting was all about-face, really. But if Jane liked the Agnews as much as Bella thought she would, it could be perfect.

She realised she could never have told Nevil about her unconventional approach — even if she didn't suspect him of almost criminal activity. He just wouldn't have understood. When she'd first got to know him she'd had to accept he had a much more businesslike approach to selling property than she did. Bella felt it was all more to do with the people and their different personalities.

She really hoped she was right in this instance. Then the Agnews would finally find a home they could love, and Jane could stop worrying about a huge great house crumbling about her ears that she would soon have to leave.

Bella took her tea out into Alice's garden, a little bit sad that she wasn't there to join her. There weren't so many mornings when breakfast in the garden was a possibility. On the other hand, Alice was in Marrakesh — with a lovely man; she could probably have breakfast any-where she liked.

Bella smiled ruefully as she sipped her tea. What had she done wrong? She was in her twenties and well up for adventure. And yet it was her sixty-year-old godmother who was halfway across the world with a wonderful man having, she sincerely hoped, the romantic weekend of her life. She sighed. Maybe when she was Alice's age things would come right for her.

After catching up with her washing, she went on to the internet again. She put in Nevil's name and tried to find a picture of every person he was linked to. The trouble was, the bit of video was so difficult to see details on. She probably wouldn't have been able to identify Nevil if she didn't know him so well. He'd also been linked with dozens of people, and none of the matey pictures had a 'dodgy property developer' tag on them.

If only she could have asked Tina! She had lived in the area all her life and seemed to know everyone in the county and beyond. But until Bella had something a bit more concrete it would be wrong to involve her. If Nevil found out, Tina would lose her job. Dominic was the only one she could consult as things stood. She wished he'd answered her email before now, so she wouldn't have to rely on him being at Jane's.

* * *

She set off for Jane's just after three thirty. The Agnews were, as usual, early. She saw them in their car, parked well out of the way. Knowing they would be, Bella was too.

'Hello, you two!' she said gaily, in spite of feeling anything but. She wanted her plan to work so much, and yet going on past experiences with the Agnews, it was very unlikely to. 'Aren't we lucky with the weather?'

Mrs Agnew got out of the car. 'Aren't we? And what a lovely house. It's just a pity we couldn't afford all of it.'

Bella chuckled gently. This had always been their problem: stately-home tastes on semi-detached money. 'You are talking several hundred thousand above your budget,' she said. 'And it isn't for sale anyway. Mrs Langley won't be selling until she absolutely has to, which won't be for a while.'

Mr Agnew got out too and they leant on the car to chat. 'So, what's the story?'

'Basically, she doesn't want to move, but the house needs quite a lot of work doing to it. She has no money apart from her house. If it could be divided in some way — and I know just the person to make a really good job of that — it would mean she could go on living here. The advantage to you would be that you could live in part of a really gorgeous house with very large level garden. You'd be able to have at least one really big reception room and a good-sized kitchen, and as much upstairs as you'd need . . . ' She drew breath. She realised she had more emotional investment in this coming off than was strictly professional.

'What we like about you, Bella,' said Mrs Agnew, 'is that you obviously care. I think you want us to have our dream house just as much as we do!'

Bella laughed. 'Well, not quite as much, I don't suppose.'

'By the way,' Mrs Agnew suddenly asked, 'have you found out any more about those two men digging in the garden of Badger Cottage?'

Bella had never admitted she was supposedly engaged to one of them. 'Not really. I am working on it though.'

'I am sorry we didn't feel we could make an offer, but in the circumstances . . . '

Bella shook her head. 'Oh no! I completely understand. Seeing two men digging when you were expecting to see badgers must have been an awful shock!' They both smiled. Put like that, it did have a funny side. 'But I think this will suit you much better actually. Apart from sharing, I think it will have every box ticked.' She twinkled at Mrs Agnew. 'Even the rose arbour — I think that was your 'sacrificial box', wasn't it?'

'It was!'

'And there are plenty of outbuildings for train

sets,' Bella said to Mr Agnew. 'Although you might need help to get them cleared out.'

Mrs Agnew sighed ecstatically. 'Is it time to go in now? I can't wait!'

Bella opened the gate. She could see Jane Langley with her hands together in the middle of the lawn. She was wearing the pretty silk dress she'd worn when she'd come to Sunday lunch for her birthday, and Bella realised she'd dressed up because she was nervous. Bella was nervous too. If this didn't work she'd have three disappointed people to console — as well as herself.

'Jane!' she said as she led the Agnews up to her. 'This is Mr and Mrs Agnew — Mrs Langley.'

'How do you do?' said Mrs Agnew. 'Oh! There's a goldfinch! How lovely! Sorry I got distracted!'

Jane Langley smiled as she took Mr Agnew's offered hand. 'They are delightful little birds, aren't they? Do you like birds generally?'

'Love them,' said Mrs Agnew. 'One of the main reasons we wanted to move to the country was because of the wildlife. We have badgers and foxes in Oxford, and I also love having them — but you get more birds here.'

'Of course I encourage all wildlife. It's why I won't have a cat. Would you like to see the garden, Mrs Agnew?'

'I'd love to! But please call me Imogen. And my husband is Alan.'

'And I'm Jane.' She smiled warmly. 'Now come with me.'

As the two women strolled across the lawn, talking hard, Mr Agnew and Bella looked at each other.

'They seem to be getting on OK!' said Mr Agnew. 'Do you know if Mrs Langley allows badgers to dig up her lawn, like my wife does?'

Bella chuckled. 'Yes, she does. For such a keen gardener she's very tolerant. Mind you, she says you might as well welcome them in, because they're awfully hard to keep out! Shall we join them?'

Bella and Mr Agnew wandered along behind the others, who were talking about gardening with a fervour they both admired but couldn't quite share.

'Oh! *Clematis armandii!* I've tried to grow one for years! I usually get them through the first couple of winters and then they die on me,' said Imogen Agnew.

'To be honest,' said Jane, 'that is my third attempt. It's been there a few years now so I'm optimistic.'

'And what's this rose? I love that little green centre!'

' 'Madame Hardy',' said Jane. 'Are you a fan of roses?'

'Oh yes. If I could only have one sort of flower it would have to be roses . . . '

As Alan Agnew went to join his wife and Jane, Bella detached herself from the back of the pack. She went to sit in the shade of the rose arbour and got out her phone. She wanted to see if there was a message from Alice. While she knew her godmother was an adult and all that, Bella felt she'd taken a big step with Michael in a very early stage of their relationship. It would be awful if it all went hideously wrong. A *having an amazing time* text would be reassuring.

No message from Alice, but there was one from Dominic. *Been away, but hope to be up this weekend. Things a bit tricky this end. D.*

It wasn't much but it sent Bella to heaven for a few moments. Jane hadn't been certain if he'd be able to come. Then she chided herself for being pathetic and went to join the others. She might be needed.

Just as she was about to head off for the vegetable garden, where she could see the others examining the broad beans, she saw Dominic's car pull up. She stayed where she was, and realised he had Dylan with him. Unable to help herself she went over to greet them.

'Hello! Hello, Dylan!'

The little boy gave her a beatific smile. 'Hello. Can we go to the swings and have ice cream?' He'd obviously remembered the last time he'd seen Bella.

'Well, probably not right now, but I do know that your — Dominic's — Aunt Jane has got an old tin bath we could put water in and use as a paddling pool. Did you bring your trunks?'

'Hello, Bella,' said Dominic and kissed her check.

Her heart flipped at the sight of him. He looked gorgeous in jeans and a casual shirt, but she realised he could be wearing a onesie and she'd probably still fancy him.

'Did you bring yours?' he went on.

Bella blushed. 'What? My swimming trunks? No. I'm working. The Agnews are here. They seem to be getting on with Jane really well.'

'That's partly why I'm here,' said Dominic. 'She told me of your plan, and although it's a bit off-the-wall I think it could be perfect. But this is a big decision for Aunt Jane. I felt I should be here to help her make it.'

'She doesn't have to decide anything today. This is just a preliminary meeting, to see if the idea is remotely possible.'

Dominic nodded. 'I got your email, by the way, but I didn't have a chance to give it the attention it needed.'

'I hope you didn't mind my using contact details I got from your file, but I didn't know who else to ask.'

'It is tricky.'

Then Bella noticed Dylan twisting Dominic's hand and realised this wasn't the moment to discuss it. She crouched down to his level. 'Shall we go and find a drink? This hot weather does make me awfully thirsty.'

Dylan nodded.

Dominic looked down at the little boy. 'If you'd be happy to go inside with Bella, Dyl, I should go and find Aunt Jane and meet these Agnews I've heard so much about.'

'They were by the veg patch when I last saw them but they might have progressed to the fruit cages by now,' said Bella. 'Come on, Dylan. I happen to know there are smoothies in the fridge. And ice lollies.' She knew this because, at Jane's request, she'd stocked her fridge earlier in the week.

'Cool,' said Dylan, and Dominic and Bella exchanged glances.

26

The grown-ups, as Bella now thought of them, seemed to be taking a long time to look round the house, but she was very happy with Dylan. She had always got on well with children — especially ones like him. She just wished she could be as sure that Dominic liked her.

Of course she knew he thought she was a nice person, or he wouldn't have dreamt of leaving Dylan with her while he kept himself on hand for his aunt in case there were any legal issues to discuss. But did he 'like' her the way Michael liked Alice? He certainly wasn't giving anything away.

Jane gave permission for the outbuildings to be explored, and Bella and Dylan had found some interesting things in one of them. One of these was a tent, which, using some rope and the branches of the apple tree, Bella managed to erect. It wasn't exactly fit for a night on a mountaintop, but it made a great den for a sunny afternoon in the garden.

The old tin bath filled with water kept them both cool. Dylan was by now wearing his trunks, sunhat and sun cream. Bella, still in her dress, was very wet. She tucked the skirt up into her knickers and borrowed some sun cream.

She was just seeing if she could still do handstands, when she became aware of her clients and Dominic all watching her. Dylan was in the tent.

'Oh, hi!' she said, getting herself the right way up. 'How's it all going?'

'It's a lovely house!' said Imogen Agnew ecstatically.

'And quite big enough for two families,' said Jane.

'We will need to do a little working out on how this can be done,' said Alan Agnew. 'Would you mind if I went and had another look round?'

'And of course it will be difficult to value,' said his wife.

'That's where your friendly local estate agent comes in,' said Bella.

'And a good lawyer,' said Dominic.

Jane laughed. Bella was pleased to see how relaxed she looked, as if the thought of sharing her home with the Agnews and being relieved of worries about the house had already had an effect. 'Take no notice of these thrusting professionals,' she said, 'you go back and have a good poke round. Take as long as you like. I'll make some tea.'

'Do you want any help?' said Bella.

'No, no. You're busy here,' she said with a distinct twinkle.

Bella felt embarrassed and was glad when Dylan emerged from the tent.

'Go upside down again!' he said. 'And go in a circle!'

Bella knew this meant doing a cartwheel, and was glad she'd had time to get in a lot of practice before showing Dominic her rare talent. She glanced at him now.

'Do go in a circle,' said Dominic. 'I'd love to see that.'

He was teasing her but she didn't mind; in fact, she realised with a moment of shame, she appreciated the opportunity to show off. It was lovely to feel carefree and joyful, just for a bit.

Jane Langley's front lawn was spacious and Bella positioned herself well. She managed to fit in four good cartwheels and then righted herself, out of breath and dizzy. Dominic and Dylan were looking at a car that had just driven up.

'Mummy!' called Dylan. 'Mummy's here!'

Dylan looked questioningly at Dominic, whose expression was rigid.

Even before Celine was out of the car Bella knew there was going to be a row. She came storming across the lawn. Motherhood hadn't changed her, Bella realised. She was still the well-groomed beauty she always had been. Bella felt like a ragamuffin with her wet clothes and hair, and decided it was no surprise Dominic didn't fancy her if the svelte and elegant Celine was his preferred type.

'Dylan!' Celine snapped. 'Here!'

Terrified and confused, the little boy ran to her side.

Celine had picked up his clothes from where they were lying on a deckchair. 'Get in the car, darling,' she went on, a little more gently. 'Daddy's there.'

Bella was watching Dominic and saw the pang as he heard the word. He must have been Daddy at first. And now he had been demoted.

Celine turned on him now. 'For goodness' sake, Dominic! Didn't you notice he had a cold? What were you thinking of, letting him get wet?' Her gaze swivelled round to where Bella was standing. Then she frowned. 'Bella? Is that you?'

Bella pulled her dress out of her knickers, wishing she could run away and hide. 'I'm sorry, I didn't notice Dylan had a cold. But it's a lovely day, I'm sure he'll be fine.'

'I'll be the judge of that, thank you!' Celine said. 'And anyway, he was Dominic's responsibility. He should have made sure he was properly looked after.' She paused, lips pursed. 'I'm not sure I can go on letting you see him if you can't take care of him.'

Bella couldn't help sticking up for him. 'Really, Celine, it's not Dominic's fault and Dylan's been having a lovely time.'

'Sorry, why are you here?' Celine said. 'I'm confused. Are you with Dominic?'

Bella blushed again. 'I'm here working . . . ' She was horribly aware of being soaking wet, her mascara probably halfway down her face, her dress crumpled and filthy. 'I was just keeping Dylan amused.'

'Have you had a career change? Are you a children's entertainer now? Maybe that's a good idea. We all assumed you'd done something wrong when you left Owen and Owen so hurriedly.'

At least she hadn't known the real reason: that she had been in love with her husband and that she, Celine, had just got pregnant. 'No, I'm still an estate agent. I'm looking after Dominic's aunt.' Celine's perfectly shaped raised eyebrow made Bella feel obliged to explain her non-professional appearance. 'I was doing cartwheels to make Dylan laugh.'

'I'm sure you didn't have to go that far — he's only two! And did you know your dress is see-through when it's wet, and if you're going to do gymnastics you need a more supportive bra.'

'Celine!' said Dominic sharply.

She looked back at him again. 'As for you, I'll be in touch, but in future I don't want you having Dylan if you can't give him your undivided attention.' Then she marched off to the car. Shortly afterwards the engine was started and the car shot off.

* * *

Neither of them seemed to know what to say. Five minutes earlier Bella and Dylan had been playing happily together. She'd been remembering what it was like to be a child, completely at home in one's body. She'd enjoyed playing with Dylan as much as he seemed to enjoy playing with her. 'I'm sorry I didn't notice Dylan had a cold,' Bella managed eventually.

Dominic shook his head. 'He didn't have a cold! It's just Celine being overprotective and neurotic. Otherwise she wouldn't have driven for forty-five minutes to check!'

Bella shrugged and then went over to the deckchair where she'd left her handbag. 'I'd better make myself tidy.' Then she gave Dominic a short, embarrassed smile and went indoors to the downstairs cloakroom to see what she could do with her unruly curls, crushed skirt and grubby face.

* * *

Bella looked out of the kitchen door to see Imogen Agnew carrying a loaded tray out into the garden, where Jane was seated at the table. Bella was thrilled that the Agnews already seemed to be keeping an eye out for Jane. Mr Agnew had a couple of cake tins and a milk jug in his hands. Feeling she couldn't just pretend the scene with Celine hadn't happened, she went to find Dominic in the kitchen. He was making tea.

'I am so sorry. I feel I've completely messed things up for you. It was my idea to play with water.'

Daniel shook his head. 'You couldn't have known he had a sniffle — I hardly noticed it myself but, now I come to think about it, Celine had told me about it.' He smiled apologetically. 'She's very overprotective when it suits her. It makes her lash out.' He paused. 'I'm sorry she was so rude to you.'

'That's OK; it wasn't your fault. But her over-protectiveness must make this very difficult for you.'

'For me and Dylan. Poor little chap, he's the one who has to put up with her neuroses.' He paused. 'It was probably to make sure Dylan wasn't having too much fun that she came to check up on me.' He pushed his hand through his hair in a gesture of frustration. 'She wants it all ways. She wants childcare when it suits her, but she holds over my head all the time that I have no rights when it comes to Dylan. I only get to see him out of the kindness of her heart.'

'Ha! What kindness? What heart? What sort of woman uses a child as a pawn like that?' Bella was incredulous.

Dominic regarded her, his expression utterly bleak. 'The kind of woman I married.'

Bella suffered a pang. Did this mean Dominic still had feelings for Celine? Was he still getting over the break-up of their marriage? It must have been dreadful — especially discovering that his beloved Dylan wasn't actually his son.

She tried to study him as he turned back to fill the kettle but could learn nothing from his back. He might still have feelings for her; even though she was a bitch, men were notoriously fixated on women's looks. How could she, Bella, compete? Celine was so beautiful, and she had Dylan. All the cards were in her hand. Bella realised she had nothing except a sort of youthful prettiness, a helpful personality and an ability to do cartwheels. Not much competition really.

'Is there anything I can do to hurry up the tea? I'm gasping after all that.'

Dominic turned to look at her. She couldn't read his expression. His handsome features were inscrutable. Then he clicked the switch on the kettle. It instantly started to rumble.

* * *

'So where has that dear little boy gone?' asked Alan when Bella and Dominic arrived with the tea. 'He and Bella seemed to be having so much fun.'

'Yes we were,' said Bella. 'Which is why I look such a mess, I'm afraid.'

'You look lovely,' said Imogen. 'I wish I could do cartwheels, but I never could, even when I was young.' She looked at Dominic. 'So where is he? I assumed he was your son — '

'His mother came to fetch him,' said Dominic.

'Let's all have some cake!' said Jane brightly, diverting unwelcome attention from Dominic. 'And talk about our plans.'

Bella knew she was changing the subject for Dominic's sake, and that he must often face people's assumption that he and Dylan were related, when the DNA test claimed they definitely weren't. It was a truly horrible situation and, completely inadvertently, she had made it a whole lot worse.

'I've been thinking,' said Jane. 'What I really want is a good sitting room and a kitchen, but I don't need one as big as I've got now. A galley kitchen as part of the sitting room, with a view on to the garden would do me just fine.'

'Are you saying you don't want that gorgeous kitchen?' said Imogen, her expression becoming ecstatic.

'As long as I have space to knock up a few cakes now and again, to keep Bella happy, I'll be perfectly content. I was watching a cooking programme the other day, and this chef had a kitchen-sitting room instead of a kitchen-diner.

It made far more sense to me. An open fire in a kitchen is a lovely thing.'

'Well, you've obviously given it a lot of thought,' said Dominic.

'When I finally realised I couldn't afford to live here on my own I started thinking about what I really wanted from my home.' She paused, possibly becoming conscious she'd said more in one go than she usually did. She *had* obviously been giving it all a lot of thought. Bella was thrilled — she'd got something right, and for one of her favourite people. 'I narrowed it down to my bedroom and bathroom as they are now, and the kitchen-sitting room as described.'

'You must need some upstairs space,' declared Imogen. 'There are lots of bedrooms. I think you should have one as a spare room and maybe one for storage?'

'I suppose that would be nice,' said Jane, 'but what about you? You wouldn't want my guests up there, getting in your way.'

'If I could have that enormous bedroom overlooking the garden,' said Imogen, 'I don't care much what other upstairs rooms we have.'

'Well, I'm very glad both parties are bending over backwards to accommodate each other's needs,' said Dominic, sounding like a lawyer, 'but we must make sure there are no ambiguities.'

'I can suggest someone who could do all the plans,' said Bella. 'I've mentioned her before, Jane. She'd arrange separate entrances so there are two clearly defined properties.'

'And I recommend we arrange things so that if

Imogen and Alan want to move, the divisions might alter.'

'Oh God,' said Bella, suddenly daunted. 'I hadn't thought of that. It's going to be more complicated than I realised.'

'I'm sure all the problems can be overcome,' said Alan, smiling kindly at Bella and making her feel better.

Bella realised that her feelings were more to do with Dominic and his situation than the house, and forced a more cheerful expression. 'I just meant it'll be a bit tricky, making it all legal,' she said.

'That's my department,' said Dominic.

'This is so exciting!' said Imogen, before taking a restorative sip of tea.

'Isn't it?' said Jane. 'Now do have more cake, everyone, or I'll be living on it for the rest of the week.'

27

Alice's job as a director of a medium-sized firm making small but vital components for industrial looms and involved going abroad meant that she had travelled a fair bit over the years, but she found the whole experience very different with Michael. Instead of it merely being the businesslike process of getting from one place to another, with him, the journey was part of the adventure. It made the airport, not Alice's favourite place, seem romantic and exciting.

Once they were through the formalities, Michael insisted on taking her round the perfume shop, making her try different scents and cosmetics until she was giggling with the silliness of it all. He bought her a bottle of something which, she realised, would always remind her of this happy time. Then they went to Smith's and he bought them both magazines, which he insisted on carrying. After that he swept her off to a bar and they had champagne.

Alice was determined to enjoy every minute. She wasn't cynical, but she couldn't really believe it was real. She was a woman of sixty being taken to Marrakesh by a man many a forty-year-old would be flattered to be with.

But although part of her didn't let herself believe it, she was aware of how well they got on. They even had the same ideas about what time to go to the boarding gate and, once settled in their seats, when was a good time to stop talking and just read.

She wasn't aware of closing her eyes until she opened them to see Michael watching her.

'You're so sweet when you're asleep,' he said.

'Does that mean I'm not sweet when I'm awake?' she said, feeling caught out and worried in case she'd snored or dribbled.

He laughed at her grumpiness. 'You are always enchanting but with your lashes against your cheek and your mouth open just the tiniest bit you reminded me of the girls when they were little and slept in the back of the car.'

Alice decided to be mollified. Sleeping together was one of the things she was both looking forward to and dreading. Would desire — and she certainly had that — take her through? She smiled at him and he put his hand on hers and gave it a squeeze. Her confidence increased. This lovely man did indeed want to be with her.

The heat and the smell of animals overlaid with the smoke of wood fires hit Alice, as she got off the plane a couple of hours later. She always looked forward to that moment, when you knew you were really abroad. The sky was indigo, and it was dark but still bustling as if no one ever slept here.

'I've always wanted to see my name on a signboard at an airport, and not just the name of my company,' said Alice when they finally emerged at the place where travellers met the outside world. People were everywhere and she was looking round for a sign leading to taxis.

'Will my name do?' said Michael. 'Over there.'

'I think it might,' said Alice a few moments later, as she was handed into a limousine. She decided solo travel was overrated.

By now, Alice was expecting a gorgeous hotel and she was not disappointed. Nor was she disappointed with the excitement of the city: the narrow, bustling streets, vendors still hard at work offering enticing treasures, carpets, spices, jewellery, ceramics. Even in the dusk Alice was delighted by the intensity of the colours, like poster paints after the tasteful watercolours of England.

The riad — a hotel to the rest of the world — was delightful; it flung an aura of calm around them like a blanket of serenity. The staff were stately but assiduous. Bags disappeared, mint tea was offered and, finally, they were shown a huge room, which was actually a suite.

'How did you organise this at such short notice?' Alice demanded the moment they were alone, looking around her in delight.

'Contact in the travel business, but we were very lucky. I'm so glad. I would hate our first time away together to be anything less than perfect.'

'You set high standards!' Alice knew he was talking about the hotel, but she was worried that he'd want everything else to be perfect too, and she wasn't sure it could be.

She wandered around the suite admiring the décor, which had a distinctively French edge to it, and found two marble bathrooms, one huge and one smaller. Both were perfectly appointed, with spa-quality towels, delicious toiletries and multiple mirrors. She could have done with fewer mirrors.

The sitting room opened out on to a balcony overlooking an inner courtyard. A pool glittered below, surrounded by carefully clipped trees. It was somehow everything Alice had been expecting but more.

'What would you like to do?' said Michael. 'Have something to eat here? Or shall we find the rooftop restaurant?'

'It might not be open,' said Alice. 'Let's have something here.' She didn't want to break the spell — just the two of them in this glorious room.

'Here's the menu. Think what you'd like and I'll call down.'

Alice ignored the card he handed to her. She felt too tired to make decisions. 'Can I be boring and have a club sandwich?'

'I always have a club sandwich if I have room service,' said Michael. 'It seems right, somehow.'

'I always do too! That or a steak sandwich and salad.'

Michael nodded. 'Yes — only I have to ask them to hold the mustard. I hate mustard.'

Alice stared at him. 'I hate mustard! We are twins separated at birth!'

Michael chuckled at her gently. 'I really do hope not. That would be wrong for so many reasons.'

Feeling foolish but not minding too much, Alice got up. 'I think I'll go and fiddle about with my belongings while you order.'

The bed was absolutely enormous. It would be easy to share, but she was still nervous. She was tired. Although there was no time difference to contend with, she still felt a good night's sleep was what she wanted more than sex with a man she didn't know very well. Even though she was in love with him, it was still a big step.

When she'd chosen her side of the bed (the lady's privilege, surely?) she unpacked a few things and then went out to join Michael. He handed her a glass of champagne.

'Oh, thank you. Shall we have a toast?'

'Here's to us, then.'

Michael smiled into her eyes, and she felt a delicious little stab of desire. Perhaps the going-to-bed thing would be all right.

They went back to the balcony and sat, sipping but not talking, waiting for room service.

'Can I make a suggestion?' said Michael after a few minutes.

'You can,' said Alice.

'When we've eaten, I think you should have a relaxing soak in the biggest bathroom, and then we both have an early night? I know that technically this is a dirty weekend, as they used to call it, but I don't think we should rush things.'

Alice sighed gently. 'I think that sounds perfect. I had been feeling a bit like an old-fashioned bride on her wedding night, nervous and jumpy, not sure what to do — ridiculous as that sounds.'

'So had I,' agreed Michael. 'Well, not a bride, obviously, but under a bit of pressure.'

Alice laughed, relieved and so much more relaxed. He was so thoughtful and seemed to sense how she was feeling, what she needed from him. 'Imagine how it must have been in medieval times, when your bride might be only thirteen and a stranger to you. You were fourteen and the entire court, including your mother, were there to watch,' she said. Alice had a penchant for historical fiction.

'Dreadful,' declared Michael. 'Let's have some more champagne!'

* * *

He was incredibly tactful. He went for a walk while she ran a bath, soaked in it and then got into bed. By the time he came back she was clean and relaxed with her hair done, sitting up in bed reading her book-group book. She felt like a very respectable sixty-year-old, if you overlooked the fact that she had put on some very discreet make-up and not yet put on her face cream.

'Hello, you,' he said and came over and kissed her cheek. 'Was I too long? I wanted to give you space but I didn't want you to feel abandoned.'

'It was the perfect length of time. And what bliss to have two bathrooms! Otherwise I'd have had to clean out the bath after I'd had mine when all I wanted to do was flop into bed.' He didn't need to know what she'd done to herself before she'd slid between the zillion-thread-count sheets, relishing their icy coolness.

'I won't be long. Unless you're gripped by that

impressive-looking bit of literature, I think we should get some sleep.'

He kissed her cheek again, and then they both switched off their bedside lights. When she heard him gently snoring, she took out her face cream and applied it liberally.

* * *

Sometime near dawn, Alice was woken by the call to prayer. She loved the feeling of foreignness it gave her, of being abroad. She was in Marrakesh, in Africa. She had forgotten how much she enjoyed travelling. Michael had awakened her sense of adventure, and she loved him for it.

For a while she lay there, enjoying the sensation. She had slept surprisingly well considering she hadn't thought she'd sleep at all. She liked the sound of Michael's gentle snoring in the bed next to, but not too near her. But then, convinced she wouldn't be able to drift off again, she got up and took her case into the bathroom. While she showered, brushed her teeth, creamed her face and wondered about washing her hair, she considered her outfit for the morning. Then she replaced the touch of make-up she'd just washed off and got back into bed.

Lying there, she thought about her choice of clothes. The maxi dress was cool and the blouse was multipurpose. Too much flesh on show wasn't appropriate in a Muslim culture, she felt, the sun would be roasting hot and she didn't want to get burnt, and, most importantly, she never showed her arms except in the privacy of her own garden. Taking off whatever covered her arms would be harder for her than taking off her knickers. It wasn't logical but it was how she felt. She was just wondering if she should add a scarf to the outfit, when she drifted off to sleep.

She awoke to find Michael looking at her.

'Good morning,' he said politely.

'Good morning,' she said back.

'You look very well rested,' he said, and Alice felt her early trip to the bathroom had been justified.

'I think if you don't mind we should make an early start. It'll get extremely hot later,' he went on.

'Fine by me. I'm an early riser anyway.'

'Good!' said Michael and got out of bed. 'I'll meet you downstairs, shall I? I might get dressed quicker than you do.' He smiled. 'On the other hand, if I don't, you can be first to get to the coffee.'

* * *

After a breakfast of thc most amazing pastries and fruit, they decided to go to the souk.

'It's either that or a camel ride,' said Michael.

'The souk. If we were here longer I might like a camel ride but for a long weekend, shopping is a priority. Before it gets too hot.'

The souk was dazzling. The clothes people wore, the things for sale, in fact anything that could be a rich and vivid colour, was. Alice had to stop herself exclaiming every two minutes about how wonderful everything was. Being appreciative was one thing, looking totally naïve was another.

The crowds meant it was natural for Michael to take Alice's arm, and together they wandered from stall to stall, amused at the antics of the owners as they tried to claim their attention. Alice stopped at one selling rugs, and discovered that she did actually need a small one to cover a patch of worn carpet on the upstairs landing.

She drew Michael away. 'How much do you think I should pay for it? The trouble is I have no idea what a good price is.'

'Well, you have to haggle; it's part of the deal. I'm afraid I don't know how much you should pay either.'

'I'll do my best,' said Alice.

After fifteen minutes of spectacular entertainment, she was the proud owner of a small rug, tightly tied with string. Alice was laughing almost hysterically as Michael took the bundle from her.

'That was worth it even if I hadn't got a rug at the end!' declared Alice. 'Really, that man is wasted selling carpets. He should be on the stage.'

'I agree. It was cheap at half the price.'

Alice put her hand to her mouth. 'You don't think I paid too much for it, do you?'

'I think you haggled like a local. Now let me try my skills.'

He led them to a stall selling scarves and bought three for less than the original price for one. He draped one over Alice's head, then took it off and replaced it with another. 'That's perfect for you.'

'Oh, thank you,' said Alice, surprised and delighted.

'Now, I think a cold drink before a bit more shopping. Are you up for it?' He managed to look concerned in a way that didn't make Alice feel old and decrepit, and she was grateful.

'An ice-cold drink and a sit-down will refresh me enough for a bit more shopping,' she said and let herself be led to a nearby café.

* * *

'Well, I think we're officially lost now,' said Michael calmly a couple of hours later. 'It says in the guide book we should now hire a small boy to guide us.'

'But how do we know he won't just take us in the wrong direction for fun?' Alice's feet were beginning to hurt.

'I'll explain he won't get paid until we end up at the right riad.' He frowned slightly. 'Are you walked off your legs?'

'My feet are a bit sore.'

'I don't think we're too far from home.' He looked around and spotted a likely guide. 'Young man? Can you guide us to the Riad Isabelle?'

He was an efficient guide, and it wasn't long before they were back in the now familiar calm of the hotel sitting on the terrace with more cold drinks and a plate of hors d'oeuvres in front of them.

'Let's go upstairs,' said Michael, when they'd eaten.

'Good idea. I want to take my sandals off. Why

is it that shoes are perfectly comfortable in England and then become agony the moment you take them out of the country?'

'It's probably something to do with you taking them out of their comfort zone,' explained Michael solemnly.

Alice giggled. 'I expect that's it.'

After he had unlocked the door, she walked across the room to the balcony, kicking off her shoes as she went. She turned back to Michael. 'Now what shall we do?'

He looked at her thoughtfully, his eyes narrowing. 'I think that now, I shall take you to bed.' Then he took her into his arms and kissed her.

Alice decided to just go with it. It would either work or it wouldn't. Pulling out now for lack of nerve wouldn't make anything better. It was time to take a chance.

The bedroom was in semi-darkness, the shutters closed against the heat of the day. It didn't take Michael long to slip off the thin muslin shirt she'd thought she'd never relinquish, and unzip her dress. He laid her down on the bed and looked at her appreciatively.

Aware he could only see a very obscured version of her nakedness, Alice smiled calmly back at him. It was going to be all right, she decided.

* * *

Alice snuggled down. It had been utterly blissful. 'Would it be rude if I went to sleep now? I've lost track of the etiquette.'

'It's fine if you want to sleep. I do too.'

'Good,' she said and drifted off.

When she awoke about half an hour later she lay still, listening to Michael breathing, thinking how relieved she was that everything did still work, and that the sex had been lovely. She sighed with pleasure, deeply enough to wake Michael.

'Hello, you.'

'Hello, you!'

'That was amazing, wasn't it?' he said.

'Mm,' said Alice dreamily.

'Fancy another go?' He smiled at her.

Alice chuckled. 'You make it sound as if you're suggesting another turn on the merry-go-round.'

He moved nearer to her and kissed her shoulder. 'I think that describes it perfectly.'

* * *

'Are you cold?' he said at breakfast the following morning. They were on their balcony and a shaft of sunshine shone down over the high walls to land exactly where they were sitting.

'Not really,' said Alice, surprised.

'I'm just wondering why you feel the need to wear a cardigan.'

'This isn't a cardigan,' she said indignantly, pulling it closer. 'It's a shrug. It's quite different.'

He raised a sceptical eyebrow. 'That's a cardigan. Why don't you take it off?'

There are times, Alice decided, when it's best to just not argue. As a man he wouldn't understand if she tried to explain how she felt about her arms. She took off the shrug and resolved to keep her arms clamped to her sides for the rest of the meal. When they went out she could justifiably put it back on again for all sorts of reasons.

'That's better,' said Michael. 'I love your arms. They remind me of eggs.'

'Eggs? Is that supposed to be a compliment?'

'Not the shape, my darling, it's your freckles. They remind me of new-laid eggs, slightly brown, with freckles.'

Alice smiled, not knowing if she should react to the compliment or to the fact he'd called her his darling. 'OK, so when you think of my arms you're reminded of a dippy egg with soldiers?'

'Exactly. And what nicer thought is there?'

'I think you're mad,' said Alice and picked up her croissant. But she didn't wear her cardigan again while they were alone.

The rest of the time both flew and stood still. Alice felt she had been away for months and yet every individual minute flew by. It was heaven. When she was tired, as was prone to happen, and the doubts crept in, she was convinced that Michael wouldn't stay in her life for long, but she decided it was worth it. She might well spend the rest of her life missing him but this wonderful weekend would keep her warm in her heart for the rest of her life.

28

Bella had gone home in a state of utter devastation. Although she knew she should have felt elated — she'd got the fussiest couple in the history of house-hunting the perfect home; a match made in heaven even — and yet she'd still felt as if her heart had been torn from her. The feeling persisted as she had breakfast and cleared up. She was just about to get on the internet when her phone went. She picked it up. It was Tina.

'Bells? Sooo sorry to bother you on a Sunday. Are you busy?'

Bella had been going to spend the day on her computer, but Tina sounded in a flap. This was so unlike her. It shocked Bella out of her gloom. She said, 'Well, not particularly. What's up?'

'My daughter. She's having a party for the little one and she's got no one to help her. Her husband's away and I can't stay long because I promised Mum I'd take her out. I've cancelled the last two times so — '

Bella used Tina's need for breath as an opportunity to get a word in. This could be just what she needed. 'I'm happy to help, but what do I know about children's parties?'

'They're not a specialist skill! You just have to keep them amused, take them to the loo, stop them crying, all those things.'

'I haven't got children, Tina. I don't know all

about those things.'

'You've got loads of common sense. It's at lunchtime which is better I think.' She paused. 'So I can tell her you'll come? It's not far from yours.'

'OK,' said Bella, thinking at least it would stop her moping, and she should have time to do a bit of research before she had to go. 'When does she want me?'

'As soon as you can get there, really. I am so grateful, Bells. I knew you wouldn't let me down.'

A rather dazed Bella put the phone down a few minutes later, directions scrawled on a scrap of paper. Still, she had recent experience of being a child's entertainer and although her experience was limited, she did like them. And being really busy would stop her moping about Dominic.

However, she had the drive to the party to think about him in, and she found she couldn't stop doing it.

It wasn't only that she was in love with Dominic and he didn't seem to feel the same about her, it was that he had to live with a situation that was intolerable. If Celine stuck to her condition that he could only have Dylan when her son could have Dominic's undivided attention, she'd be able to find a reason to stop him coming whenever it suited her. She would always have the upper hand.

And there didn't seem any way out. He wasn't Dylan's father. Dylan's mother was now married to him — they were a perfect family unit. Dominic's feelings for the boy were neither here nor there. And, even more importantly, Dylan's feelings didn't seem to matter either. It was clear that he absolutely adored Dominic. And he had quite liked her. A reminiscent little smile lifted her spirits for a moment, as she thought about his squeals of laughter as she had cartwheeled round the lawn.

* * *

That evening, in spite of being tempted by the bottle of white wine in the fridge, Bella made herself tea. She needed a clear head to try and work out what to do. The party had been a good if exhausting distraction, but now she needed to concentrate. Dominic had probably forgotten all about her email asking for help after Celine's dramatic appearance yesterday, and there hadn't been a moment to discuss it before — there'd been too much else happening. She'd just have to solve the mystery of what Nevil was up to on her own.

Taking her mug with her, she went into the sitting room to her laptop and opened it. In her heart she knew what she should do and soon — if not immediately. She should leave Nevil, leave the business and relocate somewhere else. But not, she felt, until she had worked out what he was up to and, if it was wrong, put a stop to it.

She had had several reasons for not breaking up with Nevil, but at least two of them had now gone. She had admitted to herself she hadn't loved Nevil for some time, and the Agnews, her favourite, fussiest clients, were suited. Another reason, her not wanting to up sticks from a job and area she loved, had changed. If Dominic was relocating to the area, she didn't want to stay and keep bumping into him when she was in love with him and he, plainly, wasn't in love with her.

It would be really hard for her to go back to her hometown and start again there, but possibly easier than finding somewhere completely new. But at least everyone here would be OK. Jane had the Agnews, who would keep an eye on and be company for her. Alice had Michael and wouldn't feel lonely without her. The office would survive. And knowing this would make it easier for her — wouldn't it?

She kicked off her sandals, went on the internet and put in Nevil's name.

* * *

It was nearly ten when her phone bleeped. There was a text. Bella grabbed it. Was it Alice in some sort of difficulty? She'd been so obsessed with her own problems she'd hardly spared a thought for Alice in Marrakesh.

It was Dominic. He said, *Are you at home?*

She caught her breath. Her heart soared up and then down again. *Yes*, she replied.

The moments between her sending and the reply coming seemed like hours.

Can I come over?

She swallowed and typed in quickly, *Yes*.

She forced herself to put her phone down and walk across the room while she waited. She hardly had time to fiddle with the curtains before she heard her phone bleep. She raced back to it and pressed 'open'.

I'm on my way.

Bella decided that her excitement was ridiculous and tried to calm herself down. She rushed upstairs and put on some mascara and a bit of lip gloss, and was about to find some gel for her hair when she heard a gentle knock on the door. As she flew down the stairs to answer it she realised Dominic must have been only at the end of the road when he sent the text.

She opened the door and he stood on the threshold for a few moments, looking at her, holding his briefcase.

'I'm sorry to come so late,' he said. 'As I said earlier, I did get your message a couple of days ago — I've just been so busy. You must have thought I was so rude, ignoring you.'

'Do come in,' said Bella, 'and I didn't think you were rude. I wouldn't have asked for your help if I could have thought of anyone else.'

He stepped over the threshold, looking tall and rather stern, she felt. 'Of course you should have asked me for help! Think how much you've done for Aunt Jane!'

He seemed to tower over her and Bella wished she'd put on some shoes; she felt vulnerable in her bare feet. 'What can I get you? A glass of wine? Tea?' She led the way to the kitchen.

'I wouldn't have called so late, but I had supper with Aunt Jane and had some work to catch up on,' he said as he followed her. 'Then I tried to do some research on the link you sent me.' He halted at the kitchen table with a rueful smile. 'I wanted to be able to bring you some information, but I didn't get very far. I think it's something we need to do together.'

Bella felt herself blush and went to the kettle. Boiling it would give her a reason to keep her back to him until she was a normal colour again. She was glad he'd said they were friends, of course she was, but she so wished they were something more. She turned to face him. 'I've put the kettle on out of habit. You'd probably prefer wine — or would you like tea? There *is* wine . . . '

'Some wine would be nice, but it's getting late.' He glanced at his watch.

'We'll take it through with us,' said Bella. 'You go into the sitting room. My laptop's there.'

When she brought the wine in (having opened one of the better bottles in the rack in his honour) she found Dominic had set up his laptop on a small table next to hers. It would mean they had to sit next to each other on the sofa. The thought that they would be close and probably bumping into each other was both exciting and awkward. But there was nothing she could do about it.

She put the glasses of wine down, one on each little table.

'Thank you,' he said. 'I do hope we won't disturb Alice?'

Bella laughed. 'That's unlikely, she's in Marrakesh.'

'Really?' He was satisfyingly surprised. 'How come?'

'She's gone there with Michael.' Bella adored the fact her godmother was doing something so dashing at an age when most people would assume you were past it.

'I'm impressed!' said Dominic.

'So am I,' said Bella, taking her seat next to him on the sofa.

He nodded. 'He's such a nice man.'

'He is,' agreed Bella.

'I wish I could say the same for your fiancé,' he said, turning his attention to the grainy picture on his screen.

Bella shrugged and made a face. 'I know. He's a right dodgy geezer.' She smiled, to make sure he knew she was half joking.

'So why are you still with him?' asked Dominic.

Slightly tempted to ask him what business it was of his, Bella sighed.

'Well?' Dominic went on.

'The thing is, when I leave him — and I will — I'll have to leave the agency too. His ego would never let me stay if I dumped him. And if I leave, I won't be able to investigate him so easily.'

'And how easy has it been so far?' He seemed sceptical.

Bella chuckled softly. 'Well, not easy at all, actually.'

'No reason why you should stay then,' he went on briskly.

Feeling prickly about it, Bella felt obliged to explain. 'I had to get the Agnews settled first.'

'Well, you have. And wonderfully.' He seemed

less critical now. 'Aunt Jane is very happy. She adores the prospect of sharing her house and garden.'

Bella contemplated explaining that leaving the agency might mean leaving everything else. Nevil had powerful friends. He knew all the estate agents and almost everyone in the town through one contact or another. It might be hard for her to get a job without moving away. She decided against it. He probably wouldn't be interested.

'I'm so glad,' she said. 'Shall we have a look at this film then?'

'You haven't answered my question properly. You've settled your clients and even though you share an office, you're not finding you can investigate Nevil, so why are you still with him?'

'For a lot of reasons I won't bore you with.' She paused. If he could ask intimate questions, so could she. 'Why are you so concerned?'

He frowned and compressed his mouth into a line. 'Shall we get on?'

A tiny spark of something very like hope flickered in Bella's stomach. She didn't press him and she tried not to smile, but her spirits lifted.

They both peered at their screens. 'I'm still trying to find out who that man digging with Nevil is,' she said, as if she didn't care that he hadn't answered her question.

'Have you asked Nevil about this directly?'

She shook her head. 'Up to now, I haven't thought there was any point. He'd try and tell me he was burying someone's dead cat or something.'

'Unlikely, in the middle of the night, surely.'

Bella sighed. 'He'd find a good reason why it could only be done then.' She frowned and peered at the time-stamp on the video. 'It's eleven thirty at night. That is late. Too late for it to be anything legitimate, I think.'

'I agree. Do you have any clue who the man with him is?'

Bella sighed. 'No, but I do have a suspicion about one of Nevil's golfing partners, Gerald Roberts. He's bought a few properties recently. I don't really know it's him, but as I can't get a proper look I don't know it's *not* him, either.' She paused. 'And this is all guess-work, but I found some plans in the photocopier . . . ' She went on to describe how she thought it meant the old farm and the surrounding land was going to be turned into a site for a supermarket.

He listened patiently until he'd heard all her speculations, some of which she was aware she'd already put in her email to him.

'So, tell me, Bella: what do you want the outcome of all this to be?'

'How do you mean?'

'Well, do you want them hauled off to prison? Public humiliation — exposure all over the papers?'

'Not either of those, no. I couldn't do that to Nevil. But I do want them to stop whatever it is they're doing.'

His expression indicated he thought she was being too lenient. 'I suppose a threat of all the other stuff might be enough to prevent them going on with it. We just need to find out who this man is.' He peered closer at the screen. 'You can't think of anyone?'

'The only person is this Gerald Roberts and I've met him a few times. But as I said, I don't know if it's him. I suspect not.'

'Anyone — anything else?' Dominic had minimised the link and gone on to Google. His fingers twitching, he was obviously keen to type something in.

Bella made a face. 'The trouble is, it's all just rumours and odd ideas. The only other thing I can think of, only I don't have a name, which makes it fairly useless, is that Nevil took me to a very posh housing estate. He wanted us to have one of the houses. They were vile and way out of our financial league but he said we could afford it. That must be something to do with it, but as I don't know any names, where do we go from here?'

'Right,' said Dominic, thinking aloud, 'let's put in the name Gerald Roberts and see if he's connected with any big building firms.'

Working with Dominic like this was exciting and that, coupled with her little reason for optimism, meant she could put everything else that was on her mind to one side. 'Would the Companies House website be useful, do you think?'

'Not sure. Let's just think of the obvious, big property developers first.'

Bella muttered a few names and then said, 'Agate Homes. They're not really in our area, but when I think about that house . . . '

Dominic typed in the name, scanned some returns, and then input further names. A few moments later he said, 'OK.'

'I think we've made a breakthrough!' said Bella, peering at his laptop screen.

'You made it. I'm just the typist,' said Dominic. 'But it seems that your friend Gerald — '

'He's not my friend! I've barely met him!'

' — is just an intermediary. This is the man we're after. Ed Unsworth. He's big further north, but maybe he feels it's time to extend his empire a bit.'

He brought up a picture of a smiling man accepting an award.

They both examined it. 'So what do we think the award is for?' said Bella. 'Services to the Shoddy House Building industry?'

'Unless we know they're shoddy we shouldn't slander him,' said Dominic. 'But is this captain of industry the man digging ditches with Nevil?'

They both peered at Alice's computer for a few moments.

'Well, it could be. He has more or less the same build and you couldn't say for definite it's not. He's a better fit than Gerald Roberts,' said Bella. 'But if he's the big cheese and Nevil and Gerald are lower down the pecking order, why is he doing grunt-work with Nevil? Wouldn't he get a minion to do it?'

Dominic shrugged. 'That's a good point, but maybe he was just there? If he wanted Badger Cottage and wanted to knock back the price a bit, he and Nevil could have decided to damage a drain or something? It could have been an impulse thing.'

'Certainly,' said Bella. 'If basically they want Badger Cottage for the site — which is likely because it backs on to open land — they'd want to pay as little as possible for it. If there were septic-tank issues they could get a tidy bit knocked off. Maybe Nevil took him to see the property under the cover of darkness. Obviously, they would have discussed the price and he felt it was too much. And Nevil said — just the sort of thing he would say — 'We can fix that'.'

'But we would have to prove it though. If we want to confront these guys, we need definite proof.' He looked at Bella. 'Are you sure you don't want to take it further than just a warning? If they're up to what we think they are, it's very wrong.'

Bella rubbed her face, thinking hard. 'No. I don't want to see Nevil in court. He might be a double-dealing dirty businessman, but I think he genuinely loves me, in his way. I owe him the chance to get out of this with his reputation.'

Dominic narrowed his gaze. 'You're very generous.'

Bella shrugged and sipped her wine to avoid his penetrative gaze. 'As I said, he does love me.'

'But you don't love him?'

'No.'

This answer seemed to give Dominic some satisfaction. 'You just want him to stop doing it?'

'Absolutely!'

'So we need to think of a way to make that happen.'

Bella exhaled. 'Yes.'

Neither of them spoke for several moments,

then Dominic said, 'You will probably have to tell him you're on to him, but don't let him suspect you don't know everything. Otherwise you'll be warning him but you might not stop him.'

Bella bit her lip. 'Is there any chance that we can find out the full story before I have to do this?'

Dominic nodded. 'Not sure there's anything much we can do now, but I've a few contacts I could ask.'

'They will be discreet? I'd hate it if things got out of hand and Nevil got hauled off to prison.'

'It might come to that in the end, Bella. If what he and his mates are doing is illegal — and it is looking very dodgy — you might have to face that.'

'If I try my best to prevent it — explain to him that he has to stop or he will go to jail, then at least we've given him a chance.' She got up. 'I think I need more wine or some tea, or something. I feel a bit sick.'

'Did you have supper?' he said sternly.

Bella considered. 'No, I didn't, now I come to think of it.'

'Then I'm going to make you something to eat. Come along.'

She got up to follow him. 'I can get something! You won't know where anything is!'

'You can direct me.'

Bella stopped at the table while Dominic went on into the main part of the kitchen. 'Why should you cook for me when I could do it myself?'

He turned round. 'You spend a lot of your life looking after people. I think it's time someone looked after you. Now sit down, but be prepared to guide me if I can't find things.'

Bella sipped her wine and watched while he moved around Alice's kitchen. He made her scrambled eggs on toast and Marmite.

'This is delicious, and so kind of you,' said Bella, only realising how hungry she'd been after she'd started eating.

'It's a pleasure. I like cooking for people. Aunt Jane is very good about letting me from time to time.'

Bella felt a rush of warmth towards him. She was used to wanting him, being in love with him, all that heady stuff, but this reminder of what a kind man he was felt different. She finished the last forkful and got up. 'I think I should find you something delicious to eat now. It's only fair.'

She picked up her plate and walked across to the dishwasher with it.

'Shall I put the kettle on?' said Dominic.

'Good idea. I'll just see if Alice has got some posh biscuits somewhere — '

Just as Bella had her hand on the cupboard door, Dominic stepped back from the kettle on to her bare foot.

'Oh my God, I'm so sorry!' he said.

Bella, who was trying not to make a fuss, bit her lip and hopped. Dominic came towards her. 'Can I look?'

They collided. Dominic steadied Bella as she wobbled and then their eyes met. The next moment Bella found herself crushed in his arms, his mouth on hers, kissing her for all he was worth.

She didn't hesitate, she allowed herself to be carried away by passion and pent-up yearning. Whatever he wanted from her would be fine by her. In spite of the fact every inch of her was pressed against him it wasn't nearly enough. She wanted to be under his skin, to become part of him. When lack of breath meant they had to stop kissing, the world seemed to have swung on its axis and Bella couldn't have said what day it was, she was so knocked off balance.

'That was a bit of a surprise,' she said, still breathless.

'For me too,' said Dominic. 'Oh, I knew I wanted to do that, had done for ages, but I didn't realise you'd — well, react quite like that.'

'Didn't you?' Bella was delighted her feelings for him hadn't been blindingly obvious. 'I would never have dreamt you wanted to kiss me.'

He kissed her again. 'Why not?'

'Because I'm not remotely like Celine!' she said.

'No. That what makes you a million times more . . . ' He paused as if looking for the right words. ' . . . more kissable.'

Bella refused to feel disappointed when he said 'kissable' and not something more. She was very happy to be standing in Alice's kitchen, her feet bare, one toe rather bruised, with Dominic's arms around her.

He buried his face in her hair. 'I wish we could stay here forever,' he murmured.

'Here? You wouldn't prefer somewhere more

comfortable?' This was the nearest Bella could get to suggesting they moved to the sofa. She didn't want to risk her passion overtaking his.

'I do, but I can't. I have to go. I have a meeting tomorrow I must prepare for. Big long report to write.'

'You shouldn't have come over!' Bella was immediately flooded with guilt. 'You were helping me with my stuff when you should have been doing yours.'

Dominic nodded. 'Sometimes my work ethic is just appalling.' Then he kissed her goodnight.

Bella went back to the kitchen after she had seen him off and leant against the table, blissfully reliving their kisses.

When she finally got herself together enough to go to bed, she resolved she was going to finish with Nevil in the morning. She was fed up with living a lie.

29

Bella made sure she was out of the house by just gone eight the following morning and so was waiting for Nevil when he arrived. She had hardly slept, and had mentally written so many scenarios of what she was going to say to him, all of which seemed wrong, she decided to just jump in and do it. Even if it was wrong.

She leapt to her feet and followed him into his office, ignoring the half-written property details and cup of coffee on her desk.

'Nevil, we have to talk. There's a problem.'

He took a maddeningly long time to put his briefcase on the desk, hang his jacket on the back of the door and finally turn to face her. 'Sweetheart, I'm sorry, I know I've been neglecting you but it's been for a good reason. I'm on the edge of a major breakthrough.' He paused for effect. 'I'm about to change our lives, Bells.'

Bella took a moment, and then said what was on her mind. There was no nice way to do it. 'I want to break up with you, Nevil.'

He paused, sighed and then came round from behind his desk and gently pushed her into the chair before perching on the desk. He held her hands. 'Darling, I've said I'm sorry but I've been doing it all for us — '

'It's nothing to do with you neglecting me! And anyway, you haven't been really. We've never lived in each other's pockets.'

'Whatever the problem is, I can make it right.'

'No! You can't! I don't love you any more.' She knew really that she had never remotely loved him, but she didn't want to be unkind.

'Please don't say that.' Nevil seemed genuinely distressed.

Bella felt desperately guilty, although she wasn't the one in the wrong. 'I'm sorry! And it's not only that . . . ' She paused, trying to think how to accuse him of being underhand — at best — with clients.

'There's another man, isn't there? I knew it! Bella, how could you?'

'This is nothing to do with anyone else!' (And it wasn't, really, so she felt confident saying it.) 'This is to do with us not being suited and — something else.'

'What?'

Bella took a breath and steeled herself. 'I found out that you've been doing things that border on the illegal if not actually being illegal.' Of course this wasn't strictly true: she had suspicions, but she needed more concrete evidence. It was just a matter of time before she or Dominic found such evidence — enough to convict them.

She didn't want to have to use the evidence; she wanted Nevil to admit it now and promise to stop. But if he didn't stop, well, she *would* use it to get him charged. She'd have to, or she'd be as bad as him.

He frowned. 'What have you found out, Bella?' He was angrier now and less pathetic, much to

Bella's relief. But she had to be careful. She wanted him to admit it, not clam up and just shout. Then she'd have antagonised him for no good purpose.

'It doesn't matter how I found out — '

'Have you been spying on me?'

'No! How would I do that?'

'You tell me!'

She sighed. 'Nevil, I never set out to find out things about you, but I have and I am not happy. I no longer want to marry you.'

'So you're leaving me?'

'Yes. I am.' She wasn't sure you could leave someone if you didn't live with them, but she wasn't going to get caught up on semantics.

'Do you realise what an idiot it'll make me look?'

She knew he had a large and delicate ego but she wasn't expecting this. And she'd begun to feel sorry for him! 'Nevil, I've just accused you of behaving dishonestly, which is one of the reasons I don't want to marry you, and you're worried about how it'll make you look?'

'I am the head of this firm. I prefer not to look like a jerk!'

'Would you prefer to look like a criminal?'

'I don't know what you're talking about!'

'I have seen you, on a film, digging holes outside Badger Cottage at eleven thirty at night!'

He seemed shocked but recovered quickly. 'So? And that's illegal, is it?'

'It's bloody odd!'

He took a breath. 'Listen, Bella, I don't know how you got that film but really, it's nothing illegal, and I'm doing it for us!'

'There isn't an 'us' any more, Nevil. Be quite clear about that.' There was no point in trying to be tactful about this now.

'There was then!' He paused. 'So, how did you get the film?'

'I'm not telling you, Nevil.'

'I know! It's those fucking Agnews, isn't it? It's something to do with them! Don't tell me they set up a CCTV camera on Badger Cottage to check out the area after dark?'

This wasn't a million miles away from the truth, but Bella ignored it. 'That really isn't the point. And you weren't alone!'

Nevil looked at Bella sharply. 'So who was I with?'

If only they'd managed to find out for sure who it was! If she had a name to throw at him she'd be on much firmer ground. 'It doesn't matter who you were with!' she said vehemently, wishing she believed it. 'You were not alone in digging a ditch in the dark!'

Nevil's expression hardened. 'You have no idea what was going on, do you? We could have been burying a dead cat for all you know!'

Exactly what she'd thought he'd say. 'As if! Do you fancy coming with me now, with a spade, to see if there's a dead cat there?'

'Oh, for God's sake, don't be so ridiculous.'

'Which proves my point! You were up to something — definitely something very suspicious.'

'You can't prove that though, can you?'

'Oh come on! You know that I know. I could

dump you in all kinds of trouble!'

'Could you?' He put his head on one side. 'And more to the point, would you?'

'Yes I would. Unlike you, I have ethics. I think if people do bad things they should be named and shamed!'

'You might have to be a little more specific though. You'd have to be able to say exactly what' — he made the most irritating gesture in the world to indicate speech marks — ' "bad things' I was doing.'

Bella felt very tired and not just because she hadn't slept. 'Nevil! You can bluff and bluster as much as you want. You can pick me up on the details or the lack of details — whatever you like — but we both know you've been thoroughly unethical and I want you to stop.'

'Will you marry me if I stop?'

She didn't hesitate. She didn't care about his feelings any more — he'd gone too far. 'I can't. I have tried to explain.'

'Then why should I stop doing anything I like? Why should I stop making money — amazing money — just to please you?'

She closed her eyes for a second. 'It's not just to please me! It's because it's wrong!'

'No it's not. Anyway, why should I care? This is my chance to become rich. Really rich.'

'Money isn't everything!'

He laughed. 'You are bloody mad, you know that? That is one of the most ridiculous clichés ever invented! Of course money isn't everything, but if you've got money you can buy all the other things!'

Bella felt suddenly exhausted by it all. 'Nevil, I don't know how we managed to stay together for so long. Our basic principles are so different.'

He glared at her. 'They are, aren't they? Totally bloody different. And because of that I'd like you to clear your desk and be out of here within the hour.'

Bella stood up. 'You're firing me?'

He nodded.

'On what grounds?'

'I think 'irreconcilable differences' would probably cover it.'

'We might have broken up but I'm good at my job. You know that.'

'You are but right now you're a pain in the arse so get out.'

'You loved me — '

'Past tense. Not any more. Now get the hell out.'

'I could get you for wrongful dismissal.'

He obviously didn't care about possibly being sued. 'Maybe, maybe not. But I'll worry about that if it happens. Now leave.'

Bella found herself outside Nevil's door in a state of shock. Not in any of her mental rehearsals of this meeting did it end up with Nevil sacking her. She had always been in charge.

'Are you OK?' said Tina. 'You look a bit flushed.'

'No, I'm not OK actually, Teens.'

'Cup of tea? Always helps.'

'Not sure I've got time for one. I've been sacked.'

Everyone in the room stopped what they were

doing and looked over.

'You've been sacked?' Tina repeated.

'Yes.'

'What for?' asked the sixth member of the team. 'I thought you and Nevil were an item.'

Bella felt herself blush. It sounded so impossibly sordid. 'Not any more. Which is why I've got the push, I suspect.'

Nevil's door opened and he emerged. 'If you could just clear your desk and leave, Bella. Tina, maybe you could help her.' He paused. 'I don't want to have you escorted off the premises.'

Bella still couldn't move. Fortunately Tina could. 'There's a really big box in the back I haven't crushed for recycling yet. I'll get it.'

A few moments later she was methodically packing everything on and in Bella's desk apart from her computer.

'I don't think I should steal the stapler, Tina,' said Bella.

'I think you should take everything,' said Tina, carrying on with her chosen job. She tipped up an empty drawer so all the paperclips and bits and pieces fell into the waiting box. 'You can always give it back. OK, I reckon that's everything,' she finished.

Nevil appeared again. 'Oh good, you're nearly out of here,' he said to Bella.

'I'm going to help her with her stuff,' said Tina.

'She can manage a cardboard box on her own,' said Nevil.

'Yes, but she can't manage a bottle of Pinot,' said Tina.

'You can't go with her,' said Nevil.

'It's my lunch hour,' declared Tina.

'It's ten in the morning!' said Nevil.

'So?' said Tina.

Nevil went back into his office and slammed the door.

'Come on, Bella,' said Tina. 'Let's get you out of here.'

Bella had always liked Tina and known her to be a friend, but it's only when things are really tough you actually strain-test a friendship. Tina stayed strong.

'OK, here's what we're going to do,' she said to the still-dazed Bella. 'I'm going to follow you home and we're going to dump the box. Then we're finding somewhere nice where you can get gently rat-arsed and tell me all about it. Or not, depending.'

'It's a bit early for getting rat-arsed, isn't it?'

'By the time we've dumped your things and gone somewhere, it'll be past eleven. Perfectly respectable time for getting pissed.'

Bella shrugged. She was enjoying being told what to do. She'd had so much decision-making to do lately, it was lovely to just follow Tina around like a child after its mother.

30

Tina knew of a lovely pub with a garden, and because it was early, they were the only ones in it. She ordered wine, water and chips. She pushed a glass of wine towards Bella.

'Of course you don't have to say anything . . .'

'But anything I do say will be taken down as evidence and used against me?'

Tina took a sip of her water. 'Something like that.'

Bella laughed. 'I don't suppose I should tell you any of it really. It's all such a muddle.'

'Well, of course you don't have to say a word. We can just sit here in peace and quiet and slag off Nevil.'

'Don't you like him, then?'

Tina shook her head. 'Not much. I like everyone else there though.'

Bella sipped her wine. 'Me too.' She closed her eyes, trying to take in that she had been sacked. The lovely job she so enjoyed was no longer hers. And to think she'd held off dumping him to spare his feelings. Ha!

'You'd probably rather talk to Alice about this,' said Tina, obviously desperate for all the details.

'She's away.' Bella looked at Tina. 'In Marrakesh.'

'Oh wow! Good for her!' Tina was impressed.

Bella nodded. 'With a man.'

'Double wow!'

'A younger man . . . ' Feeling slightly guilty for sacrificing Alice's privacy to save her own, Bella gave Tina a few key facts. Then she said, 'Golly, I do hope she's OK.'

'Of course she's OK! She's with a gorgeous younger man, in Marrakesh! What could possibly go wrong?'

'Anything could really. But I hope it hasn't.'

'You're worrying about Alice so you don't have to confront your own problems,' said Tina. 'She's fine; you're not.'

Bella didn't reply.

'You don't have to tell me . . . '

Bella smiled. 'But if I don't, you have thumbscrews in the car?'

Tina nodded. 'That's it.'

There was no one else she could talk to, and Bella felt maybe airing her problems out loud might help. She took a sip of wine. 'OK, so you know me and Nevil were engaged?'

Tina nodded again.

'It was supposed to be a secret!'

Tina gave the kind of laugh reserved for people who thought it was possible to keep anything like that secret in a small office. 'So why did you break it off? You found out at last he's a dickhead, or another man?'

'Actually neither,' said Bella, feeling defensive. 'I always knew — well, found out quite early on — that Nevil had his faults . . . '

'So it's another man?'

'Well, there might be, but that's not why I broke it off.'

'Why 'might be'?'

'It's complicated.' She thought about how Celine could stop Dominic seeing her if he had Dylan with him and it was a weekend.

'You mean he's married?' Tina's gaze hardened slightly.

'Not any more.'

'Custody problems?'

'Kind of. But more complicated.'

'Oh.' Tina didn't seem to have an answer for this. 'So why did you break it off with Nevil?'

'I found out he's been doing very dodgy things.'

'Like?'

'Apart from some deal I wouldn't have ever found out about if he hadn't left some plans in the photocopier — '

Tina shook her head regretfully. 'He doesn't get enough practice with that photocopier. That's a schoolboy error.'

This made Bella smile. 'Well, the really condemning thing is I caught him digging holes outside properties at eleven thirty at night! On a tape, not in real life. And before you ask, no, it wasn't a dead cat.'

Tina's quick-fire questioning stalled. 'So what was he doing?'

'I don't really know. I can only guess. And he wasn't alone, which is more significant, I think. Don't know who it is, either. It's a very indistinct video.'

'Sweetie, no offence, but how did you get a video of Nevil digging a hole with A. N. Other?'

'It is a bit of a funny one. The Agnews. They wanted to be sure there was wildlife at Badger

Cottage. They set up a camera to check. Instead of Mr Brock the Badger, they got Nevil. Thank goodness they didn't recognise him.'

Tina giggled. 'And that was what showed you the light? About marrying him?' Tina seemed to think Bella had been very slow to realise Nevil was not the man for her.

'Well, no, frankly. But I think I knew I wouldn't be able to stay with Rutherfords if I broke up with him and I didn't want to leave. I love my job! I love you lot! And I even wondered if I would have to leave town.'

'Really?'

Bella shrugged. 'Well, Nevil could tell all the other estate agencies not to employ me. It might be hard to get another job. Anyway, it's all out of my hands now. And I think the leaving-town thing is a definite.'

'It's so wrong. You're really good at your job. It should be him that leaves, not you.' Tina was thoughtful. 'We'd all prefer that.'

'Unless I can pin something definite on him, I have no power at all. Something he took great satisfaction in pointing out.'

'Would it help if I looked at the video?' asked Tina. 'I'm a local girl. I might recognise someone. If they are local, that is.'

'Well, another pair of eyes might help. I have a few ideas. You could at least rule some of them out.' She glanced at her watch. 'Your lunch hour will be running over then.'

Tina made a sound that was almost a spit. 'I think even Nevil knows he can't do without me. But I will be quick.'

* * *

Back at Alice's, Tina knew exactly who it was on the film. 'I know him! Well, I think I do! I was moonlighting as a waitress at a big awards do a couple of years ago.' She paused the video and stared at the image.

'And his name is?'

'Eeuw. Not sure. There were a few people like that at the do. A whole roomful, in fact.'

'You want multiple choice? I can do that.'

She wrote down the names of a couple of other developers she knew, and Ed Unsworth, the person she and Dominic had suspected last night. If Tina picked him out, that would make it fairly certain it was him.

Tina stared at the list. 'Can you find another picture of this one?' She jabbed her finger at Ed Unsworth's name.

'Of course! I've got pictures of them all.'

A bit of work with the cursor on Alice's computer and she summoned up the suspects.

'It's a bit like a police line-up,' said Tina. 'Oh! That's him! Look, he's winning a trophy. But I thought he'd moved up north?'

Bella nodded. 'Liverpool.'

'Looks like his time his up!'

'So what do you think they're doing? Him and Nevil?'

'Let's have another gander,' said Tina. She studied the film again, frowning. 'Damaging the drains. That'll be the soil pipe on its way to the septic tank. If they break it and make sure it fills with earth, it'll back up. I expect they'll be making sure plenty of water goes down the loo, and so when the surveyor comes there are lots of expensive problems that'll be taken off the price. They might even arrange for some slurry to end up in the septic tank too, so the house smells.'

'You know a lot about this sort of thing, Tina.'

Tina nodded. 'Yup. I used to work for a company where this sort of thing went on all the time.'

'I'm so impressed! And grateful. I so owe you!'

Tina put her arms round Bella. 'Anything for you, hon, and do let me know how it all goes.'

When Tina had driven away, Bella considered how to put this information to good use. She wasn't going to go back to Nevil with it. He'd blown his chance of being tactfully warned off. He was now going to get a much more official tap on the shoulder.

She took a walk round the garden, and before she'd got to the end she'd decided to try and deal with this on her own, without Dominic. Her feelings were a bit complicated, she realised. Although he had kissed her, wonderfully and passionately, he had rejected her suggestion they take it a bit further, and this had made her feel as if she were doing the chasing. In spite of being modern in every other aspect of her life, she didn't want that. And having loved him for so long, she had to be sure he felt the same. So she'd sort this out on her own.

She decided to go home to visit her mother, back to Whickamford, the town she had fled from nearly three years earlier. It would get her away from things for a bit, and from there she'd be perfectly placed to carry out another plan that had come to her as she walked. It might not work but she hoped it would. Then she would concentrate fully on Nevil's dodgy dealings.

She wrote Alice a longish text explaining and then she wrote a note and left it on the kitchen table in case she didn't get the text. Then she packed her carry-on case, got into her car and headed for home.

31

Bella's mother was surprised but pleased to see her. 'Hello, darling! What brought this on?'

Bella and her mother hugged hard. 'Lots to tell you. I've broken up with Nevil.'

'Oh, sweetie. Are you very cut up about it?'

Bella could tell her mother was trying to work out if she should say 'yippee' or 'I'm so sorry'. She knew perfectly well her mother had never much liked Nevil.

'I'm fine about it, but there's lots of other stuff going on. Which is why I'm here.'

'Nevil gave you time off work? Or have you taken some holiday? I'm sure you must be owed loads.'

'Actually, he sacked me, but thank you for reminding me about the holidays. He must owe me quite a lot of money. And he'd owe me more if I sued him for wrongful dismissal.'

'OK! Do you want some lunch?'

'No thanks, Mum, I'm fine. But am I stopping you doing something?' Now she looked more carefully she could tell her mother had that just-going-out-of-the-front-door look about her.

'Pilates, but I don't mind missing it. How's Alice?'

'Oh! There's lots of lovely gossip about Alice, but maybe she should tell you herself. I will give you a hint though. It involves a younger man and Marrakesh.' Aware she'd delivered just enough information to drive her mother mad with curiosity Bella smiled. 'Mind if I put the kettle on?'

Bella told her mother all about Badger Cam and Nevil, and the conclusion that he and Ed Unsworth were damaging the drains.

'So, what are you going to do about it?' her mother asked. 'This really isn't the sort of thing you should do on your own. Is there anyone who can help you?'

'There is and there isn't.'

'Oh come on, sweetie. Tell me. I might be able to help.'

'OK, it's to do with Dominic.'

Her mother sighed the sigh of the potential mother-in-law, remembering the perfect son-in-law who had got away. 'Go on. You might find saying it all out loud makes it clearer.'

'Well, you know he was married and his wife got pregnant?'

Her mother nodded. 'I remember how devastated you were by the news.'

'Well . . . ' Bella went on to explain about Dylan not being Dominic's, and how Celine was going to make it harder for Dominic to see him.

'But why would she do that?' Bella's mother asked. 'You'd think she'd be happy about having an extra responsible adult. Is it just a power thing?'

Bella shrugged. 'I think that must be it. I'm sure she doesn't have feelings for Dominic, but I expect she likes to have some sort of hold over him.'

'So what are you going to do about that?'

Bella shrugged. 'Do you think I should do something?'

Her mother nodded. 'Yes. I know I'm usually trying to stop you rushing in to solve other people's problems, but in this instance, I feel you could help.'

Bella had resolved to confront Celine and challenge her ridiculous stance, that's partly why she'd come to see her parents, but it was a boost to her confidence that her mother was in agreement. Although she slightly suspected her motive.

She smiled. 'You think sorting out Celine will stop me trying to find Ed Unsworth.'

'Sadly, I know you better than that. But leaving Celine out of it, I'd be far happier if you didn't try to tackle potential criminals on your own. If you did this for Dominic, you could ask him for help more easily.'

Bella considered. 'OK. I just have to find out how to get in touch with her.'

'Oh.' Her mother paused halfway through putting the kettle on again. 'How will you do that?'

'Facebook. It might take a while, but I'm sure I can find her.' She looked appealingly at her mother. 'Can I borrow your iPad?'

* * *

The next morning, after a cosy breakfast with her parents and a wander round the shops with her mother, Bella set off in her car to Swindon, where Celine worked for a PR company:

probably a glossy place with lots of interns. She was planning to take her out for lunch.

Thanks to her dad's satnav, which she fitted to her windscreen with the aid of a bit of spit and some firm words, she got there fairly easily. It was about an hour from her house, so she was at the offices (very glossy indeed) by twelve. However, once she'd found a space in the generous car park, she found the tide of her enthusiasm, her conviction that trying to talk sense into Celine would work, had ebbed away. She still thought it was the right thing to do, however; she wasn't going to chicken out, but it would take a fair bit of psyching up and 'you can do its' into the driving mirror.

When she had checked her appearance — she was very keen not to look like the version of herself that Celine had last seen — she got out of the car. She discovered she was shaking slightly. This might not succeed, but it was what she had to do. For Dominic, for Dylan, and, of course, herself. But Dominic was the most important. If he had to promise never to take Dylan anywhere remotely dangerous, like the swings, or never to have him when anyone else was going to be around, like Bella or his Aunt Jane, it was going to take all the joy out of life. Dominic might not feel the same way about her as she felt about him, but that wasn't the point, really.

Bella pushed open the heavy glass door and strode across to the reception desk, full of fake confidence. She asked for Celine and, possibly because it was lunchtime, was directed to her office. And her luck held; Celine was still there, working at her desk with her office door open.

Bella tapped on it. Celine looked up, initially confused and then, as she recognised her, surprised. 'What are you doing here?'

'I want to talk. Can I buy you a sandwich and a glass of wine?'

'Why should I come out to lunch with you?' Celine asked crisply. 'I'm busy. You can say what you want to say now.'

Bella smiled, trying to keep it light. 'It would be nicer to chat over lunch. We used to know each other a bit and you've got to eat. Eating while we talk won't take up so much of your time.'

Celine acknowledged this with a shrug and a dip of her blonde head. 'OK.' She picked up her bag. 'Come on.'

Bella hid her relief. She had deliberately flattered Celine by implying she was important and her time was precious. If she could get her to relax she might be more receptive.

The two women didn't speak as Bella followed Celine across a patch of grass to a pub. She didn't seem to want to chat so there was no point in Bella trying to. Part of a chain, the pub was big enough to allow them privacy, and Celine found a table and sat down.

Bella went to the bar and came back with sparkling water, wine, glasses and menus.

'I haven't got much time,' said Celine, looking at Bella as she unloaded herself.

Bella smiled but didn't comment. 'What would you like to eat?'

'A chicken Caesar salad, dressing on the side.'

'You eat here often?'

Celine nodded. This wasn't going to be easy.

When both women had their food, Bella took a sip of her spritzer. Her mouth had gone dry.

'So,' said Celine taking the croutons off her salad. 'Are you and Dominic an item?'

This topic wasn't what Bella had had in mind. 'Not really but — '

'I always thought he had a little thing for you, back in the day. And you for him.'

Bella fiddled with her napkin. 'Really? It is about him I wanted to chat.'

'So, was I right? You're blushing!' At least she seemed to find it amusing.

'Celine! That's not what I'm here to talk about!'

'But if you want me to listen, you have to say something I want to hear.'

'Well, I'm not in a position to say whether or not Dominic has 'a little thing for me', OK?'

'So, what about you?'

Really, Bella thought, this was the second confrontation that had gone completely wrong. First Nevil and now Celine. 'OK,' she snapped. 'I do have a little thing for Dominic. Happy now?'

Celine seemed satisfied and sipped her wine. She looked at Bella through narrowed eyes, and Bella suddenly had a horrible thought. If Celine thought she and Dominic had had an affair while he was still married, it would explain a lot. She had to put her straight.

'Celine! Really! Nothing ever happened between Dominic and me while you were still married. I promise!'

To Bella's surprise, this made Celine laugh. 'Oh God, no need to tell me that! He's far too upright and stuffy to do anything about his little crush. He can be very boring about things like that, I should warn you.'

Bella didn't think these things made Dominic boring. She thought he was noble and good, not stuffy. But Celine's morals were obviously very different from hers.

'OK, why I'm here . . . '

Celine crunched on a bit of celery. 'Oh, do let's get to that.'

Bella ignored her sarcasm and pressed on. 'I feel you're being unfair making it so difficult for him to see Dylan.'

'Oh, do you? And what makes you think that?'

'I was there when you said Dominic could only see him if he could focus fully on him.'

'And you think that's unfair? Why? He has no rights over Dylan, you know.'

'The thing is, if you make it too difficult he won't be able to see Dylan, and that means he won't have him for weekends and things.' Celine's expression wasn't encouraging and Bella wasn't hopeful but she did her best. 'It must be really useful having an extra dad for him when you need one.'

Celine put her knife and fork together. She'd eaten less than half of her salad. 'It is useful, but we could manage without it. If Dominic finds having Dyl interferes with his love life . . . ' She raised her eyebrow to make sure Bella got the point.

Bella blushed again. 'That's not what I meant!'

'Isn't it?'

Bella wanted to swear or cry. She'd gone to all this trouble to help Dominic with Celine, and she'd just made it all a whole lot worse. 'Dominic puts Dylan's needs and safety above everything. You didn't need to come and check up on him. You'd never find a better babysitter, ever.'

Celine exhaled. 'OK. I suppose I was guilt-tripped by a friend — you met her — into checking up on Dominic. She thinks I shouldn't let Dom have him if they're not related.' She paused to consider. 'But she's wrong. It's just sometimes I worry he's not as careful with Dyl as he should be. But I know he loves him. And not letting him have Dylan would make things tricky. We are planning a little break soon. It would be good if Dom could have him.' She thought for a little while longer and then came to a conclusion. 'You can tell him he can still see his Auntie Jane and — you — while he's got Dylan.'

'Celine! I can't tell him that! It's up to you to tell him!'

'Oh, not sure of him, are you?' Celine laughed. 'OK, I'll tell him when I've got a minute. Now, I've got to go. I've got a meeting at two and wanted to fit some shopping in first.'

Bella stayed where she was for some time after Celine left. It hadn't gone exactly to plan, but at least Celine had agreed to ease up her conditions. A pain in her heart she hadn't really been aware of ebbed away. Everything would be all right.

32

One of the many joys of Michael, Alice reflected, was his ability to be silent. She didn't want to talk, she just wanted to look out of the window and relive the magic. The fact that they could be silent together seemed more important than all the talking they had done.

While reliving each wonderful moment she came to the lowering conclusion that the most wonderful thing had been the rediscovery of sex. She would have preferred for it to be something to do with art, music or architecture. But lovely as those things were, what was so delightful was to find out she was still a woman in all senses, and being sixty hadn't changed that at all. She was still languid with remembered pleasure. The whole experience had been magical, from start to finish.

There were several cars parked in front of Michael's house as well as Alice's.

He switched off the engine. 'Oh hell.'

'Were you expecting a party?' asked Alice, anxious suddenly.

'Not really. Sort of. Never mind. Let's go in. You'll need tea or something after the journey.'

She certainly did, and the use of a bathroom. What she didn't need was to be introduced to a lot of strange people when she'd only recently got off a plane. What were they doing here? And who had let them in? Still, she wouldn't let them spoil her bubble of happiness.

'Mike!' said a loud male voice from behind the door as it opened. 'Where the hell have you been?' A large smiling man appeared. 'We've been trying to get in touch with you!'

'Sorry,' said Michael calmly. 'I've been away.'

'With this lovely creature, I assume!' said the man, taking Alice's hand in his large soft one and then kissing her cheek. 'Good choice!'

Alice faked a smile and withdrew her hand. 'Bathroom?' she said to Michael.

'Just through there,' he said, pointing. Then he was swept into the sitting room, where Alice could hear other people talking urgently.

Alice took her time in Michael's downstairs cloak-room. She did her hair, washed her face, applied make-up from her handbag kit, and rubbed the soothing hand cream she also kept there into her hands, until she felt ready for a round of introductions to people she probably wouldn't see again. She wondered if she could sneak into the kitchen and make a cup of tea first. Perhaps they would sense they were unwelcome and leave.

She tiptoed past the sitting-room door and heard: 'Mike, you know we've been waiting for your decision on this for a while.' It was the man who'd opened the door.

'Can I get you a drink of water, Dad?' That was Hannah, Alice realised, wishing it had been Lucy, who was now an ally.

'I'm OK. Really, I ought to — ' Michael's voice.

'Mike, sorry to put you on the spot, but there

are deals resting on this. We need to get you back to London ASAP. There's a lot of paperwork, things you need to sign when you're emigrating.'

'Surely . . . ' Michael sounded very fed up.

Alice felt too shocked to move. Emigrating? Michael was emigrating? And he hadn't told her? Somehow she moved away from the door, not knowing what on earth to think. She hadn't intended to eavesdrop, really, and wanted to stop doing so. But now she wondered: if she hadn't overheard that, when on earth would he have told her?

Alice stood in the hallway breathing in through her nose and out through her mouth, just as she'd been taught in the yoga classes she used to go to. She needed to keep calm. She was an adult — quite an old adult. She must be sensible.

She found a pad and pen in her handbag and, leaning on the hall table, wrote a hasty note: *Dear Michael, Can't thank you enough for a lovely weekend, but you're obviously very tied up with the next bit of your life, so won't say goodbye in person. Yours, Alice*.

Then she hitched her bag on to her shoulder and went outside. Relieved that Michael hadn't locked his car, she got out her luggage. Then she went to her own car and set off for home.

Alice found it was possible to postpone reality for a while, if you had to. She decided not to think about anything except getting home until she was home. Bella would be back from work soon and they could have tea in the garden. Bella would want to know all about Marrakesh and

Alice would tell her. She wouldn't tell her how she'd discovered sex again, of course, but an amusing account of how they'd got lost in the souk would be fine.

Then, inevitably, Bella would ask, in a tentative, indirect way, mostly consisting of 'And are you and — er — Michael — er — you know?'

And Alice would say, no, actually, as utterly lovely as the weekend had been, she and Michael were just friends really, and that was that. She wouldn't say it was because he was emigrating, until she'd had time to get used to the idea and could rely on herself not to cry. And tomorrow she'd think what to do with the rest of her life. Alice liked to have a plan.

She hadn't thought to look at her phone, and only now saw there were two texts from Bella. Then when she got into the kitchen, there was the note saying she was staying with her mother. Alice found this unexpectedly disappointing. While she and Bella often went for days without seeing each other much, she felt she needed company now. On the other hand it did mean she had lots of time to think up a good story as to why she and Michael weren't going to become anything permanent.

After tea, Alice went into her garden. She looked at every bed, then every plant and considered them all. She remembered how she'd come by each one — bought at a garden centre, sent off for from a specialist catalogue, or given in a plastic bag from a friend. Quite a few of her favourites had been bought at plant sales and fêtes, and a couple had been 'liberated' from the gardens of derelict buildings. Every plant had a little story behind it. She took the opportunity to say goodbye to each one. For, without even thinking about it consciously, Alice had come to a conclusion. Her trip with Michael had reawoken her love of travel, her need for new adventures. Even if he wasn't going to be part of her life, she still needed the change he had instigated. She had decided she needed to leave this house and move on.

* * *

Alice refused to think of herself as heartbroken, she was too old for that. But she did feel horribly betrayed, abandoned, bereft and lonely, which probably was pretty much the same as heartbreak. However, the decision she had made in the garden the previous evening still felt right.

Years ago she heard of someone who chose to give up smoking at the same time as she was going through a tricky divorce, the theory being that she was suffering so much anyway, she wouldn't notice a bit more. Thus she decided to tackle the hardest part of moving house immediately: clearing out the loft. And even if this decision wasn't entirely logical, it would be a distraction.

Alice knew from tales Bella had told her that people glibly booked removers for their furniture having taken a brief survey of the bits they could see, completely forgetting the huge amount of stuff tucked up under the insulation in the attic, in the garage and the garden shed. And her loft had all her parents' clutter in it as well as her own. The access to it had never been easy, involving pull-down ladders, cobwebs and spiders, which is why she'd allowed things to accumulate. Now, when she was so miserable, she would take all those little inconveniences in her stride.

As a gesture to Bella's demands for health and safety in the home, she left a note on the kitchen table saying where she was, in case she broke her ankle and no one could find her. She sent Bella a text saying the same thing, in case Bella didn't come home for a while. Then she opened the hatch and pulled down the ladder. Clutching a handful of bin bags she mounted the ladder, clinging to both it and to the theory that misery could be constructive.

* * *

Alice wasn't finding it easy to focus. She'd spent a lot of time peering into old tea chests and moving things from one end of the loft to the other, and then decided she needed entertainment and had gone downstairs for a radio. She wasn't remotely hungry so hadn't bothered with lunch and gradually, she managed to fill a few bin liners with rubbish. She was sitting on the floor with a folder full of old school reports on her knees, when she heard a noise over the sound of the radio. Instantly fearing rats or mice, although she'd found no sign of any, she snapped off the radio and closed the folder, ready to run if she had to. Then she saw Michael, standing at the top of the ladder, looking up at her.

Although her brain knew instantly she had no reason to be frightened her body was slower to catch on and she screamed, although not very loudly.

'Oh, darling,' he said. 'I realise I behaved appallingly, but is it that bad? I know I should have explained everything but I couldn't bear to ruin our weekend.'

Alice wanted to cry or murder him, and was not sure which, but she was determined to do neither. Instead she resorted to dignity — not easy when covered in dust and wearing very little make-up, not to mention some old linen trousers that might well have embarrassing splits in the fabric. 'What are you doing here?' she asked, in a husky voice; tears were not far away.

'Just calling by,' he said. 'The note on the kitchen table told me where you were.'

Alice stiffened. 'How did you get as far as the kitchen?'

'Through the side door. I tried the conventional ringing the bell thing first. I tried your phone. Then I hammered on the back door. I knew you were here — your car was here, and anyway I could just tell. When I couldn't make you hear me I decided something bad had happened and I broke in. Only I didn't actually have to break anything.'

'Oh,' said Alice, still dignified. 'I must have left the side door unlocked last night. Very remiss of me.'

'Very,' agreed Michael. He regarded her. 'Are you going to come down?'

'No. I'm busy.' Then she sneezed. While she was groping for a tissue, Michael arrived in the loft.

'Darling, we do need to talk and I need to apologise properly. I should have told you about the job, and I should have done it yesterday, if not over the weekend. But I had to go to London, I had meetings all day and another couple this morning. I actually suggested we had one of those where you don't sit down, to make it go more quickly.'

'Right,' said Alice, non-committal.

'Do you really want me to explain everything here?'

'I don't think we need to talk.' She gave her nose a final wipe. 'Although I expect I forgot to say thank you for a lovely holiday. Thank you.'

'Alice, my darling girl, you said thank you about a zillion times and you wrote it in the note. That's not what I meant, as well you know.'

Alice tucked the tissue in the pocket of her shirt. 'Really, there's nothing to say. I realise you have a life, a job, a career, things I no longer have, and you must pursue it.' She hesitated. 'I now have to confess to eavesdropping. I know you're emigrating.'

'Didn't your mother ever tell you that eavesdroppers never hear good of themselves?' Michael set off across the loft towards Alice, and she backed away a little; she took refuge behind a tea chest, squatting down as if to sort through it.

'You weren't talking about me!'

'No, but it did affect you.'

'Not at all! It's your life!' Alice said. She felt another sneeze coming and got out her tissue. She really hoped he wouldn't think she was crying. 'It's the dust,' she went on. 'It's making me sneeze.' The sneeze threw her off balance so she stuck out her leg to stabilise herself.

'Please, let's go downstairs,' said Michael. 'There's lots we need to discuss.'

'No. If you have anything to say, say it here, and quickly. I'm busy.'

'OK. I brought your rug. The one we got in the souk?'

'Oh.' Alice felt a glimmer of pleasure. A new rug would be cheering.

'And I meant to talk to you about everything but the moment never came up.'

'No,' she agreed, although as she hadn't known he needed to tell her he was emigrating she couldn't have spotted a good moment.

'The trouble was — is . . . ' He paused.

She was starting to get cramp and wanted to move her leg but as she didn't want to look old and creaky, she put up with the pain. 'Come on then, spit it out.'

He laughed. 'You're a bit crabby today, aren't you?'

'Yes. Possibly. So would you be if you had cramp like I have.'

'Then get up! Stop curling up like a baby gorilla.'

'Are you calling me a gorilla?'

'A baby one. It's quite different. Now get up.'

He grabbed a hand and pulled. With his help

she got upright. She rubbed her aching leg. 'That was agony.'

'I did suggest we went downstairs before now.'

Now she was in less pain she felt more belligerent. 'And I said I was busy! Now say what you want to say.' Something caught her eye and a quick squint made her fairly sure her face was smeared with dust. She was even more determined to stand her ground.

'OK. Well, as you gathered I've been offered a job abroad.' He paused.

She nodded. 'Go on.'

'One of the reasons I wanted to take you away, apart from the usual . . . '

He seemed to need prompting. 'Which were?'

He looked pained. 'Don't make me spell it out! It's embarrassing! But it's to do with perfectly normal male urges and very attractive women.'

Alice thought this was a compliment but as she wasn't sure she decided not to push it. 'OK, let's go with the first reason you mentioned. Tell me that.'

'I wanted to ask you to come with me.' He bit his lip. 'You see, it is a big ask.'

'You want me to emigrate? Where to? Outer Mongolia? New Zealand? Or somewhere further away?'

He shook his head, beginning to smile. 'I'm not sure there is anywhere further away than New Zealand, and I didn't say anything about emigrating. Bill did.'

'So where is it you're not emigrating to?'

'Brussels.'

'What, Brussels? In Europe?' She frowned. 'Who on earth emigrates to Brussels?'

'No one! Well, at least, I'm sure some people do. But I do wish you'd stop talking about emigrating, when I'm not.'

She sighed. Her devastation was seeping away a little, but slowly. 'So what are you doing?'

'I'm going to work there for three years, possibly.'

'You mean, possibly it's longer?'

'No, possibly I won't go.'

'What is it depending on?'

'Whether you come with me.'

Alice took a few seconds to take this in. 'Are you mad?'

'I do realise it's terribly early in our relationship and that I — '

'No,' Alice interrupted. 'What's the big deal asking me to go there? It's only at the end of the Eurostar line or something.'

'But it would be for three years.'

'I expect I'd get time off for good behaviour — wouldn't I?' When she thought of the agony she'd been through, and he only wanted to ask her to live in Brussels. 'You'll have the internet, won't you?'

Half laughing he said, 'I didn't feel I could ask you to leave all this . . . ' He made a gesture, serious now.

Alice started to giggle. 'What? All this?' She indicated the boxes, the bin bags, the dust and the mess.

Michael frowned. 'Obviously I hadn't pictured you in exactly this setting. I had you more in the garden, under a rose bush or something.'

'I think you mean gooseberry bush and I haven't been under one for years — well, since I was born, really.'

Michael stopped trying to explain himself. He stepped forward and took her into his arms. 'I adore you, Alice, and I want you to come to Brussels with me. If you could face marrying me, that would be all the better.'

His body against hers was exciting and familiar at the same time and she felt she could never get enough of his kisses.

When at last he let her go she said, 'Let's go downstairs. What are we doing in this dusty attic?'

He held on to her. 'I want a picture of you exactly as you are now.'

'That means I'm covered in dust, doesn't it?'

He nodded. 'And you've got cobwebs in your hair.'

'Agh! I'm getting out of here immediately.'

A glance in a decent mirror as they went downstairs made her say, 'You go and put the kettle on or open a bottle, whatever you want. I'm going to have a quick shower.'

'Don't be long.'

'I won't.'

She was back with him in five minutes and found him on the phone. 'So, are you happy now?' he was saying. Then he laughed. 'Yes, all done.' Then he ended the call.

She was desperate to ask whom he was talking to but it was none of her business. 'Are you hungry?' she said instead.

'Starving. I didn't have lunch.'

Feeding people was where she felt comfortable. 'Nor did I. Forgot.' She didn't want to say she'd been too miserable to think of food. 'What would you like?'

'Biscuits and cheese and a glass of wine,' he said promptly.

'Not a problem.' She began getting things out of cupboards.

'Alice — you are sure about coming with me, aren't you?'

'Quite sure.'

'I could easily ring them back and say you've changed your mind.'

She stopped. 'Are you telling me that you've just rung and told them you'll do the job? You really didn't before?'

'I rushed up to London and signed everything, but I said they couldn't act on it until I got back to them. I didn't want a job that took me away from you for three years — even if Brussels isn't quite as far as New Zealand.'

'So, supposing I'd said no? What would you have done?'

'Found another job in England,' he said promptly. 'Or become a consultant or something.'

'You don't seem to take your career very seriously,' she said, peering into the fridge so he wouldn't see her expression.

'Oh, I do. I have. But there comes a time in your life when you realise there are more important things. You are more important.'

Alice swallowed. 'For that I shall give you my

very best Saint Agur.'

'You mean you wouldn't have anyway?' He seemed offended.

'Of course I would!'

'So you do love me?'

'Of course I do,' she said softly. Then she exhaled. 'Now I think we should eat, otherwise we'll start on the wine and fall into a stupor.'

When they did start on the wine he raised his glass to her. 'Here's to you, my darling girl.'

She smiled in return. She found she couldn't speak. Her throat was closed up by tears of happiness.

33

Bella drove back to Alice's after leaving her mother, feeling tired and anticlimactic. All the adrenalin she had relied on as she had confronted Celine had gone. Now she didn't know what to do next. She hoped the drive would give her time to think about things.

It had been lovely seeing her parents, but she had been keen to go back to her own life. For, once she had put a stop to Nevil's nefarious dealings, she would have to find a new job.

Although she had longed to instantly receive a text from Dominic saying, 'Hey, thank you so much!' she hadn't, and she realised he wouldn't yet know Celine had agreed not to be so neurotic about him having Dylan. Celine had said she would tell him when she had a minute, but she was hardly going to rush to do that until she actually wanted a babysitter.

Bella hadn't got in touch with Dominic herself. She wanted to see if she could sort out all Nevil's evil goings-on without help. Also she didn't want him to think she'd read too much into what to him might have just been a few kisses. She had loved him too long to dare to hope he might feel the same way; she needed to be absolutely sure it wasn't just a diversion for him. And, now she'd done it, she felt awful about seeing Celine behind his back. He was bound to regard it as massively interfering, and never want to see her again.

In some ways she wished she could turn back the clock to before she had dumped Nevil, got the sack and gone to see Celine. Then she had been reasonably happy: she had a job she loved, and lived with a much-loved friend in a beautiful house. How lucky she had been!

While she could go on living with Alice, could she get a job as an estate agent in town? Would all Nevil's Round Table mates refuse to employ her out of male solidarity? Quite possibly. And if she told his mates what Nevil had been up to, they'd probably say, 'Get in, son!' or offer tips such as how flinging a dead rat in through a broken window of an empty property would create a smell that took twenty grand off the price, like the overgrown schoolboys lots of Nevil's friends seemed to be.

By the time she parked in front of Alice's house she was feeling very pessimistic about being able to stay in the area.

She met Alice in the hallway, surrounded by cardboard boxes, with a heavy-duty tape dispenser in her hand.

'Oh!' she said, startled. 'Moving house?'

Alice lowered the tape dispenser. 'Err — kind of. Would you like to come into the kitchen? I'm sure it's wine o'clock.'

It was actually tea o'clock, which increased Bella's sudden anxiety. She'd been joking when she'd asked Alice if she was moving, but something was definitely up.

She sat at the table while Alice bustled about.

'So how was Marrakesh?'

Alice turned, bottle in hand. 'Brilliant!'

'Oh? Somewhere I must go?'

'Absolutely!'

Bella looked at Alice more closely. 'I must say, it has made you look great. Was there a spa there or something?'

'Maybe. Probably. I didn't go to it.'

'So why are you looking so amazing? And why are you packing?'

Alice blushed and opened the bottle. Then Bella blushed as she realised why Alice's skin was glowing and her eyes sparkling. 'Ah! I get it! It was a *very* good holiday.'

Alice nodded in confirmation.

'So what about the packing?' Bella asked, as Alice handed her a glass.

Alice frowned slightly, disquiet flickering across her expression. 'Bella, honey, you're in for a bit of a shock.'

Bella felt it would be more than a bit of a shock, she felt it was going to be a mortal blow. Was Alice really moving? Was the house she loved, where she lived, really going to be sold, on top of everything else she'd gone through just recently? Could she somehow stop it happening? Appeal to Alice's famously kind heart? 'Did you know that Nevil gave me the sack?' she said.

Disquiet became shock. 'No! That's outrageous! Why? The bastard! How dare he?'

Bella couldn't help smiling a little at Alice's reaction. She sipped her wine, feeling marginally better. 'Well, I dumped him, and told him I'd caught him out in all sorts of wicked things.'

'He cheated on you?' Alice's outrage was like milk coming to the boil.

'No! I wish! It would be so much easier. Look, why don't you tell me your news? It's obviously immense.'

Alice sipped her wine as if guilty about something. 'Yes, but I think I should hear yours first.'

Bella took a breath and told her tale of woe. ' . . . but the awful thing is,' she finished, 'I think I probably shouldn't have gone behind Dominic's back and seen Celine. And I don't think he feels about me the way I feel about him. He left because he had work to do! Doesn't that mean 'he's not that into me', as they say?'

Alice shrugged. 'I don't think he's the sort of man who'd kiss you if he didn't feel anything for you.'

'But I really embarrassed myself! I more or less invited him to stay and he said no.'

'Because he had work to do! You told me that's what he said.'

'So you don't think I've completely messed things up with him?'

'No I don't. And I do think you need his help to sort out Nevil. It all sounds very unsavoury.'

'How can I do that if I don't want to get in touch?'

Alice sighed. Bella could tell she thought she should just pick up her phone or send an email, but she also understood why she was reluctant.

'I know,' said Bella. 'Lightbulb moment. I'll go and see Jane Langley. Then if he's there, I can ask him for help.'

'But if he isn't, you're no better off. But it is a good idea to see her. She's lovely and she's bound to say nice things about you to Dominic.'

'I feel so relieved to have made a decision.' Bella studied Alice. 'So what's your news?'

Alice looked as if she wanted to deny having news. 'Mine? Well, it is a bit embarrassing.'

'You don't look embarrassed. You look glowing,' said Bella sternly.

'Well, I might be glowing but I am embarrassed, and I wished I had more time to explain it all to you.'

Bella swallowed and pretended to be calm. 'Alice, if you want to sell the house I'd perfectly understand. I can easily find somewhere else to live. I'm an estate agent!' She frowned. 'Well, I was. But I might have to leave town to get a new job anyway. I could go back to my parents!' She smiled brightly, as if this was something she was very happy to do. Although it wasn't, really. She loved them dearly, but having left home, she didn't want to go back. There wasn't the space there was at Alice's, and she valued her independence.

'No! Bella! Darling! You don't understand!' Alice was distressed. 'I'm not selling the house. I'm just going to Brussels. If you don't stay here I'll have to rent it out . . . '

'Brussels? Why? A previously unfulfilled passion for tiny cabbages?'

Alice gave a quick smile to acknowledge Bella was making a joke when she obviously wasn't very happy. 'No. I'm going to be with Michael. He's got a job there. For three years.'

'Blimey, Alice! You don't hang around!'

'Are you shocked? I am a bit . . . but I think it's right.'

'Does it feel right?'

Alice exhaled. 'Honestly, Bella, it feels totally mad, but also just what I want to do. I want the challenge of a new country, learning a language — maybe a pâtisserie course, or even a chocolatier course — and . . . well, everything.'

Bella raised her eyebrows. 'And Michael has nothing to do with it?'

Alice put her hand up to her face. 'Michael has everything to do with it. I can't believe the love of my life, my grand passion, has come now. And I can't waste it. I have to follow my heart.'

'Alice! That's so sweet! I think we should set it to music!' She was joking but then worried that she'd sounded sarcastic. 'I really am totally thrilled. Michael is a very lucky man.'

Alice acknowledged this. 'He wants to get married, but I think it's far too soon.'

'Not too soon to relocate to a whole new country then?'

'That's different! To be honest I've had itchy feet for ages. I just didn't know how to — scratch the itch, I suppose.' She looked at Bella, frowning slightly. 'Do you think I'm mad?'

'Yes, but definitely in a good way. After all, if you don't like it, you can come home.'

'Exactly! Which is one of the reasons I don't want to sell up.' She paused. 'I was hoping you'd be able to look after the house for me. Stay here, I mean.'

'Well, I'd love to, but . . . I suppose I have to

see how things work out.'

'It would be a travesty of justice if Nevil had the power to stop you working in this town when he's the one up to no good.'

'He might not be able to, but he does do a lot of networking with other businesses.' She stared at the table. 'He'd get them on his side.'

'Listen,' said Alice after a few moments. 'You need to forget your pride and get in touch with Dominic. Soon. Immediately.'

'OK.' Bella braced herself. 'I'll send a text. And if he doesn't get back to me fairly soon I'll go to Jane's and see if she knows anything.'

The text sent, she helped Alice find some mothballs for the winter clothes she didn't want to take with her, then she looked at her phone again, feeling like a teenager. 'No reply,' she told Alice.

Alice gave her a quick hug. 'Then go and see Jane.'

'I can't go now, it's late!'

Alice glanced at the old station clock that ticked away their lives. 'No it's not. It's five thirty. I was a bit precipitate with the wine. Off you go.'

Bella set off towards Jane Langley's house hoping Dominic would be there. And hoping he wouldn't. And when she wasn't hoping she was wondering why her feelings were so contradictory.

It was because she felt she was chasing him and worried that he wouldn't like the fact that she had interfered in his personal life. He might think she was bossy and, deep down, she wanted to be the pursued, not the pursuer. She couldn't get out of her mind the fact that he hadn't wanted to stay longer after he'd kissed her that evening. And as time went on and she didn't hear from him, she thought more about his apparent rejection of her than she did about his passionate kisses.

She'd rung before she set off, and Jane was waiting for her.

'Oh, darling, I was so pleased when you said you wanted to visit.'

Bella kissed her cheek. 'Well, that's good.'

'I didn't feel I'd thanked you quite enough.'

'What on earth for?' Bella was confused.

'About the Agnews coming. I like them so much and knowing they're going to be here, in the house, means I don't have to fret about the little things that are somehow so worrying. Mr Agnew — Alan — is terribly handy round the house and can fix dripping taps, odd little leaks, things like that. And if we do need professional help I won't have to wonder if the plumber is cheating me, or if I can trust the electrician, because Alan will sort it out for me.'

'I'm so glad you feel like that,' said Bella, with a satisfaction that bordered on the smug. At least she'd been right about this. That was something. 'That's wonderful.'

'It is. I feel a whole new phase of my life has started and I'm going to love it.' Having got this off her chest, she took a breath. 'Now, is it warm enough to sit out? What can I get you to drink? A glass of sherry? Something nice? Dominic's not here this evening so I could do with the company.'

'A glass of water please,' said Bella, 'but I'll get it. Would you like some? No? I'll bring mine out then.' Now she knew Dominic wasn't going to appear, Bella felt relieved, pushing disappointment further down her list of emotions.

As Bella carried the water down the garden, taking in the beauty of the herbaceous borders and climbers, scented and luscious, she couldn't help remembering how shocked she'd been to see Dominic there. What a lot had happened since. She hardly felt she was the same person.

Jane was still enthusing about the Agnews as they sat under the rose arbour, the roses replaced by honeysuckle and jasmine. 'I feel I can really enjoy the garden now I don't have to be responsible for it all. Imogen and Alan have been up, and made a list of everything we want done. Imogen will do her bit and I'll probably get help for mine, but the really lovely thing is how completely we agree on what gardens are all about.'

'Well, that's fantastic. I am thrilled. And the house part?'

Jane flicked a casual hand. 'We'll sort that out easily. I don't need much space. Now, tell me your news. Why were you so keen to visit? Not that I'm not delighted.'

'Well, they're not the same thing, so I'll start with my news.' She paused. She'd been quite glib about leaving Nevil and losing her job when she'd told her mother and Alice but Jane would take it all a lot more seriously. And now she was in her presence, Bella felt it was indeed more important than she'd allowed herself to acknowledge up to now.

'Well, actually, it's not great news, although I am fine with it.'

Jane looked anxious.

'I've — er — left my job.' Suddenly she couldn't bring herself to say she'd been sacked.

'But, my dear, why? You were so good at it!'

'Yes, and I will go on selling houses, but I can't work for Nevil any more.'

'You handed in your notice?'

Now her squeamishness seemed like lying. 'Well, actually, he sacked me. I broke off our engagement. He didn't take it well.'

Jane spent several seconds possibly struggling not to say everything that was on her mind. When she did speak out loud again, she said, 'Well, he wasn't good enough for you, dear, and I'm sure you'll soon find another job.'

'Yes.' Bella wasn't going to tell Jane that she feared she might not be able to get another job in the same town. 'But I have other news. About Alice.'

'Good news, I do hope!'

Bella laughed. 'Yes, don't worry. It is good but I must say it is rather surprising.'

Relieved, Jane clearly felt she could make a little joke. 'Go on — don't leave me in suspense. I'm old, I don't want to die before you get round to telling me.'

Bella laughed. 'She's going to live in Brussels for three years.'

'Good Lord! What brought that on?'

'A man, actually. A rather lovely man. In fact you've met him: Michael.'

Jane looked knowing. 'I thought he fancied

her. Glad to know I can still spot a budding romance.' She looked at Bella rather sternly. 'Talking of which, have you heard from Dominic lately?'

'Err, no,' said Bella.

'Poor boy, he's been frantic! He seems to have taken on a whole lot of new work when he was busy enough already.'

'Oh dear,' said Bella, for want of something better.

'Yes! He dashed off in a tearing hurry but it's all right, I've got the Agnews I can ring now if there's an emergency.'

'Did he — um — Do you know where he dashed off to?' Bella asked, trying not to let it show how much she cared.

Her friend shook her head. 'He didn't give me any details. Really he was just rescuing his clean washing from the airing cupboard and throwing it into a bag.'

'And you don't know why he was going?'

Jane shrugged. 'Something to do with his work. But he didn't tell me the details, just that he was in a rush. I didn't ask as I didn't think it important I should know.'

'Of course not. It's not important that I should know either, but I'm a very nosy and curious person.' She smiled and got to her feet. 'Well, now I've told you my news, I'll let you get to bed, or carry on doing what you were doing before I rang.'

She kissed her friend and then walked across the lawn to the drive, hoping Jane wouldn't wonder why she felt obliged to rush over with the news of her broken engagement. She really didn't want Dominic to ring his great-aunt and be told 'Bella was asking where you were'. She personally might have come round to the idea that she was pathetic and needy, but she didn't want Dominic to know. Although she'd glanced at her phone several times while she was at Jane's, there'd still been no reply to her text.

Briefly she wondered if he'd managed to find out anything for her regarding Nevil's dealings. He had mentioned having contacts. But it was unlikely, seeing he was so busy. And if he never got in touch again, well, she'd just have to get over it. She'd done it before, after all. She should be able to do it again. Eventually.

⋆ ⋆ ⋆

Alice was still up when she got home, and was disconnecting from a phone call that had made one side of her face rather red, which indicated it had not been a short one.

'That was your mother,' Alice said. 'She wanted to hear all about Michael and going to Marrakesh from the horse's mouth.'

Bella smiled. 'I knew she'd want to ask you about it. And you are her oldest friend.'

Alice smiled, obviously having enjoyed the call very much. 'And how about you? Did you manage to find out anything about Dominic?'

'Nope. He went off in a tearing hurry and didn't say where he was going.

'Oh, you poor love,' said Alice. 'What are you going to do now?'

Bella sighed deeply. 'What can I do? I have to wait until he gets in touch with me. And he might not.'

'I'm sure he will,' said Alice with an urgency that meant she wasn't actually sure. 'He's been called away suddenly and will be in touch as soon as he can be. Don't worry.'

Bella nodded. 'OK. I'll stop thinking about him.'

Alice laughed. 'Well, I wish you luck with that one.'

Bella smiled. 'It's so silly, isn't it? When you're in love, especially with a man who probably — might not — love you back, you know the best thing you could do to help yourself is to just put them out of your mind.'

'But your mind has no intention of paying any attention,' went on Alice. 'Because minds don't work like that.'

Bella paused. 'I am going to miss you, Alice,' she said. 'Who else will talk sense to me when I need it?'

'I will! We'll Skype, and you can visit and I'll be popping home all the time to make sure you've kept up with the dusting . . . '

'It's been so great living with you, Alice.'

'I've loved it too. We turned out to be a pretty good match.'

'In spite of the fact that you are a hundred and I am seventeen . . . '

'Cheeky madam. Let's have a glass of wine!'

Bella went to bed with no clear idea about what to do, but in the morning, after a surprisingly good night's sleep, she knew exactly what her next course of action had to be.

'I'm going to Liverpool,' she announced to Alice, after tea and toast and Marmite. 'I'm going to confront the property developer who is behind all Nevil's dirty dealings.'

'Oh, love! Is that wise? Going on your own? He might have a shaved head, tattoos and a gang of heavies protecting him.'

Bella laughed. 'He's a real person, not a character in a film. I expect he'll be perfectly normal. Besides, I've seen pictures of him on the internet. He looks like a pillar of the community.'

'Always the worst kind,' muttered Alice. 'Never trust a pillar.'

'Is that your rule for life?'

Alice nodded. 'Yup, and it's never let me down.'

Bella frowned. 'I do hope you can still make jokes when you're on Skype, or I'll have to visit often.'

'You'll always be welcome.'

Bella got up from the table and went round to her friend's side. Then she hugged her.

34

As Bella set off, she did wonder if her numerous preparations were really stalling tactics. She had gone on the internet and printed out instructions on how to get there. She had also put details into the satnav her father had insisted she borrowed permanently, and Alice had made sandwiches for her.

She'd had — at last — a brief, impersonal email from Dominic saying that Ed Unsworth had definitely bought property in the Cotswolds. *My feeling is he went back to his roots in Liverpool to distance himself from dodgy dealings in the South West*. He'd signed it, *In haste, D*.

Bella had spent some moments speculating if the single initial instead of his full name made it more intimate. But then she realised that lots of people just put an initial instead of their full names. It probably didn't mean anything very much.

While having the extra information made her journey more sensible, it didn't stop her anxiety. She didn't have proof of wrongdoing, after all, only that he'd bought property. But one way or another she'd gone through a lot. It would all have been for nothing if she just let Nevil and whoever else was involved get away with it.

As the satnav and her printed instructions led her away from the recently upgraded business area of Liverpool, Bella began to wonder if there'd been a mistake. Everything she'd read about Ed Unsworth on the internet had made her expect glossy offices, like those Celine worked in. In this area, which she would describe as 'ripe for restoration', the businesses were mostly manufacturers, small or boarded up. In fact when she reached her destination (with only a few 'recalculatings' from her satnav, indicating she'd taken a wrong turning) she went on to her phone to check she had typed in the right address, really hoping she'd made some mistake. But no, this was it. Now she had to go and confront him. Alice's warning of 'heavies' didn't seem so ridiculous now.

Annoyingly, there was nowhere to leave the car remotely nearby. There was a small park with sour grass and neglected flowerbeds, with parking all round it but no empty spaces. She would have to get rid of the car and approach the office on foot.

She found a car park some distance away and hoped that the CCTV cameras were working and would mean her car would be safe. She locked up carefully, putting cvcrything except her sandwiches in the boot and then, having hooked her handbag across her body, she set off, hoping she had remembered the direction correctly.

It was hot and her sandals started to rub, and suddenly she stopped being sure of her direction. Having checked the street was empty so no one would jump out and steal it, she got out her smartphone and went on to maps.

As an estate agent she was used to less desirable parts of the world — even the leafy Cotswolds had them. But this area was worse than she'd imagined. It seemed that the way gritty thrillers represented Liverpool had its basis in fact.

Luckily she managed to remember the postcode and put it in. The results told her the offices were still quite far. She walked on. After ten minutes or so she reached her destination.

The office was a small, scruffy building next to a car body shop. There was a lot of banging going on in the shop which made Bella think about the dodgy dealers she'd seen on reality TV shows. Very thirsty now, she thought longingly of a bottle of water she'd left in the car, cursing herself for not bringing it with her. She realised her thirst wasn't just caused by heat and exercise, but by nerves that bordered on fear.

But, she told herself firmly, she hadn't driven for over three hours to drive back home again without having at least tried to confront this property magnate and tell him the game was up. But the more she thought about it the more ridiculous the idea of her doing so became. How could she, young and middle class, not to mention female, possibly bring any pressure to bear on someone who was not only successful and powerful but had very dubious morals?

Someone from the body shop wolf-whistled. That made her open the door of the offices. If she hesitated any longer there would be banter, which might be well meaning but Bella was not in the mood for it.

A woman, any age between forty-five and

sixty, sat behind a desk. Her hair was bright black and frizzy and her eyes heavily made-up. She peered at Bella shrewdly.

'Can I help you, love?'

Bella knew from experience that people were generally friendlier north of Cheltenham, but somehow this woman didn't seem to be cut from that cloth. Bella smiled before she spoke, to put off the moment when her southern vowels would make her seem even more naïve.

'Hello. I wonder if you can help me. I'm looking for Ed Unsworth? Are these his — er — Does he work here?' To her own ears she sounded idiotic, and her plans to confront anyone, let alone Ed Unsworth, seem ridiculous.

'I wouldn't call it work, love, but he's here sometimes.' She peered at Bella even more intently. 'Why do you want to see him?'

None of Bella's preparations had included rehearsing an answer to this question. All she'd thought about was what she'd say to the man himself, not to his gatekeeper. 'It's a private matter.'

'It's all right, love, you can tell me. There are no secrets here.' The woman narrowed her eyes further, making Bella feel she could read her mind, knew exactly why she was there and didn't think much of her chances of telling Ed Unsworth anything.

'Really, it's a bit awkward. I'd rather just tell him. It's — er — personal.' She stopped, hoping she hadn't given the impression that she was Ed Unsworth's love child or something. 'Is he here? I've come a long way to see him.'

'You're not trying to get money out of him, are you? I can tell you now, that won't work. I wouldn't say he's tight, but Scrooge looks very generous next to him.'

'No. I don't want money.' Bella smiled again, hoping to look pathetic — which she was, really.

Something must have worked because the woman pursed her lips. 'Well, if it's personal, I'll have to wait till Joe tells me himself. But I'm afraid you're out of luck. He's not here.'

Bella's not very high spirits sank further. She would never psych herself up to come again. If she didn't see him now she never would. She cleared her throat, horribly afraid she might start to cry. Looking a bit pathetic was one thing, weeping noisily was another. She mustn't show weakness. 'Are you expecting him back today?'

'Doesn't do to expect 'im, love. But he might be here in a couple of hours.'

'OK. I'll come back in a couple of hours then. Thank you for your help.'

'You're welcome,' said the woman.

On the street again, Bella wondered what on earth she could do for two hours. For various reasons she was reluctant to get in her car and drive off. She'd have to find somewhere to park again, and the nearby car park might be full when she returned. Then she'd have to find her way back here, which hadn't been easy. But mostly she knew if she got in her car, she'd just chicken out and drive home. Far better to stay local and on foot.

She set off and walked briskly round the block in the opposite direction to the men banging in the body shop, but even so she heard them calling after her. She walked more briskly.

The businesses that filled the streets she walked through were mainly tanning or nail salons. Wondering how on earth they could all find enough business to stay open in such a deprived area, she contemplated getting a set of acrylics to help her pass the time. That would be good for her street-cred! But she knew she was too anxious to really enjoy the process.

She had bought a bottle of water and a Mars bar from a corner shop early on in her perambulations, and these meant she managed to walk the streets, trying to keep in mind her position in relation to the offices, for an hour. Then, just as she thought she would have to sit down or die, she came across the car park and remembered her sandwiches. She could sit in the park and eat them until it was time to try Ed Unsworth again. But although her car was like an oven she was still tempted to get in it and flee, so she grabbed what she needed, ignoring the beckoning seats.

Thus, a few minutes later, the sandwiches and the drink Alice had also provided tucked under her arm, she went to the park she had seen when she first arrived.

It was bliss to sit and ease off her sandals. The sandwiches were warm from being in the car, but eating them used up some of the time. The drink was almost hot but still quenched her thirst. It had been so kind of Alice to make her a packed lunch. She got out her phone to send her a text of gratitude.

Lucky Alice, she thought, with her lovely Michael. And Jane Langley was ecstatic too, with the Agnews moving in. They were equally happy having managed to compromise at last. Alan Agnew had sent an email saying how thrilled they were to be contemplating living in at least part of the stately home of their dreams — something they never could have afforded normally. She sipped the tepid squash. What about her? Jobless, manless and, although not homeless, she was about to lose her housemate. It was hard not to feel a bit sorry for herself. And soon she would be confronting a man who was likely to just laugh at her, and she'd have to go home, after spending most of a scorching day in a place where she did not feel comfortable, having achieved precisely nothing. It would have been easier if she hadn't been sitting in a miserable little park, where the grass smelt of dog wee and only ragwort grew in the flowerbeds.

She had just put down the bottle prior to finding a litter bin to put it in, when she saw a figure carrying a briefcase coming down one of the streets that led to the park. Her first thought was that he looked totally out of place and the second that he looked like Dominic. She glanced away quickly. She didn't want to be caught staring at a strange man. Her stupid obsessed brain meant any man even vaguely smartly dressed looked like Dominic to her now. She was going crazy.

'Bella?'

35

Bella looked up and almost screamed. She wasn't going mad after all, it was him! 'Dominic! You scared me half to death! What are you doing here?' She was so shocked she forgot to be pleased.

'Never mind that! What are you doing here?' He sounded surprised and not at all pleased. 'This is not an area to be hanging around in!'

'Do you think I don't know that?'

'So why are you here?' he demanded.

'I've come to see Ed Unsworth.'

'You should have told me! That's why I've come. There was no need for you to come all the way up here, especially not on your own.'

'*You* should have told *me*!'

'I would have done, only I lost my phone and I wasn't near the office. But that's no excuse. You should never have come on your own. He could be dangerous! He probably is.'

As she'd had nearly two hours to come to a very similar conclusion, she went on the offensive. 'If it's wrong for me, it's wrong for you!'

'No it's not! I'm a man. I'm not going to get the sort of unwelcome attention that you are.'

Bella remembered the men in the body shop next to Ed's office, and realised he had a point, but she was not going to concede it. 'I should hope not! But don't worry, I can take care of myself too.'

'You don't know that. You haven't met him yet!'

She looked at her watch. 'True, but I'm just about to see him — he's due in the office around now, and I think you'll find I come out unharmed.'

Dominic made a visible effort to calm down. 'There's no need for you to go now I'm here. You go back to your car and wait in it.'

'You must be joking! I have not come all this way to 'sit in my car'!'

'Please!' he went on, tight-lipped. 'I've done research on him. I know more about him than you do. There's no point in you coming in too. Not when it could be dangerous.'

Him knowing more about Ed Unsworth than she did was very irritating, which didn't make her want to be sensible. 'Don't be ridiculous! He might be unpleasant but he won't be dangerous. He's a public figure; he wouldn't dare to do anything to me. You're overreacting.'

'I'm not, actually.' He glanced at his watch. 'But if you're absolutely determined to go through with this, we'd better go in. We don't want him to leave again.'

In silence they walked to the offices and went in more or less together.

'Hello,' said the smoky-voiced secretary, giving Dominic an appreciative once-over. 'There are two of you now, are there? I wondered if you'd meet up.'

'Yes,' said Dominic. 'Is he in?'

'He might be. What name shall I give?' She looked from one to the other.

'Bella Castle,' said Bella quickly, to get in first.

'And I'm Dominic Thane.'

'And who are you?' said the woman, looking at Dominic. 'Her lawyer or her boyfriend?'

'Both,' he said smoothly. 'I'm multi-purpose.'

The woman laughed and Bella regarded him, a spark of joy taking over from her anxiety and stress for a moment.

'Go on up then,' said the woman. 'First door, top of the stairs.'

'Aren't you going to announce us?' asked Dominic.

'All right then.' The woman got up from behind her desk, revealing a very short skirt, and shouted up the stairs in a voice loud enough to control crowds without the need for a megaphone. 'Ed! People to see you!'

Bella and Dominic left the room and when they were in the hallway at the foot of the stairs, he looked at her. 'Are you sure you won't see sense and keep out of this?'

'Quite sure.' Dominic referring to himself as her boyfriend had given her the courage of a lion. Also, she didn't want Dominic going in on his own. He might need her to cover his back.

He looked stern. 'We'd better call a truce until after this meeting. But afterwards' — he paused ominously — 'I have a bone to pick with you.'

As she went up the stairs ahead of him, Bella couldn't help smiling, in spite of what she was facing. There'd been a definite twinkle in Dominic's eye, and all that crossness because she'd been going to confront Ed Unsworth on her own — surely that was a sign he cared about her?

When Bella saw Ed Unsworth in the flesh she

was quite glad she was not facing him alone. He wasn't exactly frightening but he was somehow unpleasant. He was a large man with a shaved head, wearing a tracksuit. He was the sort of man Bella would move away from if she came across him in the gym. He would lift heavy weights and sweat a lot. He had a thick gold earring, a lot of gold chains and a Rolex to match. He might have had a shabby office, but he was still a blatantly rich man.

'Sit down,' he said and then, ignoring Dominic, turned his attention to Bella. This was not due to gentlemanly good manners or feminism or anything good, Bella suspected, but because she was obviously the weaker of the two.

'So, what can I do for you, young lady?'

'For a start you can stop doing dodgy property deals.' Bella felt she sounded like a child star of the sixties in a film, gallantly facing up to the villains; she wished she'd practised what she was going to say when she had all that time on her hands.

He smiled. He had not looked after his teeth. 'Oh?' One of his canines was gold.

Bella deliberately made her voice lower; anything to make her sound more authoritative. 'Yes. You've been buying up properties in the Cotswolds for less than they are worth. You're not only doing the vendors out of their money, but you're buying up affordable properties, which stops people on lower budgets being able to buy them.'

'And you've proof of this, have you?'

'Yes,' said Dominic.

Bella nodded. This was good. Dominic sounded very sure and he had that big briefcase. He probably did have proof. She only had some grainy stills that weren't particularly damning.

Ed Unsworth took his time. His little eyes flicked from one to the other of them. He was obviously convinced that all his tracks were covered. 'What kind of proof?'

'Video,' said Bella.

He registered this with just the tiniest flicker. 'Really?'

Bella nodded.

'To be frank,' said Dominic, 'we've got a whole trail of proof of your dubious practices. The video is just an extra. It pins you down when none of our other evidence is quite as specific.'

Ed Unsworth got up and walked to the window. Bella stood up so she could see what he was looking at. It was a big black car with two large men standing outside it. A tiny part of her was looking forward to telling Alice that yes, there had been 'heavies'. Even if, she realised, they were probably perfectly innocent night-watchmen or something. 'Heavies' would make the story better.

'I don't quite understand how you could possibly have got video footage of me doing anything more sinister than signing some forms,' he said, still very confident.

'Anyone can get careless,' said Dominic.

'Not me,' he said.

'So you're admitting to the dodgy deals then?' asked Bella, feeling braver.

'No. I don't admit to anything.'

'Very wise,' said Dominic. 'Put that off as long as you can.'

Ed Unsworth wrinkled his brow, reminding Bella of a Shar Pei dog. 'You say you have video of me doing something dodgy. How do you know it's me?'

'You have a very distinctive earring,' said Dominic.

His relaxed attitude left him. 'What do you want from me?' The fact that he hadn't asked to see any proof was almost as good as a confession. Persuading him to stop might be harder.

Bella said, 'The undertaking that you'll stop doing it.'

'And what am I doing, precisely?' He wasn't rolling over just yet, Bella realised, suddenly more anxious.

'We know that you've been damaging property to get it cheaper after the survey,' said Dominic smoothly and very confidently. 'You've been running down areas so you can buy up whole lots, generally doing everything and anything you can to build up your empire.' As most of this was news to her, Bella realised he'd been doing a lot of research lately. If only he'd told her about it! It made the whole case so much stronger.

'And who's this 'we'?' Ed Unsworth looked at Bella as if she was less than a waste of space.

'The team,' said Dominic, not bothering to elaborate.

'And who are they?'

Dominic's eyebrow flicked. 'I'm not going to give you a list of their names and addresses, but

I assure you their qualifications are excellent.' He opened his briefcase and got out a sheaf of papers and handed it across the desk. 'You might want to cast your eye on that lot. I think you'll find we know enough about you to cost you a lot in legal fees, if not a spell in prison.'

Ed snatched the papers and read them rapidly. 'OK. What exactly do you want from me?'

'We want you to sign these undertakings to cease and desist from immoral practices from this day forward,' said Dominic.

'And if I don't? Not that I'm admitting anything.'

'I don't think you need me to tell you what could happen next,' said Dominic. 'You're a man of the world.'

Whatever had been in those papers must have been fairly damning, Bella decided. The big scary man seemed to shrink a little. 'But I won't sign anything unless you show me the video.'

Bella took a breath and looked at the handbag at her feet that had the video on the iPad. This was her weak spot. It was so grainy and difficult to make out. Ed Unsworth might well just laugh, and then throw them out.

But Dominic moved first and opened his briefcase. 'Here it is.' He handed Ed Unsworth a DVD.

Ed Unsworth took a stride that brought him to the cinema-sized TV screen. He slotted in the DVD. Bella braced herself for humiliation.

But the picture that came up, while even more grainy, had been digitally enhanced. Nevil was clearer than ever, and now Ed Unsworth was unmistakeable. His increased size, his baldness and his gold earring. Bella was amazed and delighted that he was so easy to identify now.

He watched in silence and then nodded. 'This isn't the only copy, is it?'

'No,' said Dominic. 'So if we discover — and we will — that what you've been doing is illegal, we'll take steps that will land you in court.'

'I wouldn't have been able to do it if I hadn't found an agent willing — very willing — to co-operate,' Joe said.

'I'm sure,' said Dominic. 'Now will you sign the paper?'

Ed shook his head. 'Nah. But tell you what, I'm feeling generous today. I won't do it again. I think we've done all we can in that area anyway. That'll have to be enough for you.'

Dominic got up, not at all fazed by having to leave without a signature. 'Fine,' he said.

On his part, Ed didn't seem remotely triumphant. They had definitely won.

* * *

Bella felt elated as they went down the stairs as fast as possible without running. As they got on to the street she stopped to look at Dominic, expecting to see the joy of victory on his face. But no, he was grim; he took her arm and marched her down the road in double time.

Bella suddenly started to see the funny side, and bit her lip. Dominic was obviously still annoyed with her for being there but really, the thought of the two of them confronting Ed

Unsworth was rather ridiculous. By the time they got to the end of the street she was giggling.

'It's not funny!' said Dominic, stopping at the corner, possibly trying not to laugh himself. 'I am still very, very cross with you!'

'It is funny,' said Bella, laughing even more now because she didn't want to, not really. 'Us confronting that huge man and him backing down.'

'It should not have been 'us'! It should have been me, on my own. You went in there with no proper information, probably the same film we saw the first time, where only Nevil was identifiable — to his fiancée who presumably knows him well!'

Although she was still chuckling, Bella had to admit, to herself, if not to him, that he had a point. 'I'm not his fiancée any more, though.'

'No?'

'And I don't work there any more either.'

'You felt you had to leave?'

Bella nodded. 'I did. He insisted I left. With a cardboard box of my personal possessions.'

Dominic frowned. 'He sacked you? That's outrageous!'

Bella shrugged. 'I can't blame him really. I told him I knew he was up to something. He didn't like it. I knew I'd have to leave, but I didn't expect him to sack me.' She sighed, thinking of other confrontations she'd had lately that hadn't gone quite as planned. Her lunch with Celine for one. She still had to confess to Dominic about that.

Unaware of her guilty conscience, Dominic said, 'I am sorry. I know how much you loved your job — and were good at it.' Bella basked for a moment in the sunshine of his approval. But then his expression darkened. 'I am still cross with you. I don't think you know how much danger you were in just then.'

'Only about the same amount of danger as you were in, I expect.'

He closed his eyes, apparently praying for patience. 'If you'd gone in there alone — '

'But I didn't. You were there.'

'You shouldn't have been there too!'

'I didn't know you were going. I didn't know you'd done all that research, or got the video enhanced or anything.'

He sighed deeply. 'Well, that was my fault. I sent you that email — belatedly, I'm sorry — after I'd been hot on the trail, and then I lost my phone and my laptop battery died.'

'That all sounds like excuses to me,' said Bella.

He took her arm and pulled her to his side. 'I know. It would sound like that to me, too. But these things happen. I'm all over the place at the moment. Lots of work, the decision to make the move permanently to Stroud — '

'Oh!' said Bella, trying to hide her delight at this news. 'Is that so you can keep an eye on Jane?'

'No, you dilly. Aunt Jane doesn't need an eye keeping on her, she's got your friends the Agnews to do that.' He paused. 'I decided to make the move to be near you.'

Bella didn't know what to say but it didn't matter because Dominic kissed her.

'Kissing in the street?' said Bella, breathless. 'I wouldn't have thought that was what respectable solicitors did.'

He laughed. 'Come on then, let's go to the docks. You need to see what a wonderful city Liverpool is nowadays. And I warn you, I've got plans to do a lot more than just kiss you.'

'That sounds nice,' said Bella, her understatement belying the surge of happiness that welled up inside her.

'Nice?' said Dominic, affronted. 'I'll show you nice. Let's go!'

36

Bella followed Dominic. He was familiar with Liverpool and she wasn't, so she was relying on him and the satnav.

Although she knew she should be ecstatic — triumphant that Ed Unsworth and Nevil wouldn't be doing any more dirty deals together — she wasn't. And Dominic obviously cared about her a lot. Yet somehow the doubt was creeping in. Would he still like her (she couldn't let herself believe he loved her, not yet) when he found out she'd been to see Celine?

And although she knew it couldn't be helped, she was sad about losing her job. She'd loved the agency so much. In fact, if she hadn't loved it, she'd have ended it with Nevil sooner. While she knew this wasn't entirely logical — it was not absolutely definite that she'd have to work in a different town — she felt it wouldn't be her patch in quite the same way. And applying for new jobs with only old references might be tricky. There were lots of people after jobs like that. She'd just be another candidate. Her excellent house-selling record would have to be taken at her word. Nevil wouldn't tell any future employer how good she was.

Alice would tell her she needed food. She'd say that Bella's low spirits were due to the adrenalin she'd needed to confront Ed Unsworth now leaving her body, and all she needed was some chocolate to feel a whole lot better. Bella felt it wouldn't be that simple.

Dominic found a car park and was in his space when Bella slid into the space behind him. He got tickets for both cars, and then he took her arm and they set off for the docks.

It was a hot afternoon, and it was lovely to be by the water to admire the huge red-brick buildings that had once been the hub of the maritime world.

'Liverpool is a wonderful city,' said Dominic. 'A friend of mine was at university here, and I got to know it a bit when I came to visit him.'

'Rather different from where we've just been,' said Bella, trying not to sound upbeat. 'There are areas like that in the Cotswolds, but on the whole my work doesn't take me there.'

'The area wasn't so bad; it was the man who had his office there who was bad,' said Dominic.

Bella nodded. 'I think I'm only just realising how much danger I could have put myself in if you hadn't been there.'

He put his hand on her shoulder. 'But I was there, and all was well.'

She smiled bravely, feeling pathetic.

'So, what would you like to do?' Dominic said. 'Do you want to find somewhere for a drink or something?'

'Actually, could we just sit here for a bit and watch the water? It's very soothing.'

Dominic found a vacant bench, and for a while they sat in silence. Then Dominic gave Bella a quick glance. 'Would you like me to give you a potted history of Liverpool's maritime past?' he asked.

'Actually no, thank you. If you don't mind.'

'I don't, but if you don't mind me saying so, you seem a bit — I don't know — subdued. Is it a delayed reaction after confronting Ed? You should be turning cartwheels — we nailed him!'

Bella smiled. 'I couldn't turn cartwheels here. I can only do them on grass, with my dress tucked into my knickers.'

'Can we hold the thought about you and your knickers until later? Although it will be a struggle. What's on your mind?'

His gentle teasing was already making Bella feel better. 'I will tell you, but you might not like it.'

'It was me who banned discussion about your knickers, so I'm already disappointed. Tell me anyway. What have you done wrong now?'

Bella fell on this excuse to put off her confession a little longer. 'What do you mean 'now'? I haven't done anything wrong apart from this one thing!'

Dominic raised a doubting eyebrow. 'If you discount squaring up to Uncle Ed without much proof of his wrongdoing, and on your own.' He paused. 'Which actually I don't.'

Bella was indignant. 'Well, you didn't tell me you were going, so of course I had to go. The not-having-a-phone thing is just lame! By the way, where did you get all the information? I was impressed.'

'The no-phone thing was real, although I admit it was damn stupid. But with regard to Old Ed, I told you I had contacts and the internet will tell you everything if you ask the right questions.'

Bella nodded, half hoping he'd forget she'd been about to tell him something.

'So what about your confession?' He hadn't forgotten.

Bella realised she'd have to do it. 'I went to see Celine.'

'You did? Why?'

He didn't seem angry, just surprised, which was encouraging. 'Because I thought it was terribly unfair of her to imply you didn't look after Dylan properly when you obviously do.' She paused. 'I pointed out it was nice for her to have you as an extra dad.'

'Oh.'

Bella couldn't infer much from this monosyllable. 'I said that if she insisted you had to focus on only him, you might not always be able to have him when she wanted you to.' She paused. 'She hasn't been in touch to tell you this?'

He made a face and a 'what?' gesture with his hands. 'The no-phone thing?'

'I'd forgotten.' She paused. 'You're not cross about me interfering?' She studied his face. It would be so awful if she'd blown her chances of happiness because she couldn't help sticking her nose into injustice.

After what seemed like forever to Bella, but was probably just a second, he shook his head. 'No. You meant it for the best. But I'm surprised Celine agreed. She usually sticks to what she's said in the heat of the moment, however unreasonable it is.'

Bella pushed her hair back off her face. Relief

at his reaction had made her hot suddenly. 'Well, she did admit that her friend — you know, the one we met while we were at the swings, having ice creams? She sort of egged Celine on to check up on you that day at Jane's.'

He shook his head at the memory. 'It did seem more unreasonable and insane than Celine usually is, which is saying something.' Then he turned his attention back to Bella. 'So, do you feel better now you've got that off your chest?'

She laughed gently. 'That expression always makes me think of a nasty cough or something.' She felt a hundred times better.

'I'm glad. I was worried you were sad because you broke up with Nevil. From my own experience I know that breaking up with someone is always extremely painful, even if you'd stopped loving them a long time ago.'

She was horrified that he might think this. 'No! I'm not sad about that at all! We weren't really suited and I never really loved him, but I pretended to myself I did and that I enjoyed his company. I think I sort of glossed over the things that were wrong for my own convenience.'

'That happens. So how long were you together?'

'Over two years.'

He frowned. 'You must have got together fairly soon after you moved to Stroud.'

'Oh yes,' said Bella, thinking back. 'I was in such a low place, I sort of gravitated towards his cockiness. And of course the fact that he was instantly attracted to me was very good for my ego.'

'So why were you in such a low place?'

Bella realised that she'd revealed far more than she meant to. 'Well, you know . . . New job, new town, all those things . . . '

He frowned again and shook his head. 'No, those things don't make you sad, they make you excited, and you went there willingly. Why were you sad?'

Bella looked up at him, not wanting to say, even now. She wanted him to be the first to confess to love, not her.

Dominic went on. 'I never knew why you left so hurriedly. It seemed so odd. One minute you were doing well in the job and always seemed so cheerful when I saw you in the office and then — boom — you'd left! Why?'

Bella took a few seconds, thinking up every excuse she could to explain her sudden exit. She fell back on the truth. 'I was in love with someone. Someone married. I couldn't hang around. I might have done something — well, wrong.'

Bella didn't dare look at him and see his reaction. Instead she stared at the water, finding solace in the light dancing on the waves, creating sudden bursts of sunlight like camera flashes exploding.

'Was that someone me?'

Bella just nodded.

'If it's any consolation, I think it was worse for me. Celine was pregnant. I had to stand by her, or I'd have followed you sooner.'

Bella wasn't sure she'd understood. 'Sooner?'

He looked rueful. 'Oh yes. I was in love with you too. I didn't know how you felt, of course. But when I was free of Celine, well — let's just say me finding work in the same town as you wasn't a coincidence.'

'I thought it was because of Jane.'

He shook his head. 'I could have made sure she was all right without moving to Stroud and there are other members of the family who'd have done that. Although I'm so glad I've had the chance to get to know her properly.'

'If only I'd known . . . '

'You wouldn't have gone rushing into Nevil's arms so quickly?'

'No! It was definitely a rebound thing.'

'After you left I was a mess,' he said. 'I know nothing had ever happened between us, if you don't count a kiss under the mistletoe, but I knew — felt I knew — that you were mine really.'

'But you were married. And then Celine got pregnant. That was what made me go.'

'It was all horrible. Especially when Celine implied you covered up for her when she was having an affair.' He hesitated. 'I think she suspected I had feelings for you and used you just to be nasty.'

'That's horrible. I must confess I didn't think about you suffering. I thought it was just me.'

'Same here. It never occurred to me it was because of me that you left.'

'Well, that's good for my pride, at least. I think Celine suspected, even if she wasn't certain.'

'But thank goodness that's all in the past.' He put his arm round her shoulders and hugged her to him. 'So what will you do now? Confront Nevil? Tell him what we've done?'

'I already have. And if he'd agreed to stop, I

would never have gone to see Ed.'

He chuckled, still hugging her to his side. 'Although it was obviously wrong and dangerous, I'm kind of glad. I like the thought of making love to you in Liverpool.'

'Dominic?' she questioned gently.

'I think we've waited long enough. I'm going to take you to a really good hotel where we can make up for lost time.'

'Dominic! We can't go to a really good hotel without luggage or anything!'

'Oh yes we can. Trust me, I'm a solicitor.'

Bella got the giggles as she and Dominic entered the reception area of what seemed to be the poshest hotel in the city. She knew it wasn't helping but she couldn't stop.

'I feel like Julia Roberts in *Pretty Woman*!' she whispered as they crossed acres of marble to the reception desk.

'Ssh!' he said, patting her arm. 'Good afternoon,' he said grandly. 'Have you a room? Now. Just one night.' Then he tossed his credit card on to the desk and the woman opposite picked it up with a smile.

Five minutes later they were being shown into a huge room overlooking the water. The moment they were alone, Bella ran to the window to look out. 'This is an amazing view!'

'Yes,' said Dominic. 'Shame you won't have time to look at it.'

He took her into his arms and kissed her, and then without breaking the kiss he swept her up into his arms and carried her to the bed, where he dropped her.

'For a solicitor, you can be quite dashing,' said Bella, panting slightly.

'You ain't seen nothing yet,' he said, and peeled off her coat.

Bella gave a happy sigh.

* * *

The following morning, having taken advantage of the laundry services provided, as well as using all the other facilities, (spa bath, trouser press, free tea and coffee) Bella turned on her phone. She had found time to text Alice and her mother to assure them of her safety and the success of the mission, but then she'd turned it off. Now, having enjoyed a very leisurely breakfast on the balcony, she felt ready to face the rest of the world.

There were a lot of missed calls, and a text from Tina.

Get yourself into the office ASAP. Nevil is out on his ear and they want you back!

She showed the text to Dominic. He grunted in satisfaction. 'You're not the only one who can fix things behind people's backs.'

'What? But you didn't know I'd been sacked until I told you!'

'No, but I knew about Nevil. I told them at Rutherfords' head office what a star you are, but they already knew that. They must have been furious when they heard Nevil had fired you.'

'I suppose we should get back though and see what's going on.'

'I suppose we must. Shall we leave your car

here so we can travel together?'

Just for a second Bella was tempted by the thought of shooting down the motorway in Dominic's much bigger car but then said, 'No, that would be silly. It would be a pain to come and get mine later.'

He drew her to him. 'I suppose so. I just don't want to be parted from you for a minute.'

'Or in this case, nearly three hours.'

'Will you go directly to the office, or stop off at Alice's first?'

'Go straight there, I think. Thanks to this very luxurious hotel, I'm all clean and ironed. No reason to call on Alice first. If I start talking to her I'll never get to the office.'

'I'll meet you there then.'

It took them several minutes to say goodbye.

⋆ ⋆ ⋆

When she arrived back in Stroud, Bella parked her car in the office car park and let herself in the back way. Instantly there were cheers, party poppers and bottles of champagne. Through the streamers she spotted Dominic, pouring champagne into glasses.

'Here she is!' said Tina. 'Our heroine!'

'You're a heroine too!' said Bella, hugging her friend hard.

'And you got rid of Nevil,' said David, one of the other agents. 'Who was OK but he never gave any of us credit for our hard work.'

'We think you should apply for his job, Bells,' said Tina. 'We've discussed it.'

'I'm not the most senior by any means,' said Bella, shocked, taking the glass Dominic offered her.

'Apply. If you get it it'll be because you deserve it and we'd all be happy,' went on Tina. 'Wouldn't we, guys?'

There was a general chorus of 'yes!' and 'hear, hear!', even a reluctant one from Edward, who was Nevil's current second in command.

'I made a cake,' said Tina. 'Let's have some. It's practically lunchtime.'

'My perfect lunch,' said Bella, sitting on a desk, swinging her legs, sipping from her glass. 'Champagne and cake.'

* * *

Afterwards, they left Bella's car in the car park and Dominic drove back to Alice's. Alice hugged them both hard when they got through the door.

'Oh, loves! I am so pleased everything's worked out for you. And Dominic's OK about living here with you while I'm away?'

Bella looked at Dominic. 'I never got round to asking him . . . '

'As Bella has signally failed to find me a suitable property, I'm more than happy to share this fabulous house with her while you need us,' said Dominic gallantly.

Alice laughed. 'Well, that's good! And do feel free to redecorate, move stuff around, anything like that.' She put her arm round Dominic. 'Now, have you two had lunch?' she said as she led the way to the kitchen.

'Cake, mainly,' said Dominic.

'And champagne,' said Bella. 'It was lovely, but I could do with something savoury. Partly to mop up the fizz.'

'I've made a quiche,' said Alice. 'And a list of things you'll need to know about the house . . . '

'Are you sure you're OK about living here?' said Bella as she and Dominic cleared up after eating the quiche and reading the list. 'I could easily find us a nice little rental.'

Dominic took his hands out of the sink and gave her a quick hug. 'I'm all for 'love in a cottage',' he said, 'but I think I prefer 'love in an ex-vicarage, with five bedrooms and a well-kept garden'. But anywhere you are is the perfect home for me.'

Bella kissed him.

Epilogue

Bella put her arm round Dominic's waist. 'It was so sweet of you to come with me to see Alice off, especially when we had to get up quite early in the morning to get her here on time.'

They were walking through Kings Cross St Pancras station after putting Alice on the train. She was off to her new life, Michael having gone ahead. But judging by the number of texts Alice had received on the journey, there was no doubt that he would be waiting for her on the platform when she arrived.

'She did have quite a lot of luggage, and she's been so good to me,' said Dominic. 'It was lovely of her to clear out that little room so Dylan has a bedroom near us.'

'He loved it, didn't he?' Bella chuckled, remembering the weekend that Dylan had spent with them all. He had explored the house with Dominic, wide-eyed and thrilled and, later, made a den in the garden. Or rather Dominic had made it, but there was no doubt about whose den it was. Alice had been generous with rugs, cushions and pots and pans.

'He really did. Even Celine has begun to see how good it is for me and Dylan to see each other, and you.'

Bella hugged his arm a little tighter. Then she stopped in front of the statue of the couple kissing. 'Sweet, isn't it?'

'It's OK. I prefer the one of John Betjeman. Part of me longs to send for the proverbial fish knives.'

'But I don't want to be called Norman.'

He laughed. 'I don't know. I think you might get to like it.' He kissed her head. 'I do like it that you get my references, that you know that poem.'

Bella was pleased. 'Do you want to go and look at the statue before we get our train back?'

'Actually, you've got the rest of the day off. I'm taking you out to lunch.'

'Oh?' Bella had planned an afternoon in the office.

'Yes. It was a unanimous decision when I consulted your colleagues. You've been working so hard since Nevil left and you need some time off.'

Bella frowned. 'If I'm going to apply for Nevil's job, I really need to — '

'You've done it all. Tina told me. Now come on. Do you mind a bit of a walk to the restaurant?'

Bella didn't put up much of a fight. She knew it would have been a struggle to go back to work having seen Alice off. In spite of being so blissfully happy these days, she did feel sentimental about partings, and had wept just a little bit as she and Alice had hugged goodbye. A lovely lunch with Dominic would be the perfect thing to take her mind off it.

Dominic took Bella's arm and they walked along. She didn't know that part of London so she just let Dominic steer her.

'Oh!' she said after about fifteen minutes' walking. 'We're in Camden Passage! All these lovely stalls. I adore markets.'

Dominic seemed pleased. 'It was considerate of Alice to travel on a Wednesday, as otherwise it wouldn't be operating. Unless we came on a Saturday when it would be heaving.'

Bella didn't answer. She'd gone to a stall selling antique silver. She picked up a rattle. 'I suppose Dylan is a bit old for a rattle.'

'Or not nearly old enough.' Dominic found a charming little pill box with a silver top. 'This is sweet.'

'Gorgeous! I wonder if my mother would like it for Christmas?'

Dominic dissuaded her from Christmas shopping quite so early and they wandered along, enjoying the stalls and the sunshine. Eventually Dominic said, 'I'm getting hungry.'

'Mm, so am I. Have you booked anywhere?'

He shook his head. 'No, no. Haven't booked. I knew we'd find somewhere in this area though. Where do you fancy eating?'

'That pub looks nice.' She pointed to one a little way away, which seemed traditional, with hanging baskets outside. 'It might have a garden. I love London pub gardens. Not that I've much experience of them but I find them glamorous somehow.'

'The pub it is,' said Dominic. He took her arm again.

They had nearly reached the pub, and Bella had realised she was really hungry, when Dominic suddenly turned down a side street.

'Dom! Where are we going? I'm starving!'

'Sorry!' he said, not slackening his pace. 'I just

realised something.'

He came to a halt in front of a very elegant jewellery shop.

'Why are we going in here?' Bella asked as Dominic made to enter.

'We might need something,' he said, pulling her arm.

She resisted. 'Dom! It's a jeweller's. Lovely, but hardly full of life's necessities!'

'Oh, I don't know,' he said, and led her firmly inside.

Bella started to giggle with embarrassment as they arrived in the shop. She stopped when the beautiful young woman behind the counter said, 'Mr Thane? I have what you want.'

Bella's mouth went dry and she felt a bit dizzy. Was this what it looked like? A tray of five beautiful, modern rings was produced and placed on the counter top.

'Do you like any of these?' he asked her. 'If you'd rather have something more traditional . . . '

'Dominic?' she whispered.

He hit his forehead with his hand. 'I've left out a vital bit, haven't I?'

Bella nodded. She still felt dazed. This could only mean one thing, surely.

'Tell you what, you choose a ring then I can produce it when I've — done the thing that I forgot to do first.'

'If you'd like me to leave you alone . . . ?' said the assistant.

'No, it's all right,' said Bella. 'I'll just have a look.'

The rings were spectacular. Bella had always thought she was traditional in her tastes but these challenged that. 'I like them all,' she said eventually, having inspected each one.

'If you could just choose your favourite?'

'Can I try that one?' She pointed to a square diamond with a frame of gold.

'Here, let me,' said Dominic, taking the ring from the assistant. 'I think I should.' He slid it on to her finger.

'It's amazing,' whispered Bella. 'I love it.'

'Maybe you should try them all on?' said the beautiful assistant. 'Your fiancé selected them so carefully.'

'Let's not jump the gun,' said Dominic. 'I don't want to take anything for granted.'

'No,' said Bella, still hardly able to speak. 'This is the one.'

Dominic made a face. 'What? The man or the ring?'

Bella smiled shyly. 'Both.'

* * *

'I can't even imagine how expensive that ring must have been,' said Bella a few minutes later.

'Ssh. That's nothing to do with you.' He opened the door of thc pub. 'Shall we have champagne? Or a stiff drink?'

'A stiff drink,' said Bella. 'I think I might be in shock fairly soon.'

The pub did have a courtyard garden and, for some reason, they were the only ones in it. They had their drinks and Dominic had the bag with the ring box in his pocket.

'I'm sorry I've been so clumsy about doing this whole proposal thing. I felt I ought to have the ring ready but didn't want it not to be what you wanted, so . . . ' He stopped talking and Bella realised he was nervous. 'Will you marry me, Bella?'

She nodded. 'Yes please.'

'In which case . . . ' He produced the bag and the box and opened it. 'Should I go down on one knee for this bit?'

'No! Don't! Someone might come!'

Strangely, a few moments later, when some people did investigate the garden, Bella didn't notice at all. She had a beautiful ring on her finger and was wrapped in Dominic's arms.